THE MAGPIE'S RING

Angus Rose

The Magpie's Ring

ISBN: **1532792859**

ISBN-13: **978-1532792854**

1

This book is dedicated to Dr. Paul Blakemore, who has, through his endeavours and achievements, set an example for the rest of us to follow.

Dear Holly, congratulations on winning a copy of my novel. I hope it goes someway towards entertaining you over the summer!

all the best
Angus Rose

The Magpie's Ring

I would like to thank Alexandra Amor and Julie Lewthwaite for their guidance and encouragement and also for the kind words that helped me through the final hurdles of completing The Magpie's Ring.

The Magpie's Ring

Chapter One

The Magpie

How the ring had come to be caught in the highest most part of the oak tree was of no concern to the magpie. Nor did she have any concern for the people of the village, who wandered dazed and trembling, staring in fear at the vast burning crater that had appeared after the night's terrible events. A fearful night of unearthly shrieks and blinding flashes in which homes had been shaken to rubble, and balls of light had blasted from the ground high into the night sky. A night of terror that had only ended when the world about them had been torn apart by a mighty thunderclap. And as the people below began to pick through the rubble and call for their loved ones, the magpie hopped from branch to branch, cackling with glee at finding something so gleaming and so pretty to adorn her nest with.

Grasping the glittering prize in her beak the magpie had flown back to her nest in a young beech tree by the village chapel. She had carefully placed it first here, and then there, and then back here again, before deciding to put it just where she could gaze upon it when the time came to brood her eggs. When her clutch of seven young had hatched, the poor magpie had been so busy flying to and fro with beakfuls of food that she didn't notice the ring slowly slipping under the growing young and down through their tangled home. By the time the fledglings had flown in summer, the ring had come to rest in the fork below the nest.

As the years passed the tree grew around and then

swallowed the ring until it had been drawn deep, deep down into the trunk. Far away from daylight, far away from thieving magpies, and far away from the scores of children who came to play under the spread of the tree's branches, the ring lay hidden.

Almost four centuries later, the beech tree, darkened with rain and made darker still by the threatening winter sky, still harboured its treasure. It had guarded it while generation after generation in the village of Weston Pewsey had been born, had grown and had died. It had witnessed kings and queens come and go. It had witnessed wars bringing their destruction and misery to the world. It had seen the chapel become a school; quiet, sober worshippers giving way to noisy, laughing children who sought shade and shelter under its spreading branches. It had witnessed those who came seeking the ring, some with good intentions, and others with evil in their hearts. But always it had held the ring hidden deep in its bosom.

Chapter Two

Ned Penhallow

Ned Penhallow lay in his bed, tormented by a braying cough, a bunged-up nose and a sore throat that made him wince and grimace whenever he tried to speak or swallow. Ned hated being ill, hated being ill during school holidays, and especially hated being ill during the Christmas holiday, when Mum was too busy to look after him, dashing around as she was trying to keep her head above the rising tide of Christmas preparations as well as entertaining his six-year old brother, Sam. What made it worse, worse than being ill and not even being able to miss school was not being able to help decorate the tree and the mantelpiece with Mum, as he had done ever since he'd turned five years old.

Ned shifted in his bed, causing the slew of comic books that Sam had brought up to slide from the duvet and splatter to the floor, knocking over the last of the orange juice that had been lunch. Kicking his covers away, he grabbed a discarded sweater, a gift from his eleventh birthday the week before, and used it to mop up the worst of the spill before righting the glass and picking up the comics. Shoving the sodden sweater under his bed, Ned hopped back into his bed and pulled the covers up to his chin as he heard the first creak from the stairs that signalled the start of a visit from Sam. Looking up through the skylight in his attic room, Ned watched a flock of crows battling against a rising wind to reach the huge oak tree that grew next door in the school playground. The wind had been blowing all night, moaning around chimney pots and whistling through wires, tearing small branches from trees and sending them tapping and skittering across the slates of the roof.

Listening to the growing storm, Ned longed to be outside running around with Sam, splashing through puddles and catching the wind under the wings of his coat. As he lay there watching the racing clouds, the bedroom door started to open very, very slowly and the tangled mop of his brother's blond hair poked stealthily into the room, followed after a moment or two by one bright blue eye, a nose complete with rivulets of snot, and then a second blue eye.

'Hi, Sam,' Ned managed to croak.

'Hi, Ned. Are you awake?' asked Sam, as he slid round the door and closed it as quietly as he could for fear of alerting their mother to his clandestine visit.

Ned spluttered and nodded, as another bout of coughing wracked his thin frame.

'Come in, before Mum hears you.'

'Here, I've got you some tangerines. Mum's forgotten to bring them up. Shall I peel one for you?'

Ned nodded in reply, his throat flaring with pain after speaking just a few words, and watched as Sam dug his pudgy thumb into the orange skin of the fruit and began peeling.

'Mum says the wind's going to get even stronger and that we're going to have a Great-Aunt Gail overnight.'

Ned coughed and spluttered again as a laugh caught him unawares.

'What? What's wrong?' asked Sam, pausing in his peeling.

Still coughing, Ned motioned for Sam to pass him something to write with.

Dropping the peel on the carpet, and handing
Ned the now slightly mangled fruit, Sam dropped onto
his hands and knees and carefully pulled out the bottom
drawer of Ned's bedside cabinet and, feeling around
inside grasped the secret notebook and pencil they kept
hidden in there. Handing them to Ned, Sam sat and
watched as his brother pulled his knees up and, resting the
notebook on them began to write, tongue-tip poking
between teeth, face nearly touching the page.

After a couple of minutes of concentration,
interrupted only by a brief Mum-alert that turned out to
be a false alarm, Ned handed the notebook back to Sam,
who lacking any form of concentration span, had by now
eaten the tangerine that he'd peeled for his sick brother.

Sam took the notebook and, carefully following
the words with his finger, read them out loud.

'Not Great-Aunt Gail – a gale. She means a big
storm.'

As if to confirm this, the wind at that moment
chose to rise to a howling crescendo that threatened to
push the walls of the house inward, before dropping back
down. The boys looked at each other with a mix of terror
and excitement dancing across their faces as the bedroom
light flickered on and off.

'If the electricity gets cut off, can I sleep in your
room, Ned? Please?' begged Sam, his eyes like saucers.
Sam was still terrified of the dark, something that, had he
been feeling better, Ned would have teased him about,
even though he too could imagine all manner of ghouls
and beasties crawling out from under his bed when the
lights were switched off. On this occasion, however, Ned
merely nodded, feeling very much the heroic big brother
as Sam grinned and hugged his thanks.

A shout from down below made the brothers

jump guiltily.

'Sam Penhallow, where are you? Are you bothering your brother again?' their mother yelled from the kitchen.

Knowing that there were only seconds to spare, Sam jumped up from the bed, tiptoed hurriedly across the carpet and slipped out of the door, silently pulling it closed behind him, while Ned threw the notebook, pencil and the remains of the tangerines into the secret cubbyhole and pushed the drawer back into place. As the sound of his mother's sprinting feet reached his ears, he quietly slipped back into his bed, knowing that Sam by now was either about to be caught red-handed on the bottom few steps that led up to the attic, or had managed to dodge into his own room, where he could pretend to have spent the last ten minutes sword fighting a dragon.

Heart thumping in his ears, Ned waited. There was no shout from Mum, only the muffled sound of voices coming up from Sam's tip of a room, followed by Mum padding quickly up the stairs. For the second time in a matter of minutes, the bedroom door was gently and very, very quietly pushed open. Mum's wavy brown mop of hair appeared round the door.

'Poppet, you're awake,' she said, as she pushed the door open fully and strode into the room. That was very typical of Mum, never one to creep mouse-like into a room, not when the room quite obviously needed someone to be in charge of it. She stood in the middle of the room, clad head-to-toe in bright running gear.

'Horrible day – too many patients with the same bug that you've got. I'm going for a run,' she declared, just in case Ned hadn't noticed her garish outfit. 'Great-Aunt Gail's coming round in a minute to look after you both, so I'll go then. I'll go mad if I don't,' she added.

Mum said this as though her very sanity was hanging by the thinnest of threads, which if Dad were to believed, was very much the case.

'I'm going for a long one – I need to get my miles up for London,' she said, as she fussed and tucked Ned in. Every year since he could remember, Mum had wanted to do the London marathon, and last year she'd finally been given the chance.

'Dad'll be back before I'm finished, and I'm sure Great-Aunt Gail will come up and read to you if he's particularly grumpy, so don't get worried,' she continued, as to Ned's horror she picked up a piece of discarded tangerine peel that he had missed.

'Is there anything you want, my dear?' she asked, as she finished tidying up.

Ned could only shake his head as he waited, hoping that Mum wouldn't notice what it was that she was holding in her hand.

'OK, I'll tell Sam that he can pop up for a few minutes – he can finish giving you those tangerines, you pair of rat bags.' She smiled and pecked a kiss on Ned's forehead. That was the good thing about Mum, she was strict but she wasn't mean, and Sam and Ned loved her to bits.

Stooping and picking up the empty glass that Ned had knocked over earlier, she strode from the room.

'Oh, one other thing. There's going to be a big storm tonight, are you going to be alright sleeping up here by yourself?' she asked, poking her head back round the door.

Ned replied with a thumbs up to show that it was perfectly OK; if anything, it was exciting to be in the attic with the storm blowing and howling like some gigantic monster while he was tucked up all safe, cosy and warm with his duvet pulled right up under his chin. And anyway, it wouldn't do to let Sam know that he was frightened of a silly old storm.

At that moment the doorbell let out a fearsome, strident clanging. There followed almost immediately an impatient rat-a-tat-tatting on the door itself, as umbrella handle met wooden door. Another round of clanging from the doorbell left no-one in any doubt that someone was at the front door, and that someone could only be one person – Great-Aunt Gail.

'Where's the invalid?' she enquired in a voice that carried up the stairs. 'In bed, I hope, and not trussed up on the sofa watching the thinly disguised pig's offal that is broadcast to children these days.'

Great-Aunt Gail had a very dim view of television, and an even dimmer view of children's television. Listening carefully, Ned knew that the words 'David' and 'Attenborough' would soon make a grand appearance in Great-Aunt Gail's next sentence.

'These children should only be allowed to watch David Attenborough – he's simply, simply wonderful,' she proclaimed.

Ned also knew that as she said this, her hands would be clasped to her ample bosom, her eyes raised to heaven and her face a picture of rapture as she spoke the hallowed name.

'Sam-u-el Penhallow, come and see your great-aunt,' she boomed, switching from Attenborough zealot to commander of great-nephews.

'Coming,' came Sam's reply, a mixture of adoration and blind fear of his eccentric great-aunt. A thunder of feet hurtling at full tilt down the stairs followed by the impact of small child on great-aunt meant that Sam was currently having the air squeezed from him by Great-

Aunt Gail's formidably strong arms. Ned knew that his turn was imminent, and that the only advantage of being so ill was that he would avoid having his backbone nearly broken in two by Great-Aunt Gail's python-like enthusiasm for hugging them both.

'Well, Alice, you can go for your run now – I must say that outfit really is quite eye-wateringly ghastly. Does it make you run faster?'

Without waiting for a reply, Great-Aunt Gail began her ascent to Ned's room, while the boys' mother tugged on her trainers, and with a sigh of relief, slipped through the front door and trotted off into the gathering dusk. Hearing the door close, Ned stood on his bed and, opening the skylight, poked his head out and watched his mum trotting up the track that led away from the house and up to the top of the Combe, a large hill that stood like a sentinel over Weston Pewsey. Relishing the fresh air blowing on his hot face, Ned looked out over his school, longing to be climbing through the branches of the oak tree that stood at the edge of the playground. The two boys often sneaked into the schoolyard when school was closed, waiting for Mr Swanson, the janitor, to finish locking up and leave before wriggling through the thick rhododendron hedge that separated the house from the school. Once inside, they would commando-crawl their way to the climbing frame, expecting to be caught at any moment, before sneaking inside the wooden play fort where they would catch their breath and listen very carefully for the sound of grown-ups. When the coast was clear they'd run helter-skelter for the base of the oak, where Ned would give Sam a bunk up high enough for him to scramble on to the first branches and lower the rope ladder that they'd carefully hidden in a hole in the trunk.

'Ned Penhallow, what do you think you are doing? You'll catch your death of cold. Now get into bed!'

Great-Aunt Gail's salvo brought Ned crashing out of his daydream and sharply back to reality as his head, with a mighty thump, connected with the window frame.

'Now look what you've done, ' Great-Aunt Gail began. 'Oh, you poor thing, and with such a terrible cold, too. You poor dear, let's tuck you up.'

While it would be perfectly correct, and possibly life-saving, to recognise that Great-Aunt Gail was terribly fearsome, she wasn't without her soft side, especially when it came to looking after poorly children, and so she clucked and fussed around Ned, fluffing his pillows, tucking his duvet and blankets in, peeling a tangerine (and not eating it) and fetching him another glass of orange juice before leaving to attend to Sam.

A little while later, while Great-Aunt Gail clanked pots and pans around in the kitchen, Ned heard a car draw up and stop. Chewing his fingernails, he waited for the sound that he liked the least. A rattle of keys in the lock, and Dad was wiping his shoes on the doormat.

'Dear me, I can't believe how windy it is. Has that wife of mine really gone out running in this?' he complained to the house in general.

'Hello, Gail,' he called into the kitchen as he hung his coat up and hurled his briefcase into the cupboard under the stairs. 'Thanks for coming round and looking after Sam and the malingerer.'

'Hello, William,' came the terse reply. 'Ned isn't malingering – he has a nasty virus. Even Alice agrees and you know how much it takes to convince her after she's spent all day listening to poorly chests.'

'Where is he? In bed? What about Sam?'

'Sam's doing his homework in his room and

Ned's nicely tucked up in bed. Or at least I hope he is – he had his head hanging out of the window when I went up there.'

'Oh well, I'm sure a bit of fresh air wouldn't have done him any harm, dozy child that he is.'

Ned could tell by the extra loud bang of a pan on the table, that Great-Aunt Gail didn't agree in the slightest with Dad's last comment. The stairs creaked as Dad took the stairs two at a time, muttering under his breath all the way. Ned jumped guiltily and pulled his knees to his chest as Dad's head appeared round the edge of the door, breathing heavily after the headlong flight from Great-Aunt Gail.

'Still "ill" I see,' he said glaring. 'Can you talk yet?'

Ned shook his head, pointing at his throat.

'You're not going to be scared of the wind, are you? The last thing I want is you bawling your eyes out in the middle of the night.'

Once again, Ned shook his head, his eyes beginning to fill with tears.

'And you won't need this up,' Dad said, as he walked over to the skylight and banged the blind down with sharp tug. 'And don't let me catch you with your head out of the window, either.'

Ned nodded miserably, taking care not to catch his dad's eye, and flinched as the door slammed shut. The stairs shook as his dad clumped his way down to Sam's room. A squeal of joy rang through the house, as Dad burst in pretending to be a dragon and the two set about mock-fighting. Breathing a shuddering sigh of relief, Ned wiped the tears that now ran down his face and, with a silent prayer of safety for his running Mum, drifted off to sleep.

The Magpie's Ring

Chapter Three

A Storm Arrives in Weston Pewsey

The storm that arrived during the night blew with such ferocity that at times it sounded as though a choir of banshees were screaming their unearthly song on the slates above Ned's head. At first, Ned had slept deeply, but as the storm gathered strength he tossed and turned and cried out as his dreams grew into terrifying nightmares of something dark and terrible coming to lurk in the village, something that arrived with a terrible, shrieking howl and a thundering crack that ripped the air apart.

By morning, the worst of the storm had passed and the dark grey roiling clouds of the day before had started to break up, and a watery winter sun cast its rays over the devastation left behind. Ned woke slowly, still sleepy and tired from his restless night, and as he sat up in his bed and swung his legs to the floor, the nightmare that had preyed upon his sleep was already beginning to fade. Walking slowly downstairs, Ned could hear the usual morning din erupting from the kitchen. Dad was busy slapping butter onto toast to munch on while driving to work, while Mum charged from chore to chore with her usual unrelenting energy.

Sam looked up from his porridge as Ned wandered into the kitchen.

'Hi, Ned,' he shouted, bouncing up and down on his chair, 'are you feeling better now? Do you want to come out and play?'

'Hi, Sam, hi, Mum. My throat's feeling loads

better. Can I go out and play with Sam today?'

Dad grunted and waved a buttery knife in the direction of the boys' mother.

'Ask your mum, she's the doctor.'

Ned looked at his mum imploringly.

'Please, Mum, please,' he said. 'I feel loads better.'

'Not much wrong with you in the first place,' muttered Dad under his breath.

'Well, I'm going shopping today – last few presents to pick up,' said Mum, frowning at her husband. 'Great-Aunt Gail's looking after you today, so you'll have to ask her, and she's still asleep.'

Ned rolled his eyes at the way his parents neatly avoided shouldering any responsibility when they were busy, but the thought of being looked after by Great-Aunt Gail meant that someone would at least be sitting still long enough to listen to him instead of dashing around from one thing to the next or fixing him with a cold stare every time he entered the room. Sam, meanwhile, was bouncing up and down on his chair at the very mention of presents.

'How many sleeps till Father Christmas comes?' he yelled, desperate to be heard above the crash as Mum hurled clean pots and pans into an open cupboard as though something nasty and vicious were living in there.

'Five,' said Ned, feeling excited for the first time in days. 'Is there any toast left – I'm starving.'

'I'm not surprised,' Great-Aunt Gail's came voice from behind him as she sailed into the kitchen, resplendent in dressing gown and hairnet. 'You've had nothing but tangerines and grapes for the past three days. A growing boy like you needs plenty of food,' she said, skewering a battered old bamboo chopstick into her iron-grey hair. Sam immediately nestled onto Great-Aunt Gail's lap and began his habitual tracing of the characters that were engraved into the bamboo.

'Please tell me what the writing says,' he begged.

'My dear,' she teased, 'I can't for the life of me remember what it says. In fact, it's so, so old that I'm sure nobody on Earth can read it.'

'Now, William, would you be so good as to make a pot of tea, please? I had such a dreadful night, I barely slept a wink,' commanded Great-Aunt Gail as she took her seat at the table.

'Must have been someone else doing all the snoring, then,' said Dad, as he turned and filled the kettle.

'Did you say something? I do wish people wouldn't mutter – it's so rude. And by the way, William, your snoring was absolutely dreadful last night. It made the windowpanes rattle, I'm sure of it.'

Sam giggled at this while Dad turned round mouthing the words, 'Me? Snore?' in mock indignation.

Eyeing his dad warily, Ned waited until Great-Aunt Gail had taken her first sip of tea – then, and only then would he have the slightest chance of getting a favourable reply to the question that was burning on his lips.

'Great-Aunt Gail,' he asked, as the china teacup was placed reverently back on its saucer and a sigh of contentment had escaped Great-Aunt Gail's lips. 'Great-Aunt Gail, could I play outside today? Only for a little while. I'll dress warmly, I promise.'

Ned knew that even with the soothing effect that tea had on Great-Aunt Gail he'd have to keep the begging to an absolute minimum. Great-Aunt Gail turned in her seat to face Ned, brushing a stray lock of grey hair back into her hairnet.

'Yes, you may. But you mustn't overdo it, and you must come in when I tell you to,' she said, her stern blue eyes looking directly into Ned's.

'Thanks, Great-Aunt Gail, you're the best,' said Ned, as he gave Great Aunt Gail a hug and began capering round the kitchen with an energy that had long-deserted his parents.

A yell of 'Breakfast first' from Mum brought him skidding to a halt, as a plate of toast and scrambled eggs was deposited on the table as bait to end his headlong charge around the kitchen. A few minutes later, after polishing off his first proper meal in days, Ned careered out of the kitchen and charged upstairs, leaving behind a trail of toast crumbs. As he threw his clothes on, Ned bounced onto his bed and glanced out of the skylight. What he saw stopped him in his tracks. The mighty oak that had stood in the school playground for as long as anyone could remember looked as though it had been cleaved by a giant's axe. One huge branch lay where it had crashed through the play area, demolishing the swings and wooden play fort that Ned and Sam had so often used as cover, its very tips brushing against the wall of school assembly hall. The tree that remained standing looked sadly diminished; the awful tear in its trunk where the branch had split away made Ned think of a mortally wounded hero breathing his last. Ned watched as a lone magpie flew to the wound and, flapping furiously, began pecking at something caught in the exposed wood.

'One for sorrow,' murmured Ned, reciting the first line of the rhyme his mother had taught him when he was Sam's age.

Time and time again the bird hovered, scrabbling for a foothold on the split trunk, all the while pecking frantically, before flying to a branch to rest until launching its next attack. Startled, the bird flew from the tree and perched on the school roof, bobbing and flicking its tail, its raucous call rattling over the schoolyard. Ned craned his neck to see what had caused the bird to take flight and could just make out the sound of the padlock that secured the school gates being unlocked, followed by a clattering rattle as unseen hands pulled the chain through the bars and swung the gates open. A few moments later Ned spied Mr Swanson, wrapped up against the cold weather, walking briskly across the schoolyard. He watched as the old janitor stopped and surveyed the scene of destruction and, after checking that the fallen timber hadn't damaged the school, reached into his pocket and pulled out a phone; after a short pause he began speaking. Mr Swanson had always been quietly spoken and so Ned had difficulty in picking up what was being said, only catching the name 'Mrs Sharp', the head teacher, as Swanson said goodbye.

'Come on, Ned.'

Sam's shout was loud enough to make Mr Swanson look up from his survey; catching sight of Ned, he gave a friendly wave. Ned returned the wave and ducked back into his room, leapt from the bed and hopped across his bedroom floor while struggling to tug his socks on.

'Come on, Ned – let's go and play.'

Sam's impatience had by now got the better of him and he, too, had raced up the stairs to Ned's room and was jumping up and down.

'Sam, Sam, the school tree's been hit by lightning.' Ned was still hopping up and down, partly in an effort to keep balance as he continued to fight with his sock, and partly at the thought of all the things they could do on the branch that lay across the playground.

'Really? Is it on fire?' asked Sam, his bright blue eyes wide with excitement.

'No, but there's a huge branch fallen down in the

playground. It's massive – we can pretend it's a Viking ship if you want.' Ned knew that Sam's adoration of anything Viking-related would later help persuade him to join in even the most daring of plans.

Hurtling downstairs into the hallway, the boys nearly collided with Great-Aunt Gail who, summoned by the clanging doorbell, bustled from the kitchen wiping her hands on a tea towel. Pulling the door open revealed Mr Swanson, hands stuffed deep into his pockets. Seeing that it was Great-Aunt Gail who answered, he quickly pulled his hands out, and, standing upright, lifted his deerstalker hat from his head.

'Good morning, Mrs Hastings, are you looking after the boys today?' he asked, trying to brush his thick white hair into something that didn't resemble a wild shrub.

'Hello, Mr Swanson,' she replied. 'Yes, giving their mother a bit of a break. Now, how can I help you?'

'I thought I'd better tell you that the oak tree in the school playground has taken bit of a beating, and one of the big branches has split off. It's still attached to the trunk and so it could be dangerous,' he said, looking pointedly at the two boys as they hovered behind Great-Aunt Gail.

'Don't you worry, Mr Swanson, they're not going anywhere near the schoolyard today. Besides, Ned's only just getting over a nasty virus and so he won't be out long enough to cause trouble.'

'And I'd stay clear of the Dell too – I expect there'll be a fair few fallen trees there as well,' said Mr Swanson.

Mr Swanson was always warning children away from the huge, tree-filled crater that lay near the school adding to the mystery that surrounded it.

'The Devil himself burst from Hell and that's the hole he made,' he'd once told Ned and Sam as they'd

23

helped him do his chores around the school.

'And sometimes Old Nick still sends up bolts of lightning when he's in a temper,' he'd teased, when Ned had quizzed him about flashes of light he'd seen coming from the Dell in the dead of night.

Ned and Sam exchanged a knowing look, both aware that once plans had begun to hatch, they had to be carried out no matter what the risk. Great-Aunt Gail thanked Mr Swanson, and wishing him goodbye, turned to the boys and planted her hands firmly on her hips.

'Now, I'm going to make the rash assumption that you not only heard, but also listened to and understood what Mr Swanson has just said. Sam. Ned,' she said to the boys, naming them each in turn in order to leave them in no doubt whatsoever that they were being spoken to.

'Yes, Great-Aunt Gail,' the boys intoned dutifully.

'I'll be keeping a close eye on you now, so don't try anything silly.'

With Great-Aunt Gail's words of warning fading rapidly from their minds, Ned and Sam hauled on their trainers and raincoats and tumbled out of the door in a tangle of boisterous excitement. Jostling and pushing as he and his brother raced round the corner of the house, Ned was already plotting what to do with the branch. By the time they'd reached the swings at the end of the garden, he had made up his mind.

'We've got to do a dare, Sam,' he declared, as they mounted the swings and kicked off, each trying to out-swing the other. The swings creaked in accompaniment as Ned whispered his plan to Sam.

Chapter Four

The Broken Tree

Ned jabbed Sam in the ribs and hissed.

'Is she at the sink?'

'No, I can't see her anywhere,' Sam replied, peering carefully over the kitchen windowsill.

'Quick, then, let's go for the Tunnel.'

The Tunnel was, in fact, just a small hole in the bottom of the hedge that the boys used to sneak through into an out-of-bounds area of the school grounds. Once inside the Tunnel, the boys were hidden from view, giggling excitedly at their daring. Picking a twig from his collar, Ned leopard-crawled to the far end of the Tunnel, enjoying the secret world inside the hedge.

'Coast's clear,' Ned whispered over his shoulder to Sam, who was squirming and squeezing his way past Ned. 'Get off me, numpty, you're squashing me.'

Sam squirmed and fought all the harder.

'I want to go first,' he protested. 'You always go lead scout, it's not fair.'

'I'm eldest, I have to go first to make sure it's safe for you,' Ned whispered back, as he wriggled out from under his brother and scrambled out into the open. 'Wait here, soldier and keep your eyes peeled.'

Sam immediately manned an imaginary machine-gun and aimed it across the playground at Mr Swanson's cottage. A few moments later, Ned reappeared.

'All clear,' he announced, giving Sam the thumbs up. Sam returned the thumbs up and, joining Ned, followed closely on his heels to the front of the school.

Like thieves, the two boys slunk alongside walls, sneaked between buildings and froze when they heard footsteps crossing the schoolyard. They breathed out, relieved to hear the rattle of a key in the school gate lock, followed by the clattering of a chain being laced through its iron railings.

'Mr Swanson must be leaving for the day,' whispered Ned. 'The place is ours now.'

Grinning to each other, the boys dodged enemy bullets as they sprinted across open ground to the fallen branch. After a quick check to make sure they weren't being watched, the boys surveyed the new addition to their playground.

'I bet it weighs a thousand tons – look what it's done to the swings,' squeaked Sam.

'At least a thousand, probably two,' said Ned, offering his elder brother expert opinion.

'Wow, really? Two thousand tons!' Sam gasped in awe, both at his brother's knowledge and the enormous number.

'Let's see if we can climb from one end to the other without touching the ground,' said Ned, leading the way to the far tip of the fallen limb where the thinnest branches reached, grasping for the school. Threading through the crown proved difficult at first as the brothers picked their way through a mass of fine branches, but as they reached the thicker branches, they were able to monkey and shimmy their way toward the main branch with ease. Once on the branch, the boys scampered along its broad back until it grew too steep for Sam to climb.

'I can't go any further,' he complained in frustration. 'It's too hard, I'll fall off.'

Ned, being the big, brave elder brother, carried on, carefully picking his way up the last steep section to where it still remained attached to the tree by splinters as thick as a man's leg. Grasping one of the splinters in both hands, Ned hauled himself up until he was perched against the tree trunk. He could now see what the magpie had been so eagerly attacking. From the surface of the wound protruded a small curved piece of metal, gleaming dully in the winter light. As Ned hooked his finger into the semicircle of metal and tugged, he felt a warm, tingling shock spread up his arm and throughout his body. Moments later a fierce, bitter gust of wind appeared from nowhere and shrieked and tugged at him, threatening to topple him from his precarious seat and dash him to the playground below. Ned clung to the tree, reeling not just from the wind that had left his eyes streaming, but also from the sensation he had felt when he'd tried to pull the object free.

'Ned, I'm scared. That wind scared me. It all went black,' came a timid cry from below.

In his excitement and fear, Ned had forgotten all about Sam.

'It's OK, Sam, I'll be down in a second,' he called.

Again Ned reached out, more tentatively this time, and tried to free the piece of metal, which moved ever so slightly as he tugged at it. Again, a warm, glowing sensation, more powerful than before, ran up his arm and again, a vicious wind, stronger and angrier than before, blasted him with ice and sleet, stinging and whipping the exposed skin of his hands and face and driving him away from the object.

'Third time lucky,' Ned muttered to himself, as Sam once again called out in fear.

This time, as the warmth spread up his arm and the wind pummelled him, something happened that was far, far worse than the wind that had battered him.

'Ned Penhallow, what on earth do you think you are doing?'

They had been spotted by Great-Aunt Gail, who was now booming with anger from Ned's bedroom window.

'Get down from there at once!'

Ned, torn between trying once more to free his discovery and further incurring the wrath of his great-aunt, carefully clambered from his perch and, sliding and scuffling back down the branch, joined Sam, who was by now in floods of tears, but who helped him down onto the playground.

Great-Aunt Gail had by now rushed from the house and stood at the school gate, where Mr Swanson, too, had appeared, his eyes wide with alarm as he quickly unlocked it. As the only barrier between them and Great-Aunt Gail swung open, its screaming hinges adding to the feeling of doom, Ned stepped in front of Sam and stood firm.

'Don't shout at Sam,' his own eyes now filling with tears. 'It was my idea,' he added bravely as Great-Aunt Gail, who in her fury had grown to twice her normal size, bore down on them. As Great-Aunt Gail grabbed them both by the scruff of the neck and marched them past Mr Swanson, Ned glanced remorsefully at the school caretaker.

'Sorry,' he whispered, eyes dropping to the ground.

'Three bitter winds will blow, and a fourth will see it free again,' was Mr Swanson's reply. 'There will be others who come seeking it. Beware now.' Mr Swanson's words followed Ned as he was hauled from the playground. Craning his neck round, he could see Mr Swanson frowning, as though trying to remember something from the far distant past.

Chapter Five

Ned and the Ring

'I do declare that your heads do not function properly – take your ears, for instance – they only pick up three words – chocolate, Christmas and television – all the others seem to bounce off. And your mouths – permanently open with either food going in one way or noise coming out the other – both in high volumes, I may add, and quite often at the same time. And as for your noses – either snot running out or fingers rummaging in. You could have fallen from that branch and done Heaven knows what to yourselves. Or worse, it could have fallen on you and killed you.'

With Great-Aunt Gail's well-chosen but frighteningly accurate words still ringing in their ears, the boys had been dismissed from the kitchen and sent to their rooms until lunchtime, when a short, barked command of 'Lunch!' had been fired up the stairs. The meal had been a silent, icy affair as all three sat at the kitchen table and munched through the sandwiches that Great-Aunt Gail had prepared for them. The only time the silence had been broken was when Ned and Sam made eye contact and had been unable to stifle a giggle. A Medusa glare from their great aunt had reminded the boys that they were not yet back in favour.

'Right.' Great-Aunt Gail's voice had made the boys jump. 'You, Ned can clear the table and wash the dishes. Sam, I would like you to dry them, please.'

'Can't we just put them in the dishwasher?' said Ned.

Great-Aunt Gail replied with a single stern look.

Clearly, the afternoon was not going to involve much in the way of laughter and festive jollity. Ned picked up each plate, careful not to clatter them together, and began running hot water into the sink. Desperate to see if anyone had come to look for his discovery, he tried in vain to peer out of the window.

'I would imagine that by now Mr Swanson has arranged for someone to come and chop that branch up.'

With a guilty start, Ned pulled his head back from the window, leaving behind a sticky, ghostly imprint where his cheek had pressed against the cold glass.

'Once you've done those, there's the cupboard under the stairs – it needs a good tidy up. You can both help me.'

Ned groaned inwardly – the stairs were in a part of the house furthest from the school and gave absolutely no chance for him to watch for anybody climbing the tree. After endless hours of sorting through coats, boots, shoes and mouldy old rucksacks that smelt of mice, Great-Aunt Gail announced that it was time for tea and that they were to wash their hands. Freed at last from the musty confines of the cupboard, Ned and Sam raced upstairs and into the bathroom. Ned hastily washed his hands and, nearly tripping over his brother, leaped up onto the toilet seat and peered out of the small window that only grown-ups could reach.

In the light cast by a nearby street light, Ned saw that no one had set to sawing up the fallen branch. Just as he was about to step down from his vantage point, Ned spotted a movement in the shadows that lurked at the base of the tree; something, no, someone was standing looking up at the wound in the tree's side. Ned watched, his breath caught in his throat, as the figure melted back into the shadows.

'Tea is ready!' Great-Aunt Gail's shout made Ned jump, so much so that he slipped and barked his shin painfully against the toilet. Clutching his wounded leg, Ned reluctantly made his way downstairs, his face drawn into a worried frown by what he'd just seen and Mr Swanson's chilling words as Great-Aunt Gail had marched them off the playground. 'There will be others who come seeking it, Ned. Beware, now.'

'What on earth is wrong, Ned?' asked Great-Aunt Gail when Ned finally appeared and sat down quietly at the kitchen table. 'You normally charge to the table as though you haven't eaten for a week. You're not ailing again are you?'

'No, sorry, I'm fine. Just tired.'

'An early night for you, then.'

'I'm really sorry about the tree, Great-Aunt Gail. Please don't tell Dad.'

Great-Aunt Gail looked at Ned and, for the first time since hauling the boys inside, her expression softened.

'I'll have to tell your mother, but there's no need for your father to know. Boys will be boys,' she said, gently stroking Ned's fringe into a parting.

As promised, Ned and Sam were trooped off to bed at a horribly early hour, but not before receiving a severe telling off from Mum. With threats of a month of no television ringing in his ears, Ned closed his bedroom door and leaped across the room and onto his bed. Heaving the window open, Ned peered through the darkness, desperate to pick out the figure again.

Much later, when Mum and Dad had gone to bed and Great-Aunt Gail had left for the night, Ned lay awake in his bed listening carefully. In the house, no one stirred, only the house made any noises, creaking and muttering to itself as it, too, settled and began to slumber. Ned slid from under his covers and quickly dressed. After one last peek out of the window at the tree, he carefully tiptoed his way across the room and down the stairs, freezing once when he heard Sam muttering in his sleep. At the bottom of the stairs he turned left and carefully sneaked open the door of the cupboard that he, Sam and Great-Aunt Gail had cleaned out hours earlier. Under the pile of discarded coats and shoes they had come across Dad's long-lost tool box and it was this that Ned now opened, and from the jumble of tools inside, pulled a sharp chisel and a heavy mallet, and after wrapping each in an old T-shirt, slipped them carefully into his school rucksack.

Creeping through the house, Ned made his way to the kitchen and eased open the window. The cold night air nipped at him and sent goosebumps running up his arms as he clambered onto the sill and lowered first his rucksack, and then himself, onto the frosty grass below. Night-time had swathed the village in its cloak, and not a breath of wind stirred as the full moon cast the world in silver and black. The blackest, stealthiest of shadows filled the garden, each one hiding a slavering, fanged monster waiting to feed on Ned as he slunk by. The occasional rustle in the undergrowth and the mournful, lonely hoot of an owl were the only sounds to reach Ned's ears as he crouched and ducked into the Tunnel. Crawling through and emerging from the far end, Ned expected a clutching, withered hand to reach down and grasp his exposed neck as he left the sanctuary of the hedge.

The front of the school was bathed in the searchlight-bright silvery moon. Ned stuck as close to the wall as possible, squeezing himself in to what little shadow was cast by the newly repaired and painted bird tables that Mr Swanson had placed there. He paused at the corner of the school and peered nervously round. The inky shadows that surrounded the base of the tree were large and deep enough to hide not just one person but several, and it was these that Ned watched intently until he began to shudder with cold. Nothing stirred in the shadows, and in the stillness of the night it was as though the whole world was holding its breath, watching and waiting for Ned to act.

Carefully, Ned edged round the corner of the school and, as quietly as he could, darted to where the top of the branch touched the school. Once in amongst the topmost branches, Ned felt safer, and he crawled through the tangled mass and into the shadow that ran the length of the fallen branch. Nothing, not even the faintest rustle of the tiniest mouse, could be heard. Using the finger-deep cracks that ran like canyons in the tree bark, Ned scampered nimbly on to the branch and slowly wormed his way along until he reached the steep climb that led to the trunk. Like a mourner's veil, the dark shadow of the tree threw itself over Ned, immersing him in blackness as he reached up and grasped a handhold below his perch. Anything could appear from below and sink its teeth into the exposed flesh of his calf and drag him away. A dreadful grunting, snorting sound came from below him. Something was coming for him, something that had waited until he was too close to escape. From the shadow appeared a badger. Ned let out a long shuddering breath that startled the animal, which, after one curious look at the boy in the tree, continued its nocturnal foraging.

Thinking that nothing more could frighten him that night, Ned hauled himself up once more to the wound in the tree's side. There, in a patch of moonlight, lay the object that he had first seen so many hours ago.

Looking around him, Ned saw that the whole playground was now engulfed in dense shadows, and looking up he could see that a single towering cloud had eclipsed the moon's silvery light. Turning back to his discovery, Ned saw that what he had thought was moonlight was light coming from the object itself.

Shrugging his rucksack off, Ned drew out the mallet and chisel and, steadying the chisel against the wood, drew the mallet back and struck. So still was the night that the thud of mallet on chisel rang as loud as a cannon. Nervously, Ned glanced round to see if any lights were being switched on in the houses that surrounded the school. None were, so Ned once again struck the chisel, sending it deeper into the wood. He wiggled it free, then set the chisel below the object and struck again. Becoming more confident with each blow, Ned quickly hewed a moat around the object, stopping only once when a car, and a police car at that, drove slowly past the school gates. Arms straining and teeth set, Ned put all of his weight and strength into one mighty heave and levered the object clear and, as it fell from its confinement, he reached out instinctively and caught it in the palm of his hand.

The very moment that the metal touched Ned's outstretched hand, a burst of painfully cold sleet slashed across his face and from nowhere came a fierce shrieking wind that hauled at his hair and clothing with such strength that it felt as though fingers were twisting themselves out of the wind and tearing and pulling at him. With his free arm, Ned clung desperately to the shards of timber that stuck out from the trunk. Still the wind continued to shriek and howl, trying to hurl him bodily into the boiling shadows that were rising from below. Hail as well as sleet now spattered painfully against the exposed skin of his hands and face. Ned began

35

to shudder and moan with cold and terror, his hands now throbbing with the agonising cold. The fallen branch gave a sudden lurch as it too began to succumb to the brutal onslaught. As Ned began to slip from his perch, bullied and pummelled by the savage wind, heat spread from within the hand that still clasped his find and, as he watched, light began to shine from between his fingers, bringing with it a beautiful warmth. With all the colours of a summer's dawn, the light blossomed until it completely encased Ned. The cruel wind that had so nearly flung Ned to the ground still blew, beating and screaming with fury, but now shying away as the light grew stronger still, its barrage of icy hail and sleet harmlessly fizzling out as it met the edge of the light.

Uncurling his fingers, Ned looked for the first time at what he had freed from the tree. The ring that lay in his palm was battered and scratched with ancient scars, the outer rim woven with intricate figures that swarmed and flowed as though the metal was liquid. The light that burned from it gave one large pulse before falling back into the ring, leaving only the glow of the moon gleaming on its surface. The wind, now vanquished, had fallen away to nothing. Looking down, Ned could see that at the base of the tree lay a drift of sleet and hail. Elsewhere all was peaceful, the night as undisturbed as it had been when Ned had first climbed onto the fallen limb. Even the school bell, which would ring in the lightest of breezes, hung still and silent. Taking care to remove all evidence of his visit, Ned slipped the tools into his rucksack and dropped it from his perch and onto the ground before sliding down the branch and onto the playground, the ring clutched tightly in his hand.

Picking up the rucksack, Ned darted across the school grounds and once again gained the safety of the

Tunnel. Rustling through the leaves, he crawled into the garden, sprinted across to the kitchen window and scrabbled back into the house, taking care not to clang his rucksack against the sink. Once inside, Ned crept up to his room, wincing as one of the stairs grumbled at the cheekiness of this late night disturbance. In his bedroom, he clicked on his bedside light and shoved the rucksack far under his bed, along with his sodden clothes. Ned pulled the bottom drawer out of his bedside cabinet and carefully placed the ring alongside his other contraband. Before diving under his covers, Ned peered once more out into the night. The playground and the tree were once again bathed in silvery moonlight. Had Ned watched for longer, he would have seen a shadow, tall and capped by an outlandish hat, detach itself from the darkness at the base of the tree and walk away towards the village church.

Chapter Six

Darkness Gathers

A twig snapped loudly somewhere in the nearby gloom. Whatever had broken it had crashed off into the dense forest that surrounded them.

Sam's voice quavered in the gloom.

'Ned, I'm scared.'

'There's nothing to be scared of,' said Ned, trying to sound braver than he felt.

'What was that animal in the bushes?' Sam whispered.

'Probably only a little bunny rabbit. Or maybe a mummy deer looking after its baby,' Ned replied.

The two boys continued picking their way along the narrow, rutted path, occasionally snagging their feet on hidden roots. A thin mist began to smoke from the ground on either side and gradually drifted across, obscuring the path. Something to their left leapt up from the dense undergrowth and galloped away, causing the mist to swirl.

'There is something out there, Ned, and it's big,' moaned Sam.

'It was a deer, I saw it, honest,' Ned lied, trying his best to calm Sam's mounting panic. 'It probably smelled us and ran off.'

High above, in the thick pine canopy, an unseen bird screeched loudly and took flight with a rapid clatter of wings that made the boys jump.

Sam began to whimper more earnestly now, and clutched at Ned's sleeve.

'I don't like it in here, Ned. Where did Mum and Dad go?' Ned didn't know. He couldn't remember at exactly which point he and Sam had become separated from Mum and Dad, or why indeed they'd chosen to walk in these woods so far from home.

'I'm not sure, Sam, but we're definitely heading back towards the car; they'll be there for sure, or someone will be, at least.'

'OK,' said Sam in a small voice, now holding his big brother's hand and looking up at him in worship. He even managed a small smile.

'That's better, Sam, I'm sure we're pretty close – I recognise that big tree over there.'

Even in the dim half-light of the forest, Ned could make out the broad trunk of an ancient beech tree that dwarfed the surrounding conifers.

'I'll race you to it,' Sam yelled, slipping his hand from Ned's and sprinting away.

Ned tried to follow, but instead foundered in the now waist-deep mist.

'Sam, no, stop!' he yelled in panic, as Sam disappeared into the mist.

'Stop, Sam, I can't move!' Ned was now screaming at the top of his voice. Sam turned around, laughing, and shouted back to his big brother.

'Come on, slowcoach, I'm going to win.'

Ned watched, bound helpless in the mist, as the bark of the beech tree began to wrinkle and bulge and a hideous face burst from it. A pair of triumphant eyes glowed above a vicious hooked nose, and below the nose the trunk split apart to reveal a ragged mouth lined with savage teeth, each as tall as a man. Still Sam ran towards the tree, eyes alight with laughter as he looked back. Ned thrashed his body from side to side, desperately trying to pull his legs free of the mist, but no matter how hard he tried to move the mist held him fast, powerless to stop Sam's headlong rush toward the tree. Sam turned and saw what the trunk had become and his scream of terror joined Ned's. Desperately trying to back-pedal, Sam tripped and fell and, with a gleeful snarl, the tree sent a root springing from the ground to wrap itself around Sam's waist and with a lazy flick, tossed him kicking and screaming through the air and into its gaping maw.

Ned's hoarse scream echoed around his bedroom as he sat bolt upright in a tangle of sweaty bedclothes. Even as his brain fluttered awake, he could feel a dreadful malevolence within his room and as his eyes focused he saw that the ceiling had warped itself into a twisted, leering face that bulged and loomed over him, yellow eyes glinting with malice. A horrible cold voice uncoiled itself and slithered through Ned's mind, bringing with it images of terrible dark places and shadows filled with beasts that glared with shining, hungry eyes and snarled with razor teeth.

'Bring me the ring, boy,' said the voice. 'It is rightfully mine, and mine alone, bring it to me. You must give it me. You have so much that you love. So much that you could lose. Bring me the ring.'

Ned cowered against his bedstead as the terrible visage pressed itself further into the room, mimicking Sam's pitiful scream for help and filling the room with a powerful stench of rotting meat. With the drumming of footsteps up the stairs, the diabolical face swirled away, leaving the ceiling blank once more. The door banged open as Ned's father flew into the room, tatty dressing gown flapping around his pyjama bottoms.

'Ned, wake up. You're having a bad dream,' his father snapped irritably, grabbing hold of Ned and shaking him roughly.

Cowering tearfully under his father's shouting, Ned watched in horror as the wall opposite swirled briefly, and one livid yellow eye appeared that, before disappearing completely, dropped a leering wink.

Chapter Seven

After the Nightmare

Plodding down the stairs, Ned could hear his father's voice grumbling up from the kitchen, and he froze, with a familiar churning in his stomach. Today was Dad's late start at the university, and he wouldn't be leaving to deliver his only lecture of the day for another half an hour. That meant he'd probably be home early, too.

'Screaming about something. A nightmare, probably, the big baby,' his father said, disgust in his voice.

'He's eleven years old, he's still a child. I think you're being unfair,' Great-Aunt Gail's voice too drifted up. Ned relaxed slightly, knowing that while Mum was out on her morning run, someone at least would be on his side if Dad started yelling at him again.

'I didn't sleep again after that.'

'We all lose sleep over our children, it's part of being a parent.'

'You don't have any,' came Dad's terse reply.

'I've cared for those who were as close to me as though they were my own children. And lost them, too.'

The strength with which Great-Aunt Gail spoke silenced Ned's father. Ned continued his journey down the stairs, and crept into the frosty, silent kitchen. Hearing Ned mumble a timid greeting to his father, Great-Aunt Gail turned from the stove where she was stirring a large pot of porridge, and smiled warmly at him.

'Good morning, slugabed. It's ten o'clock don't

you know, and it's a bright sunny day outside.'

'I didn't sleep very well.' Ned yawned, pulling a plate of toast towards himself, flinching slightly as his father grunted at his last comment.

'Sam's not awake yet, either. Were you two cheeky monkeys up having a midnight feast?' Great-Aunt Gail asked, raising an eyebrow. Goosebumps leaped up Ned's arms as the mention of Sam's name brought back his nightmare in vivid detail.

'I'll go and see if he's alright,' said Ned, noisily scraping back his chair and earning another scowl of disapproval from his father.

Leaping up the stairs two at a time, Ned crept silently into his younger brother's bedroom. Tousled curly hair poked over the top of a dinosaur duvet and Sam grunted in his sleep, pudgy little hands clutching a well-worn cloth. After the night's events – the vicious squall that bit as he freed the ring, the light that burst from the ring driving the wind away, and then the terrible nightmare – Ned felt terror welling up inside, not just for himself, but for his little brother, who slept innocently.

'Don't wake him up,' a voice hissed from the doorway, making Ned jump. Dad had crept up the stairs and stood glowering in the doorway.

'He's still fast asleep, Dad. Shall I see if he's OK?' Ned asked.

'No, leave him alone. You've probably given him the virus that you had.'

Ned cringed under this accusation, half-expecting his father to drag him downstairs and begin shouting again. Instead, his father turned and ambled away bear-like to the bathroom for his morning shower. As Sam rolled in his sleep and grasped for his cloth, Ned saw a livid red band around his waist, purpling to a bruise in places. Ned stared in horror. In his dream, Sam had been picked up by his waist, a thick, wicked root cruelly digging into his flesh. Panic scrabbled at the back of his throat. He wanted to put the ring back, hammer it as far as he could back into the tree trunk and close his eyes and crawl under his bed, pushing himself hard up against the wall as far as possible so nothing could find him.

With a loud yawn, Sam blinked and stretched himself awake. Not wanting his younger brother to see the horror on his face, Ned backed silently out of the room before Sam was fully awake and returned to the kitchen to finish his breakfast. Picking at the porridge that Great-Aunt Gail had dolloped in front of him, Ned eyed her back as she busied herself at the sink. Having wound himself up to speak, Ned's question escaped his lips only as a sob.

'Whatever is the matter, my dear?' asked Great-Aunt Gail, turning at the sound of the cry.

Tears now breached Ned's eyes and ran down his face.

'My tummy hurts,' said Sam, as he joined them.

Ned quickly cuffed his tears away with his pyjama sleeve.

'Oh, dear, how did you do that?' asked Great-Aunt Gail, pulling Sam's pyjama top up over his belly.

'It was the tree.'

Sam's reply sent Ned's mind reeling even further.

'What tree?' Dad, now ready for work, had overheard from the hallway and his bulk filled the kitchen doorway. 'Were you two mucking around on that branch yesterday? The one that the wind tore off? You were, weren't you? Have you any idea how dangerous it is?'

All this was directed at Ned's face from just a few inches away.

'I'm sorry,' mumbled Ned, knowing only too well how dangerous their antics had been, and how dangerous things were becoming.

'And well you should cry, too; just look at Sam's bruise!'

'It was the tree in my dream.'

'What do you mean, Sam?' asked Dad, kindly.

'I had a dream that me and Ned were lost in a forest and that a tree ate me.'

'See what you've done?'

Ned flinched as his father spun round and glared at him again.

'Your stupid antics have given the poor boy nightmares now.' With that Dad stomped from the kitchen, and with a slam of the front door he left the house.

'Right. Well, then, it sounds as though you two could do with a bit of a rest today.'

Ned was by now sobbing uncontrollably, tears coursing down his cheeks.

'Ned, whatever is the matter?'

'It's not your fault.' Sam's soft hand patted Ned clumsily on the head. 'You tried to save me from the tree. I know you'll come and save me.'

'Hmm, definitely too much excitement for you yesterday, Ned. I want you two to stay close today. No charging through hedges, and certainly no climbing trees. Sam, I shall ask your mother to have a look at that bruise when she gets back from her run.'

Chapter Eight

Sam's Paper Aeroplane

'Can you make me a paper aeroplane, please? Please, please, please.' The last three words were fired off in rapid succession, along with a spatter of toast crumbs, as Sam bounced onto the sofa where Ned sat staring out of the window, the television unwatched. Ned had to smile at this; no matter how sad and upset he felt, Sam could always make the sun break through his clouds.

'OK. What do you want it to be?' he asked, switching the television off.

'A P-51 Mustang. No, no, no a Spitfire.'

When not being a dragon-fighting pirate, Sam could be found with his head in a picture book of aeroplanes, his favourite plane changing daily.

'A Spitfire it is then,' agreed Ned. Although in truth all of the paper aeroplanes he made turned out looking exactly the same, to Sam they were, in his words, 'Cool'.

'You'll have to go and fetch some paper though – Dad'll go ballistic if he finds out I've been in his study.'

'OK,' said Sam, as he slid off the sofa and trotted merrily up the stairs singing a Christmas carol at the top of his voice. As the sound of his footsteps making their way across the study above reached his ears, Ned's attention was drawn back to the television which had somehow flickered back to life. Ned watched as the comical character on the screen leaped and joked around, turning cartwheels before performing a neat back flip, landing on his feet and bowing. As he watched, the character slowly began to melt and its skin flowed and fell away, revealing a figure dressed in black that stepped neatly away from the fallen disguise. The same twisted, leering face from the night before now pressed itself against the screen, making it bulge and writhe as it spoke.

'Are you listening, boy? I can't see you, but I can sense you – you've found the ring and that ring is rightfully mine!'

As the figure spoke the last word, it forced its face hard against the screen, stretching it even further until small cracks ran from the centre and a horrible thick yellow slime oozed from each one. Ned stumbled backwards, almost falling over a small coffee table as the face continued to rant and threaten.

'I'll haunt every dream and every thought you have. I'll rip the sun from your skies, and make every day cold and black. Bring me the ring, boy, bring me the ring or you'll lose everything you've ever loved and you'll spend the rest of your life lonely and miserable.'

'Here you are, here you are.'

Ned nearly screamed aloud as Sam dashed excitedly into the room, pressing a wad of printer paper into his hand.

'Here you are,' repeated Sam, 'here's some paper.' 'Make me a Spitfire, make a Spitfire, pleeeeease,' he squeaked as he grabbed Ned's arm and dragged him into the kitchen.

'OK, OK, just let me clear the table,' said Ned, pushing Sam in front of him, desperately trying to shield his younger brother from the awful figure on the screen.

'What on earth is wrong, Ned?' said Great-Aunt Gail as Ned accidentally tore the wing off his first attempt. 'You're as white as a sheet and shaking like a leaf.'

'Nothing, just something on the telly made me

jump that's all,' Ned replied looking nervously back into the lounge. To his horror the figure was conjuring up pictures of his family – Mum running, Dad smiling on one of the days long ago before his blackness came, Sam shouting with joy in seaside waves - and turning each one into flame and laughing with insane glee as the ashes fell through the screen and drifted like dirty snow to the carpet below.

'Well, seeing as you're not watching it, I'll turn it off, shall I?' said Great-Aunt Gail and, before Ned could protest, she sailed from the kitchen. Ned turned away rigid, fingernails digging into his palms, waiting for Great-Aunt Gail's scream as she saw what the screen held. Nothing came. No terrified scream, no shriek of horror, just a single word that Ned couldn't quite catch and the television screeching furiously as it went off.

'Well, I don't think we need to see that sort of garbage, do we, now?' said Great-Aunt Gail as she returned, pausing only to look in the mirror and adjust the bamboo chopstick that kept her immaculate bun in place.

Ned stared at his great-aunt as she returned to peeling potatoes at the sink, attacking each one with such vigour that pieces of peel ended up bouncing off the window.

'I promised your mother a decent meal this evening, one that actually requires cooking. If it was down to her we'd all be eating salad – even in this weather – which I do declare is getting colder by the minute.'

Risking a glance into the lounge, Ned could see the television standing silent, no cracked screen, no yellow ooze dripping to the floor below, no pile of grey ash on the carpet. Nothing to show that mere minutes before a maniacal figure had been trying to push its way through into Ned's world, all the while screaming the most evil threats and promises of misery.

'Come on, Ned, make another one,' said Sam, tugging at Ned's sleeve.

'OK, OK. Do you want to colour it in before I fold it?'

'No, no, no just make it,' said Sam, jumping up and down with excitement and running round the kitchen table, arms stuck out on either side.

'No aeroplanes in the kitchen, young man, go for a flight around the house and see if you can burn some of that energy off,' said Great-Aunt Gail, almost tripping over the exuberant Sam as he made yet another circuit of the kitchen table.

'Message received and understood, Squadron Leader,' shouted Sam, and he promptly exited the kitchen at full pelt and proceeded to race up and down the stairs while Ned began to carefully fold a piece of paper.

'Great-Aunt Gail,' said Ned, 'do you believe in the Devil?'

'Oh, what a peculiar question. Have you been reading a book about monsters or something?'

'No, I was just wondering – I mean, Mr Swanson says the Devil made the Dell, and I was wondering if the stories were true about it being haunted by his demons.'

'Now, really, I wouldn't go listening to that rubbish – Mr Swanson's just pulling your leg. He just wants to keep you away from the Dell.'

'I like the Dell, though – it always feels safe to me when I play there.'

'Oh, I'm sure it is, my poppet, but don't stray too far into it, it goes further than most people realise.' Great-Aunt Gail turned from the sink and almost collided with the hurtling ball of energy that was banking sharply round the kitchen table. 'Samuel Penhallow, I do believe I asked

you to take your flying elsewhere, young man,' she
shouted

'Sorry, Great-Aunt Gail, I'm outta here,' shouted
Sam over his shoulder, as he exited the kitchen again.

'What about wizards?' asked Ned, as peace settled
once more and he knew that Sam's ears wouldn't
overhear.

'Hmm, what do you mean?' said Great-Aunt Gail,
returning to the potatoes and dropping them with a splash
into a pan of cold water.

'Wizards. Are there such things as wizards?
Really horrible evil ones?'

'I can assure you that there is no such thing in this
world as an evil wizard, Ned, you really have nothing to
worry about.'

'Witches. What about witches?'

'Only good ones.'

'Werewolves?'

'Ned, really, what have you been filling your head
with?' said Great-Aunt Gail, turning from her cooking
and planting her fists firmly on her hips. 'There are no
such things as werewolves, or vampires, or mummies, or
anything else you care to name. Besides,' she continued,
sighing loudly, 'we don't need devils and demons and we
don't need evil wizards and witches; there are already
enough nasty, wicked people in the world who cause
misery for others purely because they're greedy and
selfish. Those are the people you need to worry about, not
some made up monster.'

'Now what shall I make for lunch – would you
two like spinach and cottage cheese sandwiches?'

'Urgggh, no thanks.'

'Thought not – best make it bacon sandwiches and
hot chocolate to wash them down with then, hadn't I?'

said Great-Aunt Gail, ruffling Ned's hair.

'Throw it again,' squealed Sam, face glowing with excitement. Ned, trying to shake the nightmare and the morning's horror from his head, picked the paper aeroplane up from its latest crash-landing and, after straightening the nose out for the hundredth time, launched the dart high into the air. The boys, once Great-Aunt Gail had decided that they were sufficiently bundled up against the plummeting temperature, had been ushered outside after one of Mum's vases had nearly become the victim of a strafing run.

'You can come back in when lunch is ready, and if you get bored in the meantime then you can always help Mr Swanson feed the birds. Now, go, and take the Battle of Britain outside, where it belongs.'

Since then Ned and Sam had delighted in the coldness of the day. The thick layer of frozen water in the rain barrel had soon been dropped onto the drive, each lump of broken ice being smashed again and again until frozen fingers had turned them back to their original game.

'Let's launch it from the swings,' said Ned, racing round to the back garden and hopping onto one of the frost-sparkled seats. 'It'll go even further if we do.'

Kicking off and swinging his legs back and forth until he gained height, Ned readied the plane for launch. As he swung through the air, his eyes streaming in the cold, Ned heard a deep, menacing chuckle coming from the Tunnel. Leaping from the swing, paper aeroplane clutched in one hand, he backed away from the hedge, pulling Sam with him.

'Come on, we'll go into the front garden,' he said, keeping one wary eye on the hedge.

'But what about the swings? You said it'll go even further,' protested Sam, as he struggled against Ned's desperate tugging.

Another horrible laugh rattled from the Tunnel.

'Er, we might lose it in the hedge if we do,' said Ned, his voice starting to shake. 'Come on, the front garden's better – we'll be able to see Mum when she comes home from running. Race you.'

'Lunch in ten minutes, you two,' shouted Great-Aunt Gail as they charged past the kitchen window. The mouth-watering smell of frying rashers made Sam stop dead in his tracks and press his nose up against the kitchen window.

'Bacon,' he drooled, wriggling with joy at the prospect of his second most favourite food.

'Come on,' urged Ned, 'we'll have hot chocolate, too, as long as you don't pester.'

'Chocolate!'

Sam, now utterly beside himself at the thought of a meal made up of both his favourites, had to be dragged bodily away from the window, leaving a sticky smudge mark where his nose had pressed. With a sigh of relief, Ned finally brought his struggling brother to the front garden. As they started to throw the aeroplane back and forth, a robin fluttered past and landed on one of the gateposts, where it stood bobbing and calling loudly in alarm.

'Is there a cat in the back garden again, birdy?' Sam asked the robin, and began to walk round the corner of the house. 'Don't worry, I'll go and scare it off for you.'

'No, there's nothing there,' said Ned, grabbing Sam by the back of his coat and hauling him back. 'Don't worry about the cat – we can always scare it off it comes round here. Right – make a circle with your arms. Let's see if I can fly the plane through it.'

For the next few minutes, Sam giggled and squealed at every near miss as Ned tried his best to keep Sam from running back to the back garden.

Chapter Nine

Smugley Smirkens

'Oh, wow! Look, Penhallow's managed to buy a piece of paper to play with.'

A strident, crowing voice cut across Sam and Ned's giggling antics, snapping them out of their game and sending the robin, which had been watching them all the while, flying away.

'How long did it take you to save up for that?' the voice taunted.

The owner of the voice, Smugley Smirkens, leered over the front hedge, his porky face gleeful as he teased Ned. When Smugley had moved to the village with his parents a year ago, he had made life for Ned unbearable at every opportunity, stealing his packed lunch at school and tipping out the contents of his school bag whenever their paths crossed. His parents, rude, vulgar and usually arguing loudly with one another, doted on Smugley and showered him with gifts throughout the year, one of which he held aloft now in one of his fat, grabby hands.

'Look what my Mum and Dad have given me as an early Christmas present – an iPad!' he yelled triumphantly.

Ned couldn't keep the look of envy from his face as Smugley waved his prize in the air.

'Is that baby aeroplane an early Christmas present, too? I bet it's made from old toilet paper.' This from one of Smugley's cronies, Ricky Stebbings, a clever but nasty boy with a face drawn into a permanent sneer. In truth Stebbings hated Smugley, but knew that if he wanted a quiet and bruise-free life, he'd best stick close to him and take part in whatever acts of nastiness Smugley was carrying out. Between them, Smirkens and Stebbings had had more visits to the head teacher, and more detentions, than all the pupils who had ever been to Weston Pewsey Primary School in its entire history put together.

'Huh, huh, huh.' The owner of the slow, clumsy laughter that drifted from behind Smirkens and Stebbings completed the trio – Michael 'Mikey' Hassall's lumpy, dull face appeared beside them, a broad, drooling grin blooming across his face as he finally caught on to what Smugley and Stebbings were laughing and shouting about.

Ned stooped and picked the aeroplane from the ground where it had landed, glad to be able to turn his burning face away from the taunts and jeers. As he stood upright, a half-empty drink can hit him on the back of his head with a loud 'clonk'. Screams of laughter followed, as a large splash of sticky drink ran down the inside of Ned's collar and trickled down his back.

'Oh, what a shot,' shouted Smugley spitefully, and he began to hop around in a victory dance.

'Have a drink on me. Oh, so sorry, I seemed to have spilt it,' yelled Stebbings, sending Smugley into howls of laughter.

'Er, his coat's all wet.' Hassall stood frowning, trying to work out how the can had ended up at Ned's feet.

'Of course it's wet, you numpty, I just threw a can of drink at him,' spat Stebbings, landing a sharp slap on the back of Hassall's roughly shaven head.

Furious, Ned picked the can up and flung it with all his might, catching Smugley straight between the eyes and sending the last few dregs splashing over him. Silence rang out over the group. Smugley stood speechless – nobody had ever, ever stood up to him before. Ned stood speechless – he had never, ever stood up to anyone, least of all Smugley Smirkens.

Smugley growled, and he passed his iPad to a stunned Stebbings.

'You're going to pay for that, Penhallow, you little weed,' he bellowed, and tearing his coat off, began pushing his way through the front gate. As Ned began to back away, Sam burst into loud tears and ran to Ned's side.

'Leave him alone, you big bully,' he yelled, trying to stand between Smugley and Ned, despite only being half as tall as Smirkens.

'Go inside, Sam, quickly,' stuttered Ned, his voice high with terror as the advancing Smugley loomed closer.

Normally Smugley enjoyed this bit the most, the look of utter terror on his victim's face as he advanced, all the while grinning horribly and showering the poor soul who had unwittingly drifted into his view with all manner of horrible names. But not this time; this time Smugley meant business, and his business was to hurt Ned Penhallow, and hurt him badly, because nobody, but nobody, got the better of Smugley Smirkens.

Ned backed as far away from Smugley as he could, shoving a now hysterical Sam out of danger as he did so. The back of his head cracked painfully against the front door of his house as he stumbled backwards over the doorstep and landed with a painful thump that left him winded.

'Here, let me help you up,' snarled Smugley through his unbrushed teeth, foul breath blowing hot and fetid into Ned's face. Smugley's meaty hands grabbed

Ned by the lapels and with a grunt he hauled him upright before slamming him against the door hard enough to make Ned's teeth rattle in his head.

As Smugley cocked one large fist back and took careful aim at his nose, Ned could make out one noise above the loud thudding of his heart in his ears and the terrified sobbing of his younger brother – the sound of the robin once again calling in alarm.

Chapter Ten

The Garden Gate

'Oh, no you don't, laddie!'

Great-Aunt Gail's strident command made everyone jump.

'Just what in all the worlds do you think you are doing? Let go of him at once and get out of this garden. How dare you!'

Great-Aunt Gail, in full fury, strode across the lawn. Her seismic presence shook the world around them, petrifying all five of the boys. Smugley let out a cry of terror as her hand reached toward the chopstick stuck in her hair as though she were going to pluck it free and skewer him with it. Dropping Ned, he turned on his heel and promptly tripped over his own clumsy feet and fell sprawling face first onto the gravel drive.

'Waaaah! Ow, ow, ow, ow,' screamed Smugley, holding up his hands which had taken the brunt of the fall. 'Look at my hands! Look at my hands – they're bleeding, they're bleeding. I'm going to tell my mum on you.'

'Oh, shush your blubbing, you big baby, there's barely a mark on you,' said Great-Aunt Gail as, with one hand, she grabbed Smugley by the scruff of the neck and hauled him wailing to his feet.

'Get off me, get off me!' yelled Smugley, fighting free and once again falling, this time onto his rather large backside.

'Now look what you've done,' he bawled, before scrabbling back to his feet and darting through the garden gate. Dashing down the road with Stebbings and Hassall in tow, Smugley continued to shout all manner of threats and insults at Ned.

'What a dreadful, dreadful child. Where did he learn language like that?' exclaimed an outraged Great-Aunt Gail. She turned to Ned and Sam. 'Did he hit either of you?'

'No, he wouldn't dare hit Sam, it was me he was after.'

'Why was he in the garden?'

'I threw a can at him. He threw it first though!' cried Ned.

'What a horrible boy. Why on Earth did he throw it at you?'

'He was teasing me because we were playing with this,' he said, holding up the now forlorn-looking paper aeroplane, a veteran of a hundred dogfights and crash-landings.

'Well, I'd rather you played with that than fill your brains with electronic tripe,' declared Great-Aunt Gail.

Ned, though, wholeheartedly disagreed, knowing full well that he'd never own anything as flash as a computer or an iPad, and that given the chance he'd quite happily blast electronic zombies to kingdom come, even if it did mean filling his brains with tripe.

'Well, why don't you spend a little more time playing with your plane? Those boys won't dare come back and I doubt the lovely Mrs Smirkens will bother us,' said Great-Aunt Gail.

'I'd rather throw it in the bin!' snapped Ned, fighting the urge to crush the plane into a ball and stamp it into the ground. The close call with Smugley and his gang, as well as the previous night's quest and the terror that had followed, were now taking their toll.

'Now, Ned, there really is no need for that. You've had a bit of an unpleasant tangle with a rather horrible child,' said Great-Aunt Gail. Kneeling down in front of Ned, she placed her hands on his shoulders and looked him deep in the eye.

'Ned, that boy is a bully. Nothing but a nasty, spineless little bully. He is nothing to be afraid of. Believe me when I tell you I've seen much, much worse, and they were no different. All spineless once you stand up to them. Now remember this, and remember it well – you, Ned, have done nothing wrong. Nothing. You are not a horrible boy. You are not a bad person. Do you hear me? You are not a bad person. Just remember that.'

'I'll try,' said Ned, as he cuffed tears away from his eyes and sniffed loudly. 'Where's Sam gone?'

'Oh, I don't know,' said Great-Aunt Gail, as she stood up and looked around. 'He's not on the road. Perhaps he's gone to play on the swings.'

Terror snapped at Ned's heels as he hurtled around the corner of the house and to his utter horror saw Sam crouching at the entrance to the Tunnel, laughing and giggling merrily away at something Ned couldn't see.

'Sam, get away from there,' he yelled, yanking hard on the back of his little brother's coat, hard enough to pull him off his feet and send him sprawling onto the frost-hardened ground with a thud.

'Hey, what did you do that for? I was watching the funny man!' yelled Sam indignantly, tears welling up.

'Ned, really, your poor brother, why on Earth did you do that to him?' said Great-Aunt Gail, as she bustled up and carefully helped Sam to his feet, and brushed him down.

'Please don't tell Dad,' begged Ned. 'I'm sorry,

Sam, I didn't mean to hurt you. It was those boys. I thought they were coming through the Tunnel.'

Sam beamed at his big brother and wiped a single tear away with the back of his hand.

'You poor boy, Ned, I don't think anything is going to come through while I'm here to look after you,' said Great-Aunt Gail.

Ned nodded glumly and looked toward the hedge, which lay peaceful and quiet with the robin now hopping from branch to branch as though ready to fend off anything that may have been lurking in its depths.

'Right, then, lunch in five minutes, boys. Don't forget to wash your hands when you come in, although this doesn't feel like a day for miracles so I may have just wasted my breath,' said Great-Aunt Gail, as she marched off toward the house. 'We'll do something nice this afternoon once your mother gets in from her run.'

Once Great-Aunt Gail had disappeared from sight, Ned turned and knelt in front of Sam and, taking his face in his hands, looked deep into his eyes.

'Sam, you must promise me that if you see anything funny, or if someone you don't know talks to you, then you must go straight to Great-Aunt Gail or come to me and tell us. Do you promise?'

Sam gazed back at Ned, his eyes sombre. 'Ned, you're scaring me,' he said as his eyes once again began to fill with tears.

'Sam, this is really, really important. I'm not trying to scare you.'

For a second Ned thought of suggesting that Sam could sleep in his bedroom, before remembering the dreadful face that had appeared in the wall when he'd woken from his nightmare.

'If you fly the plane from your bedroom window, then I promise. And I promise not to go near the Tunnel unless you're with me.'

'OK, it's a deal. Do you want to go into the front garden and I'll go upstairs and launch her?' asked Ned kindly.

'Yeah, that'll be so cool, I bet it'll fly all the way to Australia,' squealed Sam gleefully, his wellington booted feet jumping up and down with excitement.

'OK, wait there. Don't go near the road remember,' Ned called over his shoulder as he kicked his wellies off at the back door and ran upstairs. Moments later he unlatched his window and swung it wide open and, with his head and shoulders poking through, shouted down to Sam.

'Reeeeeady when you are, Flight Captain Sam Penhallow!'

'OK, chocks away!'

'Three, two, one – take-off,' said Ned, and launched the aeroplane into the bright winter day. As it floated down towards Sam's upturned face, a sudden gust of wind picked it up and teased it just out of reach above Sam's head.

'Look, Ned, it's flying all by itself,' shouted Sam.

Ned looked down, grinning as his little brother ran joyfully after the plane as it drifted this way and then that, the gentle wind that carried it aloft playfully ruffling Sam's golden hair. Still the plane flew, sometimes falling close to Sam before darting away again. It was as Sam capered after the plane that Ned noticed that the garden gate had been left wide open as Smugley had made his desperate escape and that the wind was gradually playing the plane, and Sam, towards it and the road beyond.

Chapter Eleven

Darkness Descends

Alarm rang in Ned's voice as he shouted down to Sam, who was by now perilously close to the yawning gate as he followed the swooping and dancing plane.

'Sam, stay away from the road,' he yelled, as loudly as he could. But as the words left his mouth they seemed to deaden and muffle, as though passing through thick wool. The wind that had until now been toying playfully with the aeroplane turned cold and spiteful and snatched the plane from Sam's grasping hands and flung it towards the hedge and the road. For an instant, a fragment of dream flashed into Ned's memory – that of the tree picking Sam up and tossing him into its gaping maw.

'Sam, wait there. I'll come and get it back. Stay where you are.' But Sam, deaf to Ned's pleas, ambled innocently toward the gate. Turning away from the window, Ned found to his horror that his hands were stuck fast to the wooden frame and that the wood was sprouting shoots that crawled and snaked up his forearms, binding them tightly. Ned let out a yell of pain as cruel thorns erupted from the shoots and pierced the skin of his hands and arms. Ignoring the pain and pulling hard to free himself, Ned tried to lift a foot to push against the wall with, but looking down could only watch as thin ropes sprang from the carpet, laced themselves around his ankles and raced up his legs, tightening and biting into his legs as they did so.

'Don't go onto the road,' Ned shrieked, but again

the words were deadened as soon as they left his mouth. Sam was still oblivious to Ned's screams, a slight frown on his face as the wind now caught his hood and smacked a toggle hard against his cheek, bringing tears to his eyes. Crying out in dismay as the plane now disappeared over the hedge, Sam ran as fast as his booted feet would carry him, through the gate and straight into the middle of the road. Spying the plane on the far pavement, he darted across and snatched it up triumphantly.

'Look, Ned, it's OK, it's landed,' he yelled, and waving the paper aeroplane over his head, ran back across the road.

The bang that followed, as the car bumper struck Sam and sent him flying into the air and onto the garden hedge, would be a sound that Ned would always remember. A terrible, final crumpling sound that would always invoke the image of Sam being tossed through the air, already unconscious, body limp, hair a floating mass, and bouncing onto the hedge before landing in a tangled heap in the garden, one of his beloved orange wellington boots landing next to him. The awful frozen moment that followed, as lives passed irreversibly from one chapter to a new, painful one, was shattered by an agonised, rending scream as Great-Aunt Gail rushed to Sam's inert body.

Ned's memories of the rest of the afternoon were fragmented – the wooden frame and the carpet suddenly releasing him, the wounds from the thorns healing and leaving no trace, tottering downstairs on legs that weren't his, trying to run to Sam, but being held back by Mr Swanson, who had witnessed the accident, the driver, tearful, and crying over and over again that Sam had just run out. Mum coming home from her run, screaming and crying at the sight of her baby boy lying limp and unmoving. The arrival of the ambulance after minutes that had felt like hours. Sam's tiny body being lifted gently onto a stretcher and carried away. A last bitter gust of wind that carried the triumphant words - 'Bring me the ring, boy', and then nothing, as the world around Ned washed grey and muffled and he fell unconscious to the ground.

Chapter Twelve

The Whirlpool

As Ned blinked awake, his eyes settled on a patch of bright moonlight that shone on his bedroom floor. Outside, a full moon rode high, stars speckling the midnight sky around it, not a cloud to be seen. Voices drifted up from below – Great-Aunt Gail and another, a man, talking urgently, fearfully. Ned could only catch muffled snippets as memories of the afternoon's events tumbled into his sleep-fuddled head.

'What do you think will happen to him?' asked Great-Aunt Gail.

Sam's laughing, freckled smattered face.

'I'm not sure. He's a tough little boy, I know that for sure, but an accident like that is going to take its toll on him.'

Sam's straw-coloured mop of hair being ruffled by the wind.

'You'll need to speak to him soon – I don't think we have much time before his father gets home.'

'Too late - I think that's him now.'

The slam, that awful final slam as the car hit and sent him sailing into the air and the waiting blackness.

Ned was fully awake now, the awful crushing reality of what had happened numbing him as a terrible sense of loss and emptiness crawled its way onto his chest and lay there like a leaden stone, leaving him sobbing and shaking. The patch of moonlight on the floor began to darken as Ned slid from his bed and, kneeling in front of his bedside cabinet, carefully pulled the bottom drawer out to reveal the secret hiding place and the ring snugly tucked away inside. Reaching in, Ned gasped as his fingers touched the icy cold of the ring's metal. Standing up with his hand shoved deep into his armpit, Ned saw that what remained of the moonlight had now completely disappeared, leaving the room in deep, inky blackness. Turning to look through his window to see if the long awaited snow clouds had arrived, Ned's blood turned to ice. The night outside his window was now utterly pitch black; not a single star could be seen, no moon, not even the faintest glimmer of a street light or house light in the road outside, just the deepest, deepest, abyssal black that crushed against the window, making it bulge inward, the wooden frame splintering and cracking as the malevolent darkness tried to force its way into Ned's world. Hair crawling on his head and mouth drawn into a silent scream, Ned staggered back from the window, goosebumps erupting across his skin at the sheer evil that poured from the darkness. Ice began to form around the window and race out in all directions, spreading along the walls and crackling as it grew across the ceiling and floor like some terrible ivy. Great fangs of ice sprang from the floor and ceiling and crashed together, blocking the door in a terrible icy snarl.

As though looking down the wrong end of a telescope, Ned saw his hands fumbling at the hiding place, tearing the drawer away and clumsily pawing for the ring. Even though the iciness bit savagely into his palm, sending great shudders of cold wracking through his body, Ned held the ring out in offering and, barely aware that his feet were moving, walked towards the window on numb legs. The blackness began to swirl, becoming a screaming whirlpool that tugged forcefully at Ned, dragging him closer and closer, his world becoming a foggy haze. Now only inches away, the ring held up as a gift to the evil on the other side of the glass, the door burst open with a resounding crash and Dad, Great-Aunt Gail and Mr Swanson burst into the room. There was a loud yell from Mr Swanson, a bang, a flash and a fizzle, as for a moment the light bulb burned as bright as the sun, and then the room was plunged once again into darkness.

'Ned, Ned, where are you?' Dad shouted into the pitch black.

'I'm here, Dad,' answered Ned, shoving the ring into his pyjama pocket and wincing at the frostbite on his palm, which was already beginning to blacken and blister.

'It's absolutely freezing in here, have you had the window open or something?'

'No. What's happened to the light bulb? Has the house been struck by lightning?'

'No, it's just blown, I think,' said Mr Swanson, shining a bright white light from his hand and walking towards Ned's bedroom window.

'Here, I'll take the bulb from the landing,' said Great-Aunt Gail.

'There we are,' she said, as the bulb flickered once and then cast a steady light over the room.

With the light now shining, Ned could see that the ice that had encased his bedroom had disappeared and Mr Swanson was peering at the window, running his hand round the wooden frame and muttering under his breath as he did so, his brow creased into a stern frown.

'What are you doing?' asked Ned's dad.

'Oh, sorry. You know me, William, can't help but inspect woodwork – could do with some attention, you know,' replied Mr Swanson vaguely. 'A near-miss,' he murmured as he walked past and stood waiting by the bedroom door. 'Shall we go, Gail?' He turned to Ned.

'You won't have any more problems with that window, Ned. I'll see you at school, come and talk to me when you can.' The door clicked quietly shut as Mr Swanson and Great-Aunt Gail left the room.

Ned hadn't seen his father since he'd left for work that morning. His first thought, when he finally gathered the courage to look at his face was, That's what gaunt means. His father stood bent and crumpled, his hands buried deep in his pockets and his face sagging under two reddened eyes.

'Sam's in a coma.' Dad's unusually flat, dead voice broke the stiff silence that filled the void between them.

'What's a coma?' asked Ned, trying to avoid looking at his father's diminished figure, which he found more frightening than if he had been ranting and shouting at him.

'Hmm? Oh, it's when someone's been knocked unconscious and can't be woken up.'

'He's not dead then?' asked Ned.

'No. No, he's not dead, thank God.'

'Where's Mum?'

'She's staying with him at the hospital. She sent me home to look after you.' A hint of resentment closed Dad's reply as he turned to leave the room.

'I didn't mean it to happen,' Ned blurted at Dad's departing back.

Dad paused in the doorway and turned slightly before replying.

'Mr Swanson told me what happened, he saw the whole thing. He said that a gust of wind came and blew the paper aeroplane that you made into the road.'

'The gate ...' Ned began, desperate to say anything that would keep his father in the room, someone at least to keep him company and perhaps, for once, comfort him.

'Funny thing is,' said his father cutting across him, 'there's not been wind anywhere else today.'

And with this accusation hanging in the air, Ned's father closed the door behind him.

Chapter Thirteen

Winter's Grip

In the first two weeks of the new term Weston Pewsey Primary School had become colder and colder; indeed, the whole village had been locked in a bitterly cold freeze that blanketed the surrounding countryside in thick snow. The River Kinder, that ran through the village, had for the first time in centuries frozen over, and people from the village had been able to cross from one side to the other without any hint of the ice cracking. Temperatures had regularly plummeted to twenty below freezing. The local council were doing all they could to keep the roads open, but every time the snowplough tried to carve its way through the drifts that filled the roads, something would break – axles, the steering wheel, and once even the plough itself had mysteriously shattered into hundreds of pieces as it sliced its way through a seemingly benign drift. Attempts to drop food and medicines by the RAF had failed, as each time a helicopter or Hercules aircraft had approached, blizzards would sweep in from nowhere leaving the pilots with no choice but to turn back. Eventually, the army was able to cross the miles of snow on skis, pulling huge sledges laden with supplies for the grateful villagers and using the same sledges to evacuate those who had fallen sick and were in need of hospital treatment. Weather experts were baffled as to why only Weston Pewsey was snowbound while the rest of the country basked in the warm sun that spring sometimes lavishes upon the frozen land. Every day Mr Swanson struggled to keep the ancient, clanging heating system of the school working, only just managing to keep the temperature in the classrooms high enough for the children to work in. Mrs Sharp, the head teacher, had insisted that the school open every day even as more snow fell and parents found it harder and harder to bring their children in.

The door to the classroom slowly creaked open, making Ned jump. The year four boy who sidled round the door eyed the older class warily and froze when he spotted Smugley Smirkens occupying one of the seats. Smugley, however, was staring vacantly at a spot on the wall, nodding his head slowly up and down as though listening to a voice that no one else could hear, a line of drool starting to run down his chin.

'Can I help you, James?' asked Miss Garnham, turning from the white board.

The boy jumped and blushed as all eyes in the class suddenly fell on him.

'It's a note from Mrs Sharp,' he whispered, offering her a slip of paper in his shaking hand.

'Thank you, James, wait there a second.'

All eyes now fell on Miss Garnham as she took the note and read it out loud.

The news was greeted with cheers.

'The school is closing at lunchtime because of the cold weather,' announced Miss Garnham. 'Your parents have all been notified, and will be here to collect you at 12.30.' She handed the note back to the boy who had delivered it.

As the rest of the class jumped for joy at the thought of a free afternoon playing in the snow, Ned alone remained seated. He couldn't bear the thought of being in the cold, joyless house listening to his mother sobbing while Great-Aunt Gail did what she could to comfort her, every sob a painful reminder that Sam wasn't there, and might never be there again. Dad had been marooned outside the village, having been by Sam's bedside when the first of the blizzards had swept in and cut Weston Pewsey off from the rest of the world. Spending every possible moment by his son's side, he'd phoned through as often as he could with news of Sam's condition, each day sounding more and more despairing.

'Settle down, settle down,' Miss Garnham commanded, fixing Smugley Smirkens with a particularly stern look. Smugley was whispering behind his hand to one of his sidekicks, Hassall, whose thick, ape-like face broke into a leering grin as he slowly began to comprehend what it was that Smugley was whispering to him. Turning away from Hassall, Smugley nudged Stebbings, who had been busy wiping snot onto the plaits of the girl in front. Stebbings eyed his friend warily as he began whispering to him. Smugley, who at the best of times was someone whose behaviour was a little scary, and sometimes very scary, had been acting oddly since he, Stebbings and Hassall had been reunited by the return to school. Quite often Smugley had been spotted crouching down near the dense hedge that ran round the perimeter of the school, head cocked to one side as though listening intently, and nodding and murmuring as though in reply, and on several occasions had been caught staring up at Ned's bedroom, sometimes from the playground and sometimes staring up from the pavement in front of Ned's house, after wandering vacantly out of school.

As Miss Garnham continued her lesson, Ned risked a telling off and turned to look at Smugley, only to find that Smugley was staring straight at him. As their eyes locked, Smugley's eyes for the briefest of moments turned a livid yellow and his mouth drew back into a horrible, taunting grin as he winked at Ned.

Chapter Fourteen

A Lonely Walk

At last the dinner bell rang, spilling forth a tide of ecstatic school children into the playground, where waiting parents stood shivering in winter's bitter grip. Ned was the last to leave, slowly packing his books into his rucksack.

'How are you, Ned?' asked Miss Garnham, making him jump.

'I'm OK, thanks, miss,' lied Ned, looking down at his hands.

'Are you sure?'

For a moment, Ned nearly told Miss Garnham everything. About how somebody had posted a paper aeroplane through the letterbox on Christmas Day and how it had later disappeared from the rubbish bin, where Great-Aunt Gail had crumpled it up and hurled it. How it had later reappeared, wafting lazily around in Ned's room before screwing itself up into a ball and throwing itself repeatedly at Ned as he cowered against the door, each strike echoing the same awful bang that Ned had heard when Sam had been struck by the car. About how in the two weeks since Sam's accident his mum had spoken to him less and less until she now walked past him without seeing him, and how every time he was in the house by himself he'd jump at every creak and groan, expecting the sinister face to bulge from the wall again, or worse still, the swirling black vortex to appear outside his window and drag him in, along with the ring. How sometimes at night the wooden window frame in his bedroom would glow bright blue and sparks would leap and arc across the glass, as though keeping something terrible at bay. About the nightmares that he thrashed awake from, sweating and terrified, eyes bulging and gasping for breath. And how just last night, when he'd dare to look from his bedroom window, he'd seen a dark figure walk across the back garden. And the ring, the ring itself. How could he explain to anyone, let alone a grown-up, about how he'd found the ring and how horrible things had started to happen ever since he'd chiselled it free from the tree?

'Yes, miss, I'm sure.' He nodded, swinging his rucksack onto his back and pushing his chair under his desk.

Ned didn't bother looking for Great-Aunt Gail in the playground, knowing that she trusted him to walk home by himself. He knew, too, that Mum wouldn't be waiting either, that she would be in Sam's room, clutching his pyjamas to her red, puffy eyes, trying not to cry too much in case her tears washed away the last of Sam's sleep scent. Dad, still unable to return home through the snow, would be in the hospital, sitting by Sam's tiny and unmoving form, looking drained and ghostly grey as he read Sam's favourite stories out loud time and time again until his throat grew too hoarse to carry on.

Instead of turning left at the school gate as he normally did, Ned hesitated and, hitching his rucksack onto his shoulder, turned right and began to follow the pathway that led away from the village. He tried to make himself small and inconspicuous as he passed Smugley who was busy pleading with his mother next to a huge four-wheel drive car.

'But Mum, please. I just want to stay and play with Rick and Mikey for a while, that's all. Could you pick me up later, please?' he whined.

'OK then, my sweetie pie, I'll see you back here at half-past two – don't be late, there's a good boy,' said Mrs Smirkens dotingly, as she planted a kiss on Smugley's cheek.

'Thanks, Mum, you're the best,' he shouted, throwing his school bag into the car and running back toward the school, leaving his mother waving at his rapidly departing back.

Mrs Smirkens smiled indulgently at her son's antics but, turning round and noticing Ned staring at her, frowned and fixed him with a nasty stare as she swung her bulk into the driver's seat, causing the car to dip alarmingly.

'Stay away from my boy,' she said, as she wound down her window. 'He's been having nightmares about you. He keeps shouting your name out in his sleep, saying you're going to ring him or something.'

Ned opened his mouth to protest, anger beginning to boil.

'Don't you dare answer me back, you stupid little boy, don't you dare,' screeched Mrs Smirkens, before accelerating away dangerously, sending snow and ice splattering over several parents who had chosen to walk home with their children.

Chapter Fifteen

Smugley's Revenge

The robin had followed Ned ever since he had left the road and stepped onto the footpath that ran for miles into the countryside before looping back and entering the village next to his home. Flitting from snow-covered bush to snow-covered bush, the robin flew alongside, all the while watching him with its black bead eyes.

'You must be starving in all this cold weather,' murmured Ned.

The bird fluffed up its feathers and looked expectantly at him, its orange chest a fiery coal in the bleak day. Ned slipped his rucksack from his shoulder and unbuckled the flap.

'I've got something you can have,' he said, rummaging around for the foil-wrapped sandwich that would have been his lunch. 'Here.' He tore off a small piece of bread and soaked it in water from his bottle before dropping it onto the frozen snow. The bird flew down and, with a swift peck took the bread and flew back to its perch. The bird's performance delighted Ned, who tore piece after piece from the sandwich and threw them for the bird, being careful to soak each one first.

The stick would have struck the robin had not Ned stooped to pick up a scrap of foil that had blown from his hand. Instead, it hit Ned on the side of his head, bringing tears to his eyes as it stung his cold cheek.

'Oh, look, Ned's found a new little brother to play with,' jeered a familiar voice. 'Careful the nasty car doesn't run him over, too.'

Foul, snickering laughter echoed around the snowy clearing.

'Shut up! Just shut up about Sam!' shouted Ned, tears from the pain and the jeering filling his eyes.

'Oh, look, ickle-Ned's having a tantrum. Careful he doesn't throw Fireman Sam out of the pram.' This from Stebbings, who grinned as he emphasised Sam's name.

Smugley was beside himself with spiteful glee as Ned savagely palmed the tears away and tried to barge his way through the wall of boys.

'You're going nowhere, you cry baby,' snarled Smugley, his porky hand pushing Ned hard in the chest. Ned stumbled backwards, only just managing to stay on his feet. The boys spread out and formed an ugly circle around Ned, Hassall the next to give him a hard shove, this time in the back, sending him sprawling face first into the snow. Struggling to his feet and trying to dust the snow from his face, a kick in the pants from Stebbings sent him sprawling again, accompanied by howls of laughter as he once again fell flat on his face, his hands now cut and bleeding where they had been mauled by the cold, frozen earth.

This time, instead of getting to his feet, Ned swiftly drew one foot up, and like a sprinter from the blocks made a low dash for a gap between Hassall and Stebbings, bowling Stebbings out of the way as he did so. Just as escape was nearly his, a foot caught his heel and once again he sprawled to the ground. Rough hands grabbed the back of his coat and dragged him to his feet, twisting his arm painfully up between his shoulder blades.

'Nice try, snot nose. Here, Hassall, hold him.'

Hassall grabbed Ned's collar and hiked his

tortured arm even further up his back. Ned let out a loud scream as a sharp dagger of pain flared through his shoulder.

'What shall we do with his bag?' said Stebbings triumphantly, picking Ned's discarded rucksack and emptying its contents into the snow. 'Oops, silly me, I've dropped all your books. And now I've trodden on them,' he crowed as he stamped up and down on Ned's schoolwork, twisting his feet from side to side until all the pages tore loose and littered the ground around them. 'Ah, never mind. Here let's put some snow in – you can take it as a souvenir for Sam,' said Stebbings, cramming handful after handful of snow into the rucksack before hanging round Ned's neck and patting him hard on the cheek.

'Right then, let's see what little snot nose has got in his pockets, shall we?' said Smugley, walking round to face Ned.

Close up, Ned could see that something was different about Smugley – he looked purposeful, as though he'd been given a special task to perform. As Smugley's oafish hands began to plunder Ned's pockets, he became more and more frantic until he reached Ned's trouser pocket. A look of triumph bloomed over his face as his grubby fingers closed around the ring.

Smugley shoved his face close to Ned's and leered horribly.

'Well, well, well what do we have here then, Neddy, Neddy, wet the beddy?'

Smirking his habitual grin, Smugley held the ring up and admired it twinkling in the weak winter sunlight. With a high-pitched squeal, he dropped it and clutched the hand that had held the ring.

'It bit me!' he screamed, and sure enough a semicircle of bright red spots of blood could be seen oozing from his thumb.

'Pick it up. Pick it up now!' he yelled furiously at Stebbings, who had joined Hassall and was pinning Ned's other arm behind his back. Stebbings looked far from pleased at the prospect, but looking at the expression on Smugley's face he bent down and, after fumbling around in the snow, gingerly picked up the ring.

Nothing happened. A triumphant grin slowly broke out on Stebbings' nasty, ferrety face. Hassall let out his caveman grunt of a laugh and twisted Ned's arm higher up his back, making him scream again.

'Looks like it's ours now, doesn't it, Penhallow-maggot?' Hassall snarled, his filthy teeth almost brushing Ned's ear. A loud sizzling noise was followed by a scream that matched Smugley's, and Stebbings too dropped the ring and began hopping around, clutching his hand.

'It burnt me! It burnt me!' he sobbed, tears of pain running down his face as he shoved his scorched hand deep into the snow.

'Wuh?' grunted Hassall. As his attention turned to the howling Stebbings, his grip on Ned's twisted arm loosened as his murky brain struggled with the difficulty of doing two things at once.

Chapter Sixteen

The Dell

Ned didn't hesitate and stamped down hard, as hard as he possibly could, on the top of Hassall's foot. A third scream now rang out as Hassall, clutching his wounded foot, joined Stebbings in hopping round in a bizarre rain dance. With a mighty shove, Ned sent Hassall crashing into Stebbings, who in turn crashed into Smugley, leaving all three collapsed on the ground like three very ugly and very angry dominoes. Ned leapt over them and pounced on the ring. Clutching it tightly, he turned and sprinted away as fast as he could. Within a few short seconds, the three boys had untangled themselves from each other and were charging after him. Ned's heartbeat thudded in his ears as he desperately tried to outdistance his pursuers. Lifting his knees high, he ploughed and floundered through the deep, clinging snow. Twice he nearly fell, almost sending the ring flying from his grasp, but at last, as he rounded a corner, he could see salvation in the form of the Dell – a huge crater hundreds of years old, left by mining. Risking another fall, Ned turned to see how near the boys were. They, too, were finding the deep snow hard to run through, but they were still doggedly in pursuit, two of them now close enough for Ned to see the sweat pouring down their red, angry faces and hear their rasping, panting breath. Hassall was limping far behind, and behind him was something that stopped Ned in his tracks – the same shadowy figure that had terrified him just the previous evening. It was a triumphant howl that snapped Ned out of his trance, and with Smugley's clawing fingers brushing the back of his coat, he again turned and ran for his life. Ned dodged off the path and threw himself through a small gap in the hedge. Bursting through, he could see the thick bushes crowned with snow that marked the lip of the Dell. Loud, screaming curses told him that Smugley had tried to fit through the hole Ned had made and, risking a glance behind him, he could see Smugley's very red and very angry face poking through the hedge. A yell of laughter escaped Ned as he pictured Smugley's fat behind jammed in the hedge and his two friends pushing as hard as they could to free him. A last dash through a waist-deep snowdrift saw Ned reach the bushes and he crashed through the clutching branches and rolled head over heels down the steep drop that led into the Dell. There was less snow in the Dell and so, taking care to run only on bare patches of ground, Ned fled further into safety and cover. After a short while, he stopped and listened, holding his breath, which had been so loud from his headlong dash that he was certain Smugley and the others would hear it. Sure enough he could hear them thrashing around behind him, the air filled with yet more swearing as Smugley and the other two became ensnared in brambles and tripped over branches that had somehow not hindered him as he ran. Ned knew from all the times he had played in the Dell with Sam, or escaped there by himself when Dad was in a particularly foul mood, that in the deepest part there grew a thicket of bushes that reached from one side of the Dell to the other. So dense and thorny was this thicket that only someone thin and agile would be able to wriggle their way into its dark depths, where eventually it grew too dense to go any further. Once there he, and more importantly the ring, would be safe from his pursuers.

Chapter Seventeen

The Standing Stone

Silently, taking great care not to tread on the winter-brittle branches that littered the ground, Ned crept deeper into the Dell and, just as the crashing of Smugley and his friends seemed to be on top of him, he spotted the dense thicket. Sprinting the last few metres, he dived into safety, a shout from Smugley snapping at his heels as he did so. Wriggling desperately, Ned snaked his way between branches that at first seemed knitted together, but as he reached them he found that they moved easily enough and allowed him to pass. His pursuers were having no such luck, however, quickly becoming entangled and yelling in pain as thorns pricked and scratched them. Soon their cries were joined by Smugley's bellows of rage as he berated his friends for allowing Ned to escape. Ned continued wriggling into the haven of bushes until, to his surprise, he crawled out of the other side and into a small, perfectly circular clearing. At the very centre was a tall, grey standing stone that tapered to a narrow point. Climbing to his feet and brushing himself free of twigs and old leaves, Ned ran to the far side of the clearing and began hunting for an escape route that would lead him out of the thicket. Despite searching long and hard, Ned could find nothing, not even the narrowest of gaps between branches or trunks that would allow him to wriggle through. Even the thorns which he'd managed to avoid during his escape into the thicket grew denser and longer on this side, soon leaving his hands cut and bleeding. Despairing, he turned away from his search and looked around the clearing, glad at least that the Dell was now quiet, Smugley and his friends having slunk away home, pulling thorns from themselves and bickering over whose fault it had been that Ned had somehow managed to escape.

Returning to the centre of the clearing, Ned walked slowly around the stone before warily approaching it. The stone looked as though it had stood for thousands of years, moss and lichen obscuring its surface in large patches and a thick layer of dead leaves surrounding its base. As the last few glimmers of sunlight turned the world pink and orange, Ned could see that the stone was marked with patterns that reminded him of Norwegian runes he had seen in a book at school. Reaching out to brush away some of the lichen, Ned jumped with fright as a crackle of light leapt from its tip, briefly lighting up the clearing with blue-white light. In his pocket, the ring jumped slightly and began to radiate warmth. Pulling it free, Ned could see that the markings on the ring matched those on the stone, and as he cupped it in his palm, the ring began to glow, sending its warmth tingling though his frozen hands. Dropping the ring back into his pocket, Ned reached out and brushed away more of the lichen and moss, this time with both hands. Immediately there was an almighty shove in the small of his back and for one awful moment, Ned thought that Smugley had somehow managed to squeeze his bulk through the impenetrable thicket.

What happened next chased all thoughts of Smugley from Ned's mind. The world grew brighter and brighter as a hissing, crackling light once again filled the clearing and for a split second Ned could see his hands sinking into the stone. In an instant Ned was sucked in up to his wrists, followed by his forearms, and before he could draw breath to scream for help he was completely swallowed by the stone. After a moment of cold, suffocating darkness Ned stumbled out of the other side of the stone and stood blinking in bright daylight, at the bottom of a deep crater with the ground around him dappled by hot summer sunshine that shone through the leaves of the tree canopy high above.

Chapter Eighteen

Ned Goes Travelling

Where the Dell had been was instead a smaller, but still deep crater, ringed by a circle of twenty immensely wide trees that reached into the heavens. Carpeting the ground at his feet were hundreds of small white flowers, the buzzing of insects that flew around them being drowned out by the cries of dozens of brightly coloured feeding birds that burst up in alarm at Ned's sudden arrival. Panting slightly, Ned climbed to the crater's rim, and looking out, could see the land that lay all around was covered with tall, green grass that swayed back and forth as the warm wind sent ripples running through it. To Ned the air had never smelled so clean and so pure, the scent of the flowers and the grass so much richer than he had ever smelled before. Walking round the circle of trees, he could see that from south to west, the ground looked as though it had been scorched dry and lifeless by molten rock that had spewed from the crater that Ned had arrived in. Huge, twisted rocks lay blackened and scattered and in places deep scars had been scoured into bare rock as though the claws of some mighty beast had slashed the earth. Wherever here was, it was very quiet; no rumble of traffic, no sign of aircraft overhead, not even a crackle from the stone. Turning round and looking back into the crater to see if the stone had markings on this side, too, Ned saw to his utter horror that the stone was nowhere to be seen. With mounting panic, he ran tripping and stumbling back down into the crater and scrabbled around in the soft earth trying to uncover any trace of the stone, but to no avail. He scrambled back up to the lip of the crater and ran from tree to tree, searching behind each one, desperate for even the slightest trace of the stone that had brought him here. There was no trace to be found. There was no means by which Ned could return to the Dell, and to his home.

Desperate and utterly terrified at what he might find, Ned walked out a little way from the trees and continued surveying the landscape around him. To what would have been the north in his world lay a vast stretch of dark green forest that rolled all the way to the foot of a jagged range of mountains that barred its way like the teeth of a savage animal. From east to south were more gentle, rolling plains, scattered here and there with clusters of trees, and due south, on the very margin where lush countryside met the first barren, blasted rocky outcrops, Ned could see a cluster of buildings in the near distance. From this homestead, he could see smoke drifting gently from a chimney and a brood of chickens pecking and scratching in the dust. And capping all of this was a beautiful dome of blue sky that arced from horizon to horizon, punctuated only by the bright sun.

After one last hopeful look behind him to see if the stone had appeared, Ned plucked up his courage and, leaving the sanctuary of the trees, made his way cautiously out onto the open ground that stood between the trees and the homestead. A few metres out, Ned paused and looked behind him, back to where the trees stood tall and towering like monuments to fallen heroes. At least they haven't disappeared, thought Ned to himself, pausing only to shrug off his thick winter coat as he continued on his way through the tall swaying grass. As he reached halfway between the trees and the settlement, Ned began to relax slightly. Even though the events of the afternoon had started with a terrifying flight from the school bullies and had ended in a bewildering journey through a standing stone, Ned couldn't help but feel that whoever, or whatever, lived in the homestead would, in some way, be able to help him return home. With each step the sun's rays warmed him, chasing away the needling, bone-deep chill that the bitter winter gripping Weston Pewsey had brought with it. Marvelling at the beauty of his surroundings, Ned stopped as the ground under his feet began to rumble slightly as though a huge herd of beasts were on the move.

Turning, Ned gasped in awe at the sight that met his eyes. In the distance, from within the depths of the forest that lay to the north, a thick, black cloud boiled high into the sky as though a long-rumbling volcano had finally erupted. The air around Ned now began to lose its warmth, and even though the sun still blazed down, his skin began to pimple with goosebumps and he began to shiver as an icy cold squall whipped across the grass. Pulling on his coat, Ned watched as the cloud grew higher and higher, and for a moment he fancied that he could see a gigantic face form briefly in the billowing cloud, a once kindly, bearded face that now looked as though it were screaming in torment. Another gust of icy wind brought tears to Ned's eyes and, as he blinked them away, the illusion disappeared. But just as Ned was about to turn and continue on to the homestead, another face appeared, this one again locked in a frozen scream, and then another and another, some the faces of men and some of women, but all sharing the same tortured features. And as the cloud filled the heavens and began to blot out the sun, the faces as one fixed upon Ned and began boiling and rolling slowly towards him, mouths twisting and snarling as though cursing him. Desperately Ned backed away, stumbling as he did so and falling with a thump that knocked the wind from him. With the monstrous cloud now tearing towards him at a terrifying pace, Ned scrambled to his feet and for the second time that day ran as he'd never ran before.

Chapter Nineteen

Bryn Sayer

With only a short distance to go until he reached the settlement, Ned was suddenly struck and almost bowled over as something strong grabbed him by the scruff of his neck and lifted him off his feet. Ned let out a yell of terror and began to fight and struggle with all his might.

'Don't fight so,' roared a terrified voice.

Turning in surprise, Ned was shocked to see that it wasn't the black cloud that had him in its grasp, but instead, teeth gritted with effort as he sprinted with Ned under one of his tree trunk thick arms, it was a man. Ned stopped trying to free himself and was carried across the last stretch of ground so swiftly that the man's feet barely seemed to touch the ground. Even as they reached the sanctuary of the settlement, the ground beneath them had already turned inky black. A last burst from his rescuer, who by now was badly winded, and they burst through an open doorway and into what was clearly a kitchen. Pots and pans rattled as a huge shoulder crashed against the door, slamming it shut against the darkness that had so very nearly engulfed them.

'It's alright,' gasped the man between breaths as he lay slumped against the door, 'they can't come into a building unless they've been invited and I don't intend to do that anytime soon.'

'Who can't?' asked Ned, listening as the world outside became a roaring, sinister hiss.

'Why, the Gravemen, of course.'

The man wiped a large, work-worn hand across his face, flicking drops of sweat away as he did so, and pushing a mass of wild, black hair out of his eyes. He regarded Ned with tawny, gold-flecked eyes, taking in what to him was Ned's rather odd appearance.

'Did you come through the stone, then?' he asked, as he dragged himself up from the floor and staggered to a beautifully carved wooden chair. Ned didn't reply.

'Thought so, I could tell by the way you jumped when I mentioned it. You must have something about you if the stone let you see it. Even if they could get past those bushes, most folk could walk right up to it and not know it was there.'

Again, Ned said nothing, but continued to stare silently at the man. Eventually, he spoke. 'I don't suppose I could have a drink of water, could I, please?' His voice sounded very small and frightened.

'Well, you are polite, I'll give you that, and while we're on the subject of being polite, I'll introduce myself. My name is Bryn, Bryn Sayer. And yours?'

'Ned. Ned Penhallow.'

'Well, Ned, I'm very pleased to meet you. Now bear with me while I fetch you some water.'

Rummaging through a cupboard, Bryn brought out a delicate bowl, glazed in the most brilliant blue. Dipping the bowl into a large stone basin, he handed it to Ned, who took it carefully in both hands. Ned thanked him and drained the bowl in one go.

'By the stars, you are thirsty, aren't you? Would you like another?'

'Yes. Yes, please.'

This time, Ned took his time drinking the water, taking in Bryn's home as he did so. A large unlit lantern hung from an ornate wooden peg that had been carved

into a thick wooden beam that ran overhead, and it was
this that Bryn had turned his attention to, touching a
lighted taper to it and carefully adjusting the wick so that
light was cast into every corner of the room. The only
other source of light was the flickering flame from the
hearth of a giant open fireplace that spanned the entire
width of one end of the room.

'Is this your house?' Ned asked.

'Certainly is. Built her with my own two hands,'
Bryn said proudly. 'See these walls? Four feet thick.
Quarried every stone myself.'

Ned turned and looked at the windowsill where
Bryn was pointing.

'It's a great house. My mum would love it,' said
Ned admiringly. 'Why did you paint the window panes
black?'

'I haven't. That's the Gravemen. They turn the
very air black so that not even the sun can shine through.
Look.'

Bryn took the lantern down from its peg and
carried it to the window. Light shone all around, but
where it fell on the windowpane, it reached no further.

'If this were nighttime, the light from this lamp
would shine outside and you'd be able to see the oak tree
that stands next to the house.'

'Who are the Gravemen?' Ned asked, staring at
the writhing, living shadows that swarmed and swirled,
pressing themselves against the glass.

'They're what happens when ancient magic is
used by the wrong person.'

'Did you say magic?'

'Yes, I did, and this was a particularly evil spell
that was nurtured on the evil thoughts and black deeds of
the sorcerer who cast it, making it all the more powerful.'

'Were they people once? I saw faces just before they started chasing me.'

'Sadly, yes, they were people once, and good people at that. Honest and kind. The most decent people you could ever hope to meet.'

'How long do you think they'll stay here for?'

'Oh, not too long, I shouldn't think. Look, even now they're starting to thin out,' Bryn said, pointing to a window on the far side of the room through which they could now see a dense, dark grey fog. 'They've been riding abroad for some weeks now, haven't seen them this active for a long, long while.'

'Don't they scare you at all?'

'Nah, they're more of a nuisance than anything, especially at the moment – lots of toing and froing. You can't stray from your house for too long and you have to keep one eye open for them all the time.'

'Why did they come after me?'

'Because you were out in the open, that's when they like to take their victims. You were lucky today, young Ned, for the last few weeks I haven't dared wander out past the stone. Well, we don't need this anymore, do we now?' Bryn turned the lamp's wick down until the flame extinguished. Soon, bright sunlight shone through the windows and Bryn pulled the door open, motioning Ned to join him.

'What happens if you can't get away from the Gravemen? Do you die?' asked Ned, eyeing the retreating black cloud as it swarmed and billowed over the forest before streaming back down like birds going to roost.

'No, but you'll wish you had. They leave a freezing wisp of themselves feeding and spreading through you, draining you of every happy memory you've ever had, and so all you're left with is bitterness and hatred. And when that's all you can remember, when everything you see or think or feel is dark and dismal, and when they've had their fill of your despair, you become a Husk; an empty, desolate shadow of what you once were. The sad thing is, you don't notice becoming bad, but those around you do – your friends and loved ones – and in the end it spreads to them, too, like a plague.'

'But who made them? I mean, who cast the spell that made them?'

'Hmm, ancient legends, I'm afraid, and I'm not the one who's best suited to tell such a sad tale,' answered Bryn, glancing quickly at Ned and then looking away at something in the distance. 'Tell you what, I'll show you around the place shall I?'

Birdsong greeted them as they stepped through the back door and into bright sunlight.

'Takes more than a visit from the Gravemen to stop them,' said Bryn, as he tipped clear water into a bird bath.

'Do you like birds, too?' asked Ned, as they watched a flock of brightly coloured finches land and begin drinking.

'Oh yes. Wonderful things, birds, just look at these springfinches. Aren't they beautiful? They come back here every year and bring the warming sun with them. Did you know,' Bryn continued, 'that if you show kindness to one bird, just one then birds everywhere will help you. It's got to be proper kindness though – they can tell when you don't mean it.'

'Is that why you've grown all these flowers?' asked Ned, as Bryn opened a gate into a walled garden. 'For bird seed?'

'Indeed. Winters are very harsh around here,

difficult to believe on a day like this, I know, but if you'd been here three months ago you'd have been standing up to your chin in snow.'

'It's been horribly cold back home, especially around Weston Pewsey – that's where I live, by the way – and it's been like that since ... since the storm before Christmas. Where exactly is here by the way? I mean what is your world called?' asked Ned, peering quizzically up at Bryn.

'This world is called Elgarolyn, and the country upon whose fine soil we're standing is Fynordern. What's your world called?'

'Well, we just call it the world. Or planet Earth. David Attenborough calls it planet Earth quite a bit.'

'David Attenborough? Who's he?'

'He's a man on the telly. He likes wildlife. He really likes birds.'

'Must be a good chap, then,' said Bryn, flicking small pieces of bread to the hens that had come running at the sound of his voice. 'What's a telly?'

'It's a bit like a window that shows pictures, and you can hear people talking on it, too.'

'A bit like a Farseer globe, then.'

'What's one of those?' asked Ned.

'Well, you won't find them anymore – but they could show you what was happening miles and miles away. Very useful if you could handle them – tended to fly off and do their own thing sometimes. Well, most of the time actually, in my experience. Now, are you hungry? You look half-starved to me.'

'I'm famished,' said Ned, glad to be diverted from the Gravemen.

'Thought so. Do you like eggs?' asked Bryn reaching into the hen house.

'Not half.'

A few minutes later, Ned was tucking into a plate of scrambled eggs, sausages and toast that Bryn had rustled up. Nothing had tasted this good before, and while chewing his food, Ned gave Bryn a thumbs up.

Bryn looked up at the ceiling. 'Something wrong with the roof?' he asked, confusion on his face.

Ned shook his head trying not to laugh. 'Mumph, mumph,' he mumbled around a mouthful of egg and toast. 'No, I'm giving a thumbs up,' he said, after swallowing his food. 'It means it's good, everything's OK.'

'Oh, good,' said Bryn. 'Nothing wrong with the roof, then.'

Ned grinned and speared his last sausage.

'Nope, nor the food.'

Chapter Twenty

A Surprise Visitor

After finishing his last mouthful, Ned placed his knife and fork neatly on the plate and thanked Bryn. Bryn, who had been leaning against the open doorway, occasionally staring intently out toward the forest, turned and beamed at Ned.

'That's quite alright, young man, a growing chap like you needs his grub.'

'Bryn?'

'Yes, Ned?'

'Did you say that the Gravemen were made by magic?'

'Certainly did.'

'Really? I mean were they really made by a wizard waving a wand around and saying "Abracadabra" or something?'

'A nasty piece of work by the name of Belastung cast the spell, but I don't think the spell was "Abracadabra" or anything like that. A senior mage who knew the ancient magics was duped into taking Belastung on as a student, and it was one of the oldest and most evil ancient magics that Belastung used to bring the Gravemen into being.'

'What are the ancient magics?'

'They're the first spells and curses that were formed when the world was still new and chaotic and magic flowed from the ground and the air and the sea and weaved itself into all manner of spells and curses.'

'Are there still witches and wizards alive today?'

'Hmm, I've heard that there are one or two left, but most folk tend to steer clear of them.'

'Have you ever met one?'

Bryn smiled and let out a chuckle. 'Yes, I've met one or two. Not as bad as folk make out, but definitely a little odd, if you ask me. They love tinkering with magic and just can't stop themselves from enchanting things that really don't deserve to be enchanted.'

'Is there one near here, one that could help me get home through the stone? I mean, it's really nice here but Great-Aunt Gail will be getting a bit worried by now.'

'I don't think you'll need to go looking for one to do that,' Bryn replied, as he pushed himself off the door frame and waved his hand out of the door in greeting.

'Is someone here?' asked Ned, scraping his chair back and joining Bryn at the door.

'Hello, Bryn. Hello, Ned. Sorry I couldn't come through sooner, but the Dell was somewhat busy today. Three rather unpleasant boys were hiding near the thicket, waiting for young Ned here to come out. I had to, er, use some gentle persuasion to get them to leave.'

Ned stood open-mouthed as Mr Swanson, his white hair gleaming in the sun and a tall, wooden staff in his hand, strode across the yard to where they stood.

'It's so good to see you again, Bryn, thanks for looking after Ned,' continued Mr Swanson, oblivious to Ned's bewilderment. 'Oh, before I forget, I've bought you some tea bags - your favourite - Yorkshire Tea.'

'Thank you kindly, Charlie,' said Bryn, catching the red and green box that Mr Swanson had tossed to him. 'Good thing you didn't come through straight after Ned. The Gravemen were out and about and gave the poor chap quite an unpleasant welcome.'

'Oh, dear, must have been a bit of a shock for you,

Ned, but at least you're in one piece, eh? And what beautiful weather! We could do with some of this back home, couldn't we?'

Ned stared, still open-mouthed.

'I take it from the birdsong that the springfinches have arrived.'

'Mr Swanson,' began Ned.

'They're just like our swallows, you know,' said Mr Swanson, gazing in delight at the birds that fluttered about them, 'they'll fly hundreds of miles a day when they're migrating.'

'Er, Mr Swanson,' said Ned, looking to Bryn for help.

'Mind you, I don't think we'll being seeing swallows for a while, will we? Horribly cold on the other side at the moment, Bryn, worst it's been for years.'

'Don't worry, Ned, he always gets a bit carried away when he comes over here,' whispered Bryn behind his hand.

'Sorry, Bryn, did you say something?' asked Mr Swanson, turning his attention away from the birds.

Bryn coughed politely and cocked his head towards Ned.

'Hmm? Ah, yes, Ned. Right, um. Yes, bit of a shock I imagine, travelling through an innocent-looking stone to another world and nearly falling foul of the Gravemen,' said Mr Swanson.

Ned nodded uncertainly at Mr Swanson.

'Nicely done, Charlie,' said Bryn rolling his eyes.

'Is this real? I mean, am I having a dream or something?' said Ned, laughing nervously and looking first at Bryn and then back at Mr Swanson.

'A dream? Oh no, you're not sleeping, Ned. This is as real as the nose on your face,' said Mr Swanson. 'Or as real as the thing you have in your pocket,' he whispered, leaning close to Ned's ear.

Ned jumped guiltily and put his hand protectively on the ring.

'And anyway,' he said straightening up, 'I dare say that if you were dreaming you'd have been woken up when that dreadful Smirkens boy was bitten, don't you? He made such an awful racket over a such little nip – think what he'd have done if he'd met the Gravemen, eh? Probably wet himself, I expect.'

'Hmm, I suppose so,' said Ned, shrugging, 'but Mr Swanson, where are we? Bryn says we're in somewhere called Elgarolyn. Is it really a different world? What's the stone? How does it work? Why has it disappeared? Has all this got anything to do with Sam?'

A flood of questions spilled from Ned, his earnest face staring intently at Mr Swanson.

'That's a lot of questions, and answering them is thirsty work.'

'Would that be a roundabout way of asking for a cup of tea, old friend?' asked Bryn.

'Well, we don't want those teabags going to waste, do we now?' said Mr Swanson.

Bryn disappeared inside and, as the hiss of a kettle being placed on hot fire coals reached their ears, Mr Swanson turned to Ned. 'There's much to tell you,' he said, his brow creasing, 'but I think that if I told you even a fraction of it here and now and after what you've already been through today, it would frazzle your poor head. And not only that, there are some things I can't tell you here, the wells have ears, don't you know.'

'Walls, not wells,' corrected Ned, remembering the World War Two topic Miss Garnham had taught them the year before.

'No, I was right the first time,' replied Mr Swanson, frowning and nodding toward a small well that stood in Bryn's yard. 'No telling what lurks in there, or who it runs to.'

A little while later, all three were sitting in the shade of the oak tree that stood by the end of Bryn's house, Bryn and Mr Swanson swigging tea while Ned threw pieces of bread and delighted in the way the chickens ran after each piece.

'Well, that makes sense now,' said Bryn.

Ned and Mr Swanson had been talking about Sam and the accident, and how exceptionally cold the winter was in Ned's world.

'What makes sense?' asked Mr Swanson, flicking the remains of his tea onto the dusty roots of the tree.

'The Gravemen were abroad for most of that day, made quite a racket, too, more shrieking than hissing. Awful, it was, thought I was going to go mad with the noise alone. Bitterly cold it was, too, absolutely bitter. No matter how much I got the fire roaring, I couldn't get warm,' said Bryn, shivering at the memory.

'Do you think they caused the accident?' asked Ned, throwing his last piece of bread.

'It can't be coincidence that on the day of the accident, the Gravemen were so active, and so strong too,' said Mr Swanson, 'but no, they're not able to cause something like an accident to happen in a different world, although I wouldn't mind betting they're responsible for Weston Pewsey freezing over.'

Chapter Twenty-One

Return to Weston Pewsey

'Well, that's enough sitting around. We'd best be getting you home, Ned,' said Mr Swanson, getting to his feet and reaching for his staff.

'Will we be going back through the stone?' asked Ned, looking toward the ring of trees.

'Indeed we will. They're the only known way of moving between worlds.'

'But will it be there?' asked Ned, frowning.

'No need to worry, Ned, this stone knows if it's safe to come across, and just as importantly it knows when to close this world off from yours. Wouldn't do to have the Gravemen pouring through into Weston Pewsey, now, would it? Have you got everything that you brought with you? Coat, scarf, gloves?'

'Only my coat. I lost my scarf and gloves when Smugley got me. And my rucksack, too.'

'Luck is with you – I found them and left them on the other side of the stone – no excuse not to do your homework now,' said Mr Swanson. He turned and strode out across the meadow toward the circle of trees, face raised to the sun. 'Oh the beautiful, beautiful sun. Feel its heat on your skin, let it warm your bones, Ned. And breathe in the clean, clean air of Elgarolyn,' he sang out as he led the way.

Ned trotted along behind him, desperate to keep up lest they become separated. Bryn followed a short distance behind, laughing quietly.

'We'd better hope he doesn't start skipping and

dancing,' he whispered loudly to Ned.

Ned stifled a giggle as Mr Swanson continued, oblivious to Bryn's teasing.

'Make the most of the sunshine, Ned, it's a horribly cold home we're returning to – and going to get colder too, I think,' he called back over his shoulder.

Ned tried hard to smile at this but the words 'horribly cold home' struck deep, reminding him painfully of what lay on the other side of the stone. As they reached the circle of trees, Ned slipped past Mr Swanson and ran to the lip of the crater.

'Is it still there?' asked Mr Swanson, as he caught up.

'Yes, right there. Right there in the middle,' said Ned with a shaky laugh, pointing down into the depths of the crater.

'See, no need to worry after all,' said Mr Swanson. 'We'll be back home in the blink of an eye.'

'But what about Smugley and the others? What if they came back? What if they ambush us?' asked Ned.

'I wouldn't worry about them for a while; the last I saw of them they were running hell for leather out of the Dell screaming about seeing a polar bear.'

'A polar bear? In the Dell? What on earth made them think that?' asked Ned, incredulously.

'Hmm, I wonder what sort of person would set a bear loose on a group of young lads?' said Bryn, giving Mr Swanson a stern look.

'I've absolutely no idea,' said Mr Swanson, suddenly looking a little shifty and fiddling with his coat buttons.

'I'm sure you haven't,' muttered Bryn.

'Besides, it wasn't a real one. Just some very lively snow. Shall we be off then, Ned?' said Mr Swanson ly, as he turned and bade farewell to Bryn.

Ned, too, held out his hand.

'It's been really nice meeting you. Thanks for rescuing me and for looking after me, Bryn,' he said. 'And thanks for the lovely food, too.'

Bryn smiled and engulfed Ned's small hand in his.

'An absolute pleasure to have met you, young man. I'll see you again soon enough, I'm sure.'

Together, Ned and Mr Swanson climbed carefully down into the crater following a well-trodden path that Ned hadn't noticed in his panic.

'I'd pop your coat back on now,' said Mr Swanson, as they stood side-by-side at the stone. 'It's going to be a bit of a shock.'

Ned shrugged his coat on and hastily buttoned it up, fingers nervously fumbling.

'I'll go through first – I don't expect a welcoming party, so count to five and then follow me.'

He gulped and looked up at Mr Swanson.

'OK.'

'Right, let's go home, then.'

Mr Swanson placed one hand on the stone's carved surface and waved to Bryn with his staff.

'Bye, Bryn!' he called, as he touched the stone with his fingertips.

There was a loud crackle, a flash of blue-white light that left Ned blinking and Mr Swanson disappeared into the depths of the stone.

Silently counting to five, Ned copied Mr Swanson and placed one hand nervously on the stone, before turning and waving farewell to Bryn. As he touched the stone with his other hand there was a loud crackle, a push in the small of his back and then the sensation of being pulled in, a clutching, suffocating cold, and then he was standing in the Dell, the sudden cold making his eyes water.

'Ah, good, you made it. Thought for a second you were going to enjoy Bryn's hospitality for a little longer.'

Ned jumped slightly as Mr Swanson spoke out of the gloom.

'It's snowed again, hasn't it?' asked Ned, as Mr Swanson handed him his rescued things.

'Yes, it was one of the worst blizzards we've had so far. It started just as I was about to follow you through the stone,' said Mr Swanson, unrolling his deerstalker hat and pulling it down snugly onto his head.

'It must have been when the Gravemen were chasing me,' said Ned. 'Have they really caused all this bad weather?'

'Quite possibly,' said Mr Swanson. 'Bryn did say that they'd been particularly active over the last few weeks.'

'They're after the ring, aren't they?' said Ned.

Mr Swanson let out a deep sigh, his breath turning to fog in the cold air around them. The moon, full and glowing brightly, shone down as the snow clouds passed. In the silvery light that washed the clearing, Ned could see the grim expression on Mr Swanson's face, his normally smiling mouth turned down at the corners.

'There's a lot that we need to talk about. Some of it has to do with the Gravemen, but not all of it.'

'But it's all to with the ring, isn't it? All the strange things that have happened? Even Sam's accident?' said Ned.

'Now is not a good time, nor a good place, to talk of these things,' replied Mr Swanson, shaking his head. 'We need to get you home before someone sends a search party.'

'When – ' began Ned.

But without waiting, Mr Swanson had already begun to plough his way through the deep snow.

'Now, I think there is little chance that those boys will still be here, but nevertheless, we'd best be careful,' said Mr Swanson, as he beckoned Ned to follow.

Ned struggled after Mr Swanson as he moved silently to the edge of the clearing, where he had pushed through earlier.

'But you won't be able to get through, will you?' whispered Ned, tugging at Mr Swanson's coat. 'I mean, you're too big.'

Smiling, Mr Swanson winked at Ned and reaching out a hand, began to gently stroke one of the thick, thorny branches that barred their way. Ned watched in amazement as thorns as thick as his little finger melted back into the branches, and the branches themselves slowly pulled apart with only the quietest of rustling, revealing a track through the bushes.

Ned gasped in surprise.

'How did you do that?'

'I saved these bushes many years ago – they still feel indebted to me,' replied Mr Swanson, a hint of sadness in his voice.

Carefully, the two figures made their way along the path, the bushes behind them revealing their thorns and entwining themselves as they passed. A short distance further and they climbed up and out of the Dell, Mr Swanson kicking steps into the deep snow, Ned following close behind, occasionally glancing back over his shoulder as clouds covered the moon, once again plunging their world into eerie darkness.

'I'll escort you back to your house, Ned. I've no

doubt that your parents will be concerned about you now.'

Ned, now bone-tired and shivering, didn't answer, but did all he could to keep from stumbling. As they reached the end of the path, they heard a metallic clang as someone passed through the iron gate that stood at the end.

'Ned, is that you?'

Great-Aunt Gail fumbled with a torch that flickered on and off before cutting out for good, leaving them in pitch black darkness.

'Allow me, Gail,' said Mr Swanson, and a bright light filled the path.

'Mr Swanson, thank you. Ned – what has happened to you? Your clothes are a mess and you look sunburned! Are you coming down with something?'

Ned and Mr Swanson exchanged a secret grin as Great-Aunt Gail clucked and fussed over Ned.

'He ran into a little trouble, I'm afraid. I found him wandering around the Dell, hiding from Smirkens.'

'Not those dreadful boys again,' exclaimed Great-Aunt Gail. 'I saw them running past the house screaming something about a bear in the Dell. Such a racket, Mr Swanson, such a racket.'

'Well, goodnight, Ned. Remember to pop round whenever you want. You're closer to helping Sam than you realise,' he said, and with that Mr Swanson turned and walked his own path home.

Chapter Twenty-Two

Mr Swanson Tells a Story

'So what does the ring do? Who made it? Who does it belong to? How did it end up inside the tree? What are the Gravemen? Bryn said they were made using evil magic. Is that true? Who is Belastung? How did I get to Elgarolyn?'

Questions cascaded from Ned as he sat at the table in Mr Swanson's kitchen, hands cupped gratefully around a steaming mug of hot chocolate. Two days had passed since Ned had been pulled through the stone and into another world as he fled from the school bullies. Two days since he'd met Bryn, encountered the Gravemen and been brought back to his own world by Mr Swanson, the school caretaker. Two long days in which he'd been burning to speak to Mr Swanson about the ring and what he'd meant when he'd spoken of helping Sam. Two long days in which blizzard after blizzard had swept down upon Weston Pewsey, besieging everyone in their homes. Between storms people had valiantly tried to clear paths and roads to the outside world only to have their hopes of rescue dashed as yet more snow fell from clouds that to some bore more than a passing resemblance to howling, anguished faces. In the evening of the second day the storms had suddenly stopped, the few people who had been brave enough to be outside at the time claiming to have seen a mighty flash of fiery orange light flying from the top of Pym's Chair, the hill that overlooked the village, a mighty flash that had disappeared into the clouds and sent them boiling and seething to all points of the compass, leaving a star-encrusted sky twinkling over Weston Pewsey.

Mr Swanson was sitting facing Ned carefully skewering monkey nuts with a vicious-looking bodkin and threading them onto a piece of string, deft hands working quickly. Mr Swanson finished his task and laid the string of nuts with the pile of others that he had been in the midst of preparing when Ned had tapped timidly at the frost-laced window. He regarded Ned with his deep-set grey eyes as though looking into the depths of his soul. Ned fidgeted uncomfortably and looked down at the steam curling from his drink. It was some minutes before Mr Swanson spoke, making Ned jump.

'The ring,' he began, his eyebrows bristling as he frowned, 'is old. Very old. We never discovered exactly how old as there were no written accounts of it coming into existence, only legends of who has held it, and how they used it for either good or bad. We all have the ability to use the ring for our own ends, and how we choose to use it very much reflects our true nature. A saint, for example, would use the ring's power for good, while a bully, a coward, would use it to create discord and to cause great misery to others.'

Mr Swanson paused briefly, looking out through the window as though watching something in the far distance.

'The ring has been lost for centuries – a curse wounded the last Ring Guardian terribly and their last act was to try and destroy the ring rather than let it fall into the hands of their enemy. Sadly, the attempt, although incredibly powerful, did no harm to the ring, but it did blast it from that world into this one, where it promptly disappeared.

'I'm not boring you, am I?' Mr Swanson asked

Ned, who had listened agog as the tale had unfolded.

'No. No, not at all. Is it true?'

Mr Swanson finished the last of his tea and set the mug down.

'You have every reason to doubt what I'm telling you, and I'm glad that you have the courage to question me. As for whether it's true or not, you have seen plenty for yourself – one boy bitten, another burnt. No ordinary ring could have done that, and the injuries they received could have been far worse but for the fact that the ring has started to attune itself to you, and not to someone with a meaner nature. Besides witnessing the ring protecting you, you also travelled through a portal stone to the beautiful world of Elgarolyn, encountered the Gravemen, and enjoyed the hospitality of one of the most loyal and decent people you'll ever meet, Bryn Sayer.'

'Has this all got something to do with Sam? Is it Belastung who's taken him? Was it Belastung that tried to take the ring from me?'

Mr Swanson sighed deeply and rose from his chair.

'Come, now, the birds will appreciate these in weather like this,' he said.

Pulling on his deerstalker hat and picking up the bundle of monkey nuts, Mr Swanson gestured to Ned.

'Here, you take half and make sure that you hang them as high as you can. We don't want the local cats fattening themselves up on our already suffering bird population, do we now?' he said, a forced smile fleeting across his lips.

Blowing onto his rapidly numbing fingers, Ned picked up a string of monkey nuts and fumbled a clumsy knot onto a tree branch. From where he stood, he could

see the oak tree that had borne the ring for so long before
the storm had ripped a branch from its trunk. He
remembered the day, only weeks ago, that he and Sam
had been playing on the fallen branch when he had first
found the ring, Sam bouncing around on the branch with
him, squealing with joy, his cheeky freckled face split by
the huge grin that lived there.

'Mr Swanson, who is it who wants the ring?
Whose is the face in my nightmare and in the wall?
They've taken Sam, somehow, haven't they? Will I be
able to rescue him?'

Mr Swanson drew himself up to his full height,
filling his lungs with frigid air, before exhaling in one long
drawn out whistling breath that hung as a white cloud in
the frozen day. With a shadow hanging on his face, he
stared down at Ned.

'You'll have to be immensely brave if you want
Sam back. He is being held, or I should say, his soul is
being held, by dark forces who will stop at nothing to
possess the ring now that it has been discovered again
after all these years.'

'But who is it that appears in my nightmares?'

Mr Swanson took Ned's last string and tied it
high in a branch. With a weighty sigh he turned to Ned.

'Best we return to the kitchen. It's warmer, has a
teapot and a plentiful supply of hot chocolate, and there
are fewer eavesdroppers.'

Back in the warmth of the kitchen, Mr Swanson
placed a fresh cup of hot chocolate in front of Ned and
poured boiling water onto a teabag. Stirring slowly, Mr
Swanson watched as the water darkened before
continuing his story.

'Back long ago, centuries in your world, I joined

the court of King Shepent as an apprentice mage to Elpet the Greater, an arch sorcerer the like of which hadn't been since the ancient magics were tamed for our use, and which hasn't been seen since. Under his tutelage, I became a Learned Mage, and in due course a Senior Sorcerer.'

'You're a wizard?' interrupted Ned, mouth gaping.

'I am, but please, let me finish, and don't ask me to pull a rabbit out of a hat. Why are you grinning like that?' said Mr Swanson.

'Oh, it's just something Bryn said about wizards.'

'Is it now? Hmm, I have endured a lot of leg-pulling from Bryn over the years, so I won't ask what he told you. It's probably not true anyway,' said Mr Swanson, squeezing out the teabag and tossing it toward a compost bin that sat in the corner. The compost bin flicked out what looked like a very long tongue and expertly snapped the teabag out of the air as it sailed by. Ned stared at the bin as it settled back down with a clatter of its lid and let out a loud, contented burp.

'Er, Mr Swanson, did your compost bin just-'

'Burp? Yes, I'm afraid so, disgusting thing. Absolutely no manners. I've tried everything, but to no avail. Now, listen, there is much to tell.

'After becoming a Senior Sorcerer, I was sent by Elpet on a quest. Being sent on a quest is how a Senior Sorcerer, or Sorceress, of course, traditionally earns their staff. The quests are deliberately challenging and long, some taking decades to complete. My quest was to seek out and research the portal stones – stones that according to legend could move a person from one place to another in the blink of an eye.

'It took many decades of searching, and more nasty scrapes than I care to remember, but finally I located a source of these stones, and with much careful study managed to move a short distance through one. Quite a shock, I can tell you, especially as I ended up standing with one foot in a fire. Despite one rather singed boot, I was delighted with the result. I continued my experiments with these stones and became somewhat adept at moving, always to destinations that I could see, and eventually to destinations that I had visited before, some of them many, many miles away. Would you like a biscuit, by the way?'

'Oh, er, yes, please,' said Ned.

Mr Swanson reached for a biscuit jar and placed it on the table between them. Before Ned could touch it, the jar sprouted a pair of arms, and as though doffing a hat, lifted its lid. Dipping a hand inside it pulled forth a biscuit which it presented to Ned with a flourish.

Ned stared at the biscuit in his hand and just about managed to speak. 'Thank you.'

The biscuit jar bowed and smiled at Ned. 'You're welcome, young sir.'

Mr Swanson smiled warmly at Ned.

'Much better manners, don't you think? Where was I, now? Oh, yes, singeing my boot, wasn't I?'

Ned dragged his eyes away from the jar and nodded.

'Good. After several more experiments, I felt confident enough to travel back to King Shepent's court and present Elpet the Greater with one of the stones.

'I chose a clearing in the woods that surrounded the King's castle, and arrived there safely – no fires, no dogs or wild boar to greet my sudden arrival. I knew at once something had happened at the court. Something bad.'

Mr Swanson paused for a moment and sighed.

'By disguising myself as a wandering musician, I

was able to enter the castle and move freely about court. To my dismay I discovered that a particularly unpleasant character by the name of Belastung Caryosus had turned the King against Elpet, who had subsequently been thrown from the court, his staff taken from him and destroyed by Caryosus. After a brief battle with Caryosus, I used the portal stone to escape and sought the aid of a master craftsman to help me mine and craft the portals, something which only one man was capable of doing.'

'Bryn?' asked Ned.

'You catch on quickly.' Mr Swanson smiled.

'Yes, Bryn and I were the first two members of what became the Circle of Light. Together we built a number of portal stones using rocks that Bryn quarried and carved. As we built more of these, we discovered another ability of these stones - the ability to travel from one portal stone to another. It was purely by accident that one day we travelled not from one part of Elgarolyn to another, but from one world to another. I'd subtly altered the spell that I'd used to enchant the portals with and lo and behold we found ourselves in a totally different world.'

'But how did you get back?' asked Ned.

'The portal stones appear at the destination, as well as existing in the place you've just departed from, so we were able to move freely between worlds, and a good thing it was, too. The world we had travelled to was a sorry place, harsh and barren, with much war, misery and disease. We were able to approach some of the people we met there - refugees desperately fleeing the nearby fighting - and we taught them how to build their homes again, how to grow and harvest crops and how to prepare the correct herbs to use as medicines. I even placed a charm on their village such that it would be invisible to any warring bands.

'As we created more and more portals, so we discovered more worlds, some in need of help, others not. But the worlds that did need aid became too many for just two to help, and so in secret we began to recruit others who held the same ideals as us – to heal, to teach and bring peace where war and misery thrived - and so the Circle of Light was formed.'

'How many joined the Circle?' asked Ned

'At its peak, we numbered more than twenty of the finest mages, healers and craftsman Elgarolyn had to offer.'

'What happened, though? Why did the Circle end?'

Mr Swanson sighed again. 'Sadly, not everyone shared our vision.'

'Belastung?'

'Yes, Belastung had discovered the existence of the Circle of Light and while disguised as a healer, tried to join its ranks in order to discover the location of the portals. What Belastung would have done in the worlds we'd been helping doesn't bear thinking about.'

'So Belastung destroyed the Circle?'

'Not straight away, no. Instead Belastung worked at weakening the Circle by manipulating a fiery young mage by the name of Malverfuhren, who, though highly talented, was proving to be too ambitious for the Circle and had grown to resent his minor role within our ranks.

'Secretly, Belastung trained Malverfuhren as a disciple, slowly but surely nurturing the resentment he felt toward the Circle and filling his head with dreams of ruling an empire that spanned worlds.'

'Is it Belastung or Malverfuhren who appears in my nightmares?'

'Malverfuhren – I glimpsed his face in the vortex. Besides, I believe Belastung's final battle with the Circle took its toll. Such magic is now beyond Belastung, or at least I believe so. Such a dreadful waste of talent.'

'What do you mean?' asked Ned.

'Everyone has talents, Ned, the worst thing they can do is not to put them to good use. Instead of using their great talent, Belastung and Malverfuhren became consumed with greed. Greed for the wealth they'd seen and greed for the power they could wield. They were utterly blind to the happiness and peace that the Circle had brought to so many thousands of people.'

'But where did you find the ring?'

'We didn't find it. It was brought to us on a world that we'd been nurturing for some time, a world that had once been beautiful and peaceful and filled with great cities and ancient places of learning, but had become war-torn and ravaged. One night, as we sheltered in an underground sanctuary that we'd built, one of our number entered carrying a pathetic, sorry bundle. The bundle was a poor slip of a girl about as close to death as it is possible to be, and she held in her hands a wooden casket.'

'Who was she? Couldn't the healers help her?'

'We never found out who she was, so far was she beyond help that even the combined efforts of our best healers couldn't save her. Her final act was to put the casket in my hands and then she breathed her last. Such a shame, such a dreadful, dreadful shame. Even in death she had the beauty of an angel.'

Ned looked at his hot chocolate while Mr Swanson pulled a large white handkerchief from his pocket.

'The ring was in the casket?'

'Yes, along with a leather-bound manuscript that

eventually yielded its secrets and told us tales of good deeds and tales of terrible evil done by those who had been Ring Guardians.'

'What happened to the world that it came from?'

'Alas, it was one of the few worlds that we couldn't help; so poisonous and desolate had it become that we left shortly afterwards and returned to Elgarolyn. We brought the body of the girl back with us and laid her to rest in a place of beauty with the casket at her side.'

Ned stared silently out of the window, watching as birds flocked to the food in the garden.

'I have to go to Elgarolyn and find Malverfuhren, don't I?' he said, his voice trembling and thick with fear.

'You have little choice, I'm afraid,' said Mr Swanson.

'But can't I just give you the ring? Can't you go by yourself? I mean, you're a Mage, a Senior Sorcerer – you said so yourself. You can beat Malverfuhren and bring Sam back, can't you? You don't need me; I won't be any use.'

Mr Swanson let out a sad sigh. 'You have the ring though. You're the Ring Guardian.'

'I don't want the stupid ring – can't I just give it to you? You can be the Ring Guardian then,' said Ned, his voice frantic and pleading.

'The ring can only be given willingly, and accepted willingly,' said Mr Swanson. 'That is the only way that it can be passed from one Ring Guardian to the next.'

'Why can't we do that, then? I'll give you the ring – here, you can have it,' said Ned, digging the ring from the depth of his pocket. 'Here, take it. Please take it. Please.'

Mr Swanson leaned forward and rested his chin on his hands. 'What would you expect me to do with it?' he asked quietly.

'Go to Elgarolyn. Fight Malverfuhren. Rescue Sam.'

'Why would I, though?' Mr Swanson shrugged.

'What? What do you mean? You'd rescue Sam, wouldn't you?'

'If you hand me that ring and I take it willingly, then you'll have condemned your brother to an eternity of pain, fear and loneliness – unless, of course, Malverfuhren takes pity and destroys his soul. Naturally, were Malverfuhren to do this, Sam's physical form here in this world would then perish, horribly and painfully. It's unlikely though, as Malverfuhren doesn't understand what pity is; he is a being utterly devoid of remorse or sympathy.'

'Well, so are you! Why won't you rescue Sam for me?'

Mr Swanson frowned sternly at Ned, who glared back through eyes brimming with tears.

'Because I would be risking the lives of millions to save one. If you offered me the ring and I willing took it, I know the ring would be safe with me as its Guardian. I wouldn't then go and battle Malverfuhren and risk it falling into his hands. It's a terrible choice, one that would weigh heavily on my shoulders until my final breath, but I wouldn't flinch from sacrificing Sam to save millions of souls.'

Weeping and sobbing, Ned looked imploringly at Mr Swanson.

'But he's a little boy. He's the family baby. He's my little brother. You can't just leave him there.'

'I can and I will if you offer me the ring again.'

Ned dashed the tears from his eyes.

'Here, please use a tissue – sleeves really aren't made for that,' said Mr Swanson.

'Don't tease me!' yelled Ned. 'I can't believe you'd be so horrible. I thought you were on my side.'

'It has obviously escaped you, Ned, but I am on your side,' said Mr Swanson.

'No, you're not.'

'If I wasn't on your side, if I didn't want to help you, then I would have taken the ring from you when you offered it me not two minutes ago.'

'But you wouldn't have rescued Sam. You said so.'

'Correct, I wouldn't, and now that you are aware of that, I dare say that you would refuse to offer me the ring ever again. Now, as it stands, Sam still has a chance of being rescued. A slim one, admittedly, but a chance nonetheless. A chance that I didn't take away when you gave me the opportunity. That isn't the action of somebody who is your enemy.'

Ned snatched the tissue from Mr Swanson's hand and angrily wiped his nose.

'Well, I'm going to go and find him. You've no idea what it's like at home, watching Mum crying over him. It's like she's turning into a ghost.'

'Yes, predictably, and utterly understandably, you have put me in a difficult situation,' said Mr Swanson.

'What do you mean?'

'Nothing can stop you from returning to Elgarolyn – ,'

'Nothing is going to, either,' said Ned. 'I'm going to get my rucksack and go there as soon as I can. I'll buy a map from somewhere and find Malverfuhren and fight him.'

'Let me finish, please, Ned,' said Mr Swanson, motioning Ned to return to his seat. 'Nothing can stop you from returning to Elgarolyn, but even if you got past Bryn, who I have instructed to keep an eye out for you, you wouldn't last five minutes. Elgarolyn is a beautiful but dangerous world, populated with all manner of creatures that could send you mad with fear, plunge you into the darkest despair, or, if you're lucky, make you their next meal.'

'But I can't sit here and do nothing,' said Ned, planting his elbows on the table and burying his fingers deep into his hair.

'Quite right, you can't. Before too long Malverfuhren will do something that would persuade you to part with the ring in exchange for Sam, and who knows? Perhaps he'd keep his word and you'd have your brother back. But your peace would be short-lived, because Malverfuhren and Belastung were never previously given the opportunity to travel to this world in person. I'm sure they'd love to visit.'

'So what do I do?'

'I? Like I said, there's little chance of an "I" lasting for very long. The "I" will have to be a "we",' said Mr Swanson. 'Now, let me explain a little more.'

'Sam's soul is being held by Malverfuhren in a remote castle in our world. We shall have to travel back through the portal stone, and from there make our way on foot to Port Cadarn – it's an old smuggling port that not even Belastung would dare enter.

'I hope to hire a ship in Port Cadarn that can take us as close to Malverfuhren's castle as is possible. Once there I shall face Malverfuhren in magical combat. Malverfuhren's failing is his arrogance. He will believe that he has outwitted us and that he outnumbers us.'

'What do you mean?' asked Ned.

'Let's just say that I have trick or two up my sleeve that he will be unpleasantly surprised by.'

'Will you win?'

'If we don't then we are doomed, but if we don't face him, then Malverfuhren will only find other ways of wresting the ring from you and becoming the next Ring Guardian. The repercussions of this are unthinkable. Facing him is our only hope.'

'Right, then. How do we get to his castle?' asked Ned, his brow stern and his jaw set firm.

Mr Swanson nodded with approval.

'Come, I'll show you a map of our intended route.'

Following Mr Swanson from the kitchen, Ned paused to marvel at the ornaments that lined the hallway.

'In here, Ned.'

The sitting room was very much like the hallway. A large, richly patterned carpet covered the floor, its patterns swirling and chasing each other as Ned walked across it. Ornaments elbowed each other for space between bookshelves that were struggling to contain huge tomes.

'Ouch,' yelped Ned, sucking his stinging fingers.

'Oh, sorry, I should have warned you – that's the Dark Magic section. They're an unfriendly set of books that don't take kindly to being touched. I find oven gloves the best for handling them.'

Ned edged away from the shelves and turned his attention to the object Mr Swanson was standing by.

'That's a pretty old television, isn't it?' he asked. 'Does it still work?'

'No other television in the world can get the

pictures this one can,' said Mr Swanson, as he tapped the top of the screen. 'It's a Farseer globe – an enchanted orb that lets me look at what's going on in Elgarolyn.'

'Oh, wow! Bryn mentioned these when I told him about televisions.'

'Yes, I suppose they are like televisions, but without those awful adverts.'

'You sound just like Great-Aunt Gail,' said Ned, smiling and shaking his head.

As Ned watched, the television slowly folded in on itself and from it rose a beautifully ornate stand, at the top of which flowered a large pearly orb that stood as tall as the room. The orb gradually cleared and Ned gasped as he recognised the circle of trees that stood guarding the portal stone. With a spin of the orb from Mr Swanson, the trees became tiny as the orb took them high into the sky, and below them a vast wilderness of desert fanned out from close to the portal stone.

'You see there, Ned, the desert? That was caused by the Ring Guardian trying to destroy the ring. Very nearly destroyed Port Cadarn, too. Look, see how it peters out as it reaches the sea,' said Mr Swanson, pointing to the ragged fingers of desert that clutched at the deep green land surrounding the port.

'Where is Malverfuhren's castle?' asked Ned, scanning the landscape in front of him.

'Here, let me move the orb for you. The castle lies roughly three days by sail from Port Cadarn, here amongst these mountains. You see where the sea cuts far in-land – follow that until it becomes a river and climbs into the mountains. You'll come to castle soon enough.'

'Can the orb show us now?' asked Ned eagerly.

Mr Swanson shook his head. 'I'm afraid not, Malverfuhren would very quickly sense it and would probably turn it against us.'

'When do we travel back to Elgarolyn, Mr Swanson? I want to go soon. I don't want to leave Sam in Malverfuhren's hands a moment longer than I have to.'

'We will have to move soon whether we like it or not. I fear the storms will return within a few days and when they do, they'll be even more powerful than the last ones. Malverfuhren will be growing impatient, and we can't afford to wait and see what his next act will be. I'll meet you at your kitchen window at midnight tonight, and we'll begin our journey.'

'What shall I tell Great-Aunt Gail?'

'Leave Great-Aunt Gail to me. With the help of a little magic, I'm sure she'll understand,' replied Mr Swanson, with a slight smile.

Chapter Twenty-Three

The Journey Begins

A silver-white moon cast its glow over the still-frozen village of Weston Pewsey. Spectral clouds swept across the night sky as two dark figures, one tall and moving with ease trailed by a smaller shadow, made their way across the open ground that led to the lip of the Dell.

Ned had spent the rest of the day since leaving Mr Swanson's cottage flitting between utter terror about what was to come and excitement at the thought of embarking on a quest to find and rescue his brother's soul. The hours and minutes had crawled by and when not checking his watch, he'd be checking again that the ring was secure in his pocket. By the time Great-Aunt Gail had cooked tea for them, Ned had gnawed his normally neat fingernails into tatters. Several times he'd tried to speak to his mum and somehow say goodbye, each time being faced with the same grey, vacant mask left by the sleeping tablets the doctor had prescribed. Finally, Ned had taken to sitting on the floor of Sam's room, taking in as much of his little brother's life as he could. The collection of pebbles by his bed, each one a souvenir from the long walks they'd taken together with Mum; the clumsy attempts at pottery that sat in misshapen clumps along his bookshelves, and the carefully ordered rows of books, each and every one of them about aeroplanes.

'I'll lead the way down,' said Mr Swanson, turning to Ned for the first time since he'd tapped on Ned's kitchen window and beckoned him into the night. Far behind them a pale, grieving face looked out from

between the curtains of Sam's room as the two figures
began their descent into the pitch black Dell.

'Stay close, we won't meet anything down here,
but there may be a branch or two that could snag a foot.'

Ned nodded, his chattering teeth stopping any
words from coming out. Peering up, he tried in vain to
read Mr Swanson's face, hidden as it was in the depths of
his hood. Mr Swanson turned, the swirling of his long
cloak merging with the whisper of the wind through the
bare branches above. Despite all his efforts, Ned stumbled
frequently on the descent into the blackness, each time
being fielded by Mr Swanson's careful hands.

'A little too dark, I think,' said Mr Swanson, as
they reached the bottom of the Dell. 'A friendly light will
help us.'

'But what if someone sees our torch?' asked Ned
in alarm, as a sudden brilliance bloomed from the
sorcerer's hand.

'Don't worry, it's not that sort of light.'

Although dazzled, Ned could sense the grin in Mr
Swanson's voice.

'It's a light just for us,' declared Mr Swanson, and
without waiting to hear the question that was forming on
Ned's lips, he strode across the floor of the Dell, taking the
route that Ned had taken on his flight from Smugley.
Ahead, the dense bushes that Ned had sought refuge in
rustled and moved aside before they reached them,
revealing once again a well-used path.

'Mr Swanson,' Ned hissed, 'the bushes have
moved. Someone must be coming through.'

Mr Swanson's reply did nothing to settle Ned's
jittery nerves.

'Something certainly has agitated them; I've not
seen them like this. Stay close now, Ned.'

Treading warily, Ned followed Mr Swanson's silent footfall, his fear-widened eyes scouring the shadows for any movement or for any peculiar shape. Nothing met their eye and no sound reached their ears as they stood at the edge of the clearing.

'Put out the light, please put out the light,' begged Ned.

'It's a light just for us,' repeated Mr Swanson, this time his voice hard and alert. 'No-one else can see it.'

Ned felt Mr Swanson's hand grasp his arm and pull him sharply to the left.

'We'll stay here for a while and watch,' Mr Swanson whispered, crouching beside Ned.

For what seemed an eternity, they knelt stock still, the biting cold clawing its way through their feet and numbing their lower legs.

'I can't sense anything,' murmured Mr Swanson, making Ned jump, 'I think we're safe to go through.'

'Now? Together?' asked Ned.

'Yes, together. I'd intended to go first and make sure all was well on the other side, but something dark is abroad tonight and we'd do well to stick together. Come now, let's say good-bye to Weston Pewsey for the time being.'

Mr Swanson and Ned approached the portal, a single black finger pointing to the heavens.

'Do we do anything to go through together?' asked Ned.

'No, just hold onto my cloak, only one of us needs touch the stone. Ready?'

'Ready,' replied Ned, his voice steady for the first time that bitter winter's night.

Ned watched as Mr Swanson placed his hands flat on the portal, heard the familiar crackling and felt himself tugged through, stumbling slightly as they arrived in Elgarolyn. A dull grey mist greeted them. Mr Swanson immediately scanned the lip of the crater, the ring of trees towering high over them.

'Good,' he said after a moment, his voice sounding muffled in the mist. 'If there was anything unpleasant waiting, then we'd know by now.'

'Are we going to see Bryn?' asked Ned, as they panted their way up to the ring of trees.

'Yes, he's made ready a few things we'll need for our journey.'

'Where is his house? I can't see it in this mist.'

'No need to worry, I've trodden this path many times. I could do it blindfolded,' said Mr Swanson, as they exited the trees and made their way through the grey. A short while later, just as the rising sun began to burn off the mist that blanketed them, they glimpsed a tall, waiting figure.

'I was beginning to think you'd changed your mind,' came Bryn's greeting.

'Hi, Bryn.' Ned grinned and gave the craftsman a thumbs up.

'Hello, Ned, something wrong with the ceiling?' Bryn laughed, returning the thumbs up. 'I'll stick some breakfast on for you both, you look perished,' he said, as he turned and led them into his home.

After Mr Swanson and Ned had between them polished off a mountain of toast, scrambled eggs and sausages, Bryn presented them each with a large cloth sack.

'What are these?' asked Ned.

'Something to help you blend in,' said Bryn, as he tipped out the contents of Ned's sack. Ned rummaged amongst the pile in front of him and held up a roughly-woven white shirt.

'Is this for me?' he asked.

'Well, I don't think it'll fit Charlie now.' Bryn winked.

As Ned pulled on the last item, a sandy coloured cloak of a light fabric, he looked across at Mr Swanson.

'Are you going to change?' he asked.

'No need, I'm already prepared,' Mr Swanson replied, and with a flourish he flicked back his cloak to reveal a deep red shirt, and legs clad in a pair of dark brown breeches.

'If you're wondering, Ned, I'm a farmer and you are my grandson and we have decided to see a bit of the world. They're bound to ask.'

'Who are?' asked Ned, suddenly worried.

'The svartelves.'

'Svartelves? What are they?' Ned recoiled at the unfamiliar name.

In the world that they had just left, something small and leathery carefully climbed down from a tree where it had hidden itself hours before. Still blinking from the blue-white flash that had filled the clearing as Ned and Mr Swanson had moved through the stone, it huddled itself, muttering and cursing against the cold, as it prepared to wait the long hour that its master had commanded before it, too, could return to Elgarolyn.

Chapter Twenty-Four

A Farewell to Bryn

'Svartelves? Svartelves are creatures of the dark places, the dank caves underground and the freezing crags high in the mountain passes where the unwary travel,' said Bryn, dumping two bulging rucksacks onto the table, one small, one large. 'You don't want to tangle with svartelves if you can help it. They'll strip you of all you have and take you to their stinking lairs where they'll keep you as a slave. You'll never see daylight again if a svartelf takes a like to you.'

'Are there any near here?' asked Ned, glancing out of the door.

'Hardly any, but I've caught sight of one or two and I've seen their tracks all around the place recently. Upset my poor hens quite a bit, too. Sneaky little devils, though; scurried away as soon as I caught sight of them,' growled Bryn. 'Word has it that Belastung and Malverfuhren have been using them as their own personal army again for some time now.'

'What do you mean by "again"?' asked Ned.

'Svartelves have always been wary of humans, but when Belastung was gaining in power and trying to destroy the Circle, they made an alliance,' said Mr Swanson. 'When the end came for the Circle, Belastung used svartelves to great effect to betray our whereabouts and help catch us unawares.'

'A terrible night that was, terrible for so many good friends and for so many people on so many worlds,' said Bryn, shaking his head and letting out a deep sigh.

Mr Swanson sat silent at the table, his chin resting on his thumbs. When at last he spoke, his voice sounded thick and strained.

'There isn't a day that goes by that I don't think about that night. All those friends, all those good, noble people lost forever. Their loss left a terrible emptiness that can never be filled,' he said, staring out of the door, his normally twinkling eyes filled with an aching grief.

'Have the svartelves been seen anywhere else?' asked Ned.

'Well, I've heard that the poor folk of the eastern farmlands have had a terrible time of them recently – forever pestering the farmers for "gifts", stealing their cattle and ruining their crops,' said Bryn

'Why aren't there more of them around here, Bryn?' asked Ned.

'They've kept a wide berth of this area for as long as I can remember – probably something to do with what happened here when the ring was lost. But wary of the place or not, they're up to no good, that's for sure.'

'Do you think they know about the ring? Do you think they know that I have it?'

'Whether they know about the ring or not, I don't know, but I wouldn't mind betting they've been told to keep an eye out for you and Charlie.'

'But won't they be able to find us when we're travelling to Port Cadarn?'

'Unlikely; they don't like sunlight in the slightest, so as long as you steer clear of dark places you should be safe. But mind you keep an eye out all the same,' said Bryn, wagging his finger at the two of them.

'Same old Bryn,' said Mr Swanson, a slight laugh escaping his lips, 'always worried that I'm going to get into trouble.'

'When do we leave for Port Cadarn? Shouldn't we go soon while there's lots of daylight?' asked Ned.

'You're absolutely right, Ned, no time like the present. It's time to bid our farewells to Bryn and continue our journey into Elgarolyn. We've at least two days of tough walking ahead of us, and the sooner we get started, the sooner we'll reach our first stop.'

Ned turned to Bryn, suddenly feeling very scared and already very far from his home. An ache rose in his throat as he thought of Sam and the unknown perils of the journey that lay ahead.

'Now, don't you go looking so worried, Ned,' said Bryn, kneeling down and placing his hands on Ned's bony shoulders. 'You're safe just as long as you stick with Charlie – there's a lot more to him than meets the eye. He's been in some tight corners and had more than his fair share of narrow escapes and he's still here to tell the tale.'

Ned nodded silently, and to Bryn's great surprise, he reached out and hugged Bryn as hard as he could. Turning to Mr Swanson, Ned shouldered his pack feeling the unfamiliar weight dig into his shoulders.

'I'm ready,' said Ned, looking up at Mr Swanson who was busy cramming a white handkerchief back into his pocket.

'Goodbye, old friend and safe journey,' said Bryn, shaking Mr Swanson's hand

'Keep the home fires burning for us, Bryn,' replied Mr Swanson, 'We'll be back before you know it, so don't use up all those teabags. Right then, Ned, let us begin,'

Without further ado, Mr Swanson stepped through the door of Bryn's house with Ned at his side.

'Are we going to Port Cadarn now?' asked Ned.

'Yes, and if we ask the right person then we can hire a ship to take us as close to Malverfuhren's castle as is safe, possibly closer if we can find someone with a thirst for adventure. Or a thirst for gold, of course.'

'But if it's closer then, surely it'll be more dangerous?' asked Ned.

'Quite so, Ned, you're catching on,' replied Mr Swanson, marching off with a final wave to Bryn.

Chapter Twenty-Five

Knowledge Shines On All

As they crested the first hill that led from Bryn's house, Ned turned and looked back. Bryn was standing by his front door, still watching them, and he returned a wave as Ned lifted his hand. Looking further beyond Bryn, Ned could make out the twenty trees that stood guarding the portal back to his world, and beyond that the dark line of the forest he had seen on his first visit, stretching from one edge of the horizon to the other. Towering high over the forest, a huge bank of angular white clouds seemed to stretch from heaven to Earth.

'They're mountains! Oh, my word, they're huge,' gasped Ned as he realised what he was looking at.

'The Vygryn Eira Mountains. Magnificent, aren't they?' said Mr Swanson who, like Ned, had stopped to wave a last farewell to Bryn. 'It would take you a day to walk from the portal to the forest that you can see there, and making your way through the forest would take another two days, as long as nothing untoward happened.'

'Have you been through the forest?'

'Through the Forest of Myrkmyddel? I've entered three times, but only got to the far side once. Not the most pleasant of experiences, I can tell you.'

'Because of the Gravemen?'

'Oh, that was long before the Gravemen came to be, long before. I'll tell you all about it one day.'

'How long does it take to get from the forest to the mountains?'

'Have a guess,' said Mr Swanson.

'Three days?' Ned shrugged.

'On foot, it would take three weeks,' said Mr Swanson.

'But they look so close,' said Ned, awed.

'That's because they're so high. Only a handful have managed to travel through Myrkmyddel. Always in search of Tryddys Dalyn, a hidden valley that the legends say leads through the mountains. Some come back with wild tales of what lies between the forest and the mountains. Some never come back at all.'

'And no one knows what lies behind the mountains?'

'To my knowledge, nobody on Elgarolyn has managed to find Tryddys Dalyn, let alone pass through it.'

As they continued their journey, the sun climbed ever higher, burning off the last of the mist that had greeted them as they had come through the portal. Halting only once to fold their cloaks into their packs and sip water from the leather flasks Bryn had provided, Mr Swanson and Ned toiled through the day, following a stony track that wound through the blasted land around them, the only sound that of their footfalls and the tap of Mr Swanson's staff on the hard ground. When the sun was at its highest, Mr Swanson drew them to the shade of a small stand of trees that grew huddled in the shelter of a large cliff face. Shrugging the pack from his aching shoulders, Ned collapsed onto the ground in the blissfully cool shade. Taking a long draught of water from his flask, Ned rubbed his shoulders and neck where the straps had dug in. Leaning back against his pack, he yawned mightily.

'Tiring work, but you've done well,' said Mr

Swanson as he, too, dropped his pack and sat down with his back against it, laying his long staff down close to hand.

'Mum used to take us on long walks before Sam's accident,' said Ned. 'She took us everywhere and made us walk for miles. Fed us on chocolate and bought us fish and chips on the way home if we didn't complain too much. Sam always used to fall asleep with a chip halfway to his mouth. He made us laugh so much.'

'Well, I can't promise you chocolate and fish and chips, but have some of Bryn's bread and cheese – it's very good. What was your favourite walk?'

'Hmm, I loved the Brecon Beacons – they were great. We stayed there once over Christmas and walked up Pen-y-Fan on Christmas Day in the snow. I like the Howgills, too. We let Sam carry the map and compass last time we went there. He was chuffed to bits. Mum said Sam looked like he was leading an expedition.'

After resting a while longer, Mr Swanson climbed to his feet and after shouldering his pack, helped Ned up from the ground.

'No time to dawdle, we'd better get a move on, Ned. I want to reach shelter before dark, and it's still a way off yet.'

With a heave, Ned shouldered his pack, wincing as the straps bit down into his already sore shoulders, and followed Mr Swanson's steps out of the shade of the oasis. Had the companions looked back as they walked away, they would have seen a slight movement within the rocks against which they had just rested. Small, dark, wizened figures slipped from a narrow crack that ran down the face of one of the largest rocks and slithered their way to the edge of the clearing. Blinking and grimacing at the bright sunlight, they watched as Ned and Mr Swanson continued on their journey under the fierce heat of Elgarolyn's sun.

After what seemed like hours of trudging, Mr Swanson turned to Ned.

'You see up ahead, there in the distance – that's home for the night,' he said, pointing with his staff.

Ned squinted into the distance, blinking painfully as the wind flicked dust into his eyes.

'I don't see anything,' he croaked wearily. 'There's only that small lump over there. I can't see any houses.'

'That small lump is a house of sorts – nothing out here would survive unless it was very well hidden.'

'Hidden from what?' asked Ned, looking around nervously.

'Everything – sun, wind, sandstorms, freezing temperatures. We should be glad of this lovely spring weather.'

'This is spring?' exclaimed Ned. 'I've never been so hot.'

'It's certainly a warm one, I'll grant you that. Come, now, we'd best not linger any longer than we have to. Once night starts coming in, all manner of things come to the surface,' said Mr Swanson, ominously scanning the darkening horizon.

As they approached the small lump, which as they drew closer looked no different to the rest of the baked land that lay around them, Ned scoured it for signs of a door, but nothing resembling an entrance could be seen.

'Mr Swanson, how do we get in? And who lives here anyway?'

'That will become clear in just a moment,' Mr Swanson replied, and as they stood at the top of the lump, he brought the tip of his staff down with a sharp crack on one of the many rocks that littered the ground. No sooner had the staff touched than the rock began to rumble and grow until before them stood a small portal stone.

'Something you've come across before, I believe?' asked Mr Swanson with a smile. 'Now, hold my sleeve and let's see who's at home, shall we?'

With a familiar crackling, a sudden push in his back and a feeling of being very, very cold, the portal tugged Charlie and Ned through and with a grinding sound shrank back into the ground. Blessed coolness soothed the heat away from Ned's aching limbs as he stood next to Charlie, still clutching his sleeve. Looking about him, Ned could see that they stood upon a small raised dais, several of which lined the perimeter of a small circular room, each one set back in its own alcove.

'Are we still in Elgarolyn?' asked Ned, his voice the only sound in the perfect silence that greeted them.

'Oh, yes, we've just travelled through a short portal – very useful if you know where to find them. We're underground now.'

'It's so beautiful and cool down here. Funny to think that it's like a furnace just a few feet above our heads.'

'More than a few feet,' replied Charlie, as he dropped his pack. 'We're about two hundred feet underground here.'

Ned gulped and looked around and the small chamber.

'But what about the svartelves? Bryn said that they liked caves, didn't he?'

'Well remembered. They do, indeed, like caves, but this isn't strictly a cave. The Circle created it to use as a retreat and a place of learning. More of a temple than a cave, and the only means of entering it is through the portal. No cracks or tunnels for our leathery little friends to come through. Come, let me show you.'

As they stepped down, Ned for the first time could see a beautifully ornate arched doorway that lead out into a vast, vaulted hall. Following Mr Swanson through the archway, Ned stopped and gazed in wonder. The walls of the temple flickered and glowed with a light that seemed to shine from within the rock itself. In places the walls were covered in swathes of books that reached up to the very heights of the ceiling. Shimmering tapestries and maps hung from ceiling to floor on others, and in the very centre of the hall stood a stone fountain, clear water spouting from between four carved, kneeling figures each holding out a small object in an outstretched hand. Above the statues floated a slowly rotating globe.

'Is it a planet?' he asked, after drinking his fill of the deliciously cool water.

'A sun. The inscription reads "Knowledge shines on all",' replied Mr Swanson, pointing out a line of intricate script that ran around the edge of the fountain.

'That's the ring isn't it?' Ned burst out excitedly pointing at the object one of the statues was holding out.

'Yes, it is – exact in every detail. Look closely and you can see it has even got the same scratches and dents that the real one has.'

Ned took the ring from its hiding place in his pocket and held it next to the carved one.

'That's odd,' he said, frowning.

'Hmmm, what is?' asked Mr Swanson, who had been gazing around hall.

'Well, when I chiselled the ring from the tree, I accidentally dented it – my hands were shaking quite a lot.'

'Yes, go on.'

'If you look there, you can see that the one the

statue is holding has got exactly the same mark, too,' said Ned, pointing.

'So it has – how peculiar. Someone must have put the iungo charm on it. Very difficult to do,' said Mr Swanson, stroking his chin and peering at the ring.

'Who would have done it? What does the charm do?'

'As to your first question, I have no idea, certainly not me. As for the charm itself, it's a coupling charm – used to tell if something or someone is genuine or an imposter.'

'How do you mean?'

'Well, let me explain how it came into being. It was devised by a rather clever king who had four advisers. However, word got to him that one of the advisers was going to be kidnapped and replaced with an assassin, but he had no idea which one, so he had four statues carved, and without telling his advisers, commanded his Mage to place a charm on the statues that coupled them to the appearance and actions of the advisers.'

'How did that help?'

'Before meeting his advisers he would place something on each statue, such as a feather, or a leaf blown from a tree. If the advisers were the real ones, then they too would have the same on them.'

'And did they catch the assassin?'

'Much to everyone's relief, yes.'

'Is anyone here?' asked Ned, 'It's just that on the surface you said, "Let's see who's at home".'

'No,' said Mr Swanson, shaking his head slightly. He sighed a breath of ghosts and sorrow as he paused and looked around. 'No, there hasn't been anyone here for a long time, not since the Circle was destroyed. Even Sophos, the temple keeper, was with us when we were betrayed.'

Sadness hung in the air as they crossed the floor to a stone staircase that rose swan-like from the ground to a gallery high above them.

'You know who made these, don't you?' asked Mr Swanson.

'They're incredible, so beautiful. Who made them?'

'Why, Bryn, of course. Crafting stone is what he does best. He made most of this temple, as it happens, including the living quarters.'

At the top of the staircase, Mr Swanson led them along the left hand arc of the gallery, past several very solid-looking wooden doors, before finally stopping and pushing one open.

'My old living quarters – you are welcome to use them as my guest, and I shall take Bryn's – they're just next door.'

Ned stepped into a large, circular room with a spiral staircase running through its centre, joining the upper floor to the room that he stood in. A number of doors led off to other rooms, one of which he could see contained a tall arched glass door that looked out into a beautiful woodland landscape where birds and butterflies flew in their hundreds.

'I thought we were underground?' exclaimed Ned.

'We most definitely are. What you see there is a rather sophisticated enchantment that creates the illusion of anything the spell caster wants. As you know, I happen to like woodlands, birds and all things in nature's wonderful world.'

'How far does it go? I mean, those hills over there look as though they're miles away.'

'Oh, you could step into the enchantment and walk all the way there and stand on their summits. It's one I'm rather proud of.'

'You mean you invented, I mean wove, the spell?'

'"Olusum" is the incantation. It has many uses, and sadly many misuses, too.'

'But what if you got lost in the woods, or fell over and hurt yourself? What then? Who would find you?'

'Good question. All you have to do is utter the word "terminus", which is the incantation to end the spell, and voilà, you find yourself right here.'

'"Terminus". Like a bus station?' asked Ned, picturing a noisy, fume-filled bus depot with queues of people waiting to board.

'Yes, well, I suppose they mean the same thing – end or finish. Now, feel free to look around, Ned – you'll find everything you need in here, and when you're ready we'll eat.' With that Mr Swanson turned and left his old quarters.

Ned dropped his dusty pack by the staircase and set about exploring his new home. Mr Swanson's study was as Ned expected – a large, comfy armchair next to a fireplace in which a crackling blaze burst into life as Ned approached, and as he tested the armchair for comfort, a small table laden with a large plate of biscuits and a pot of tea waltzed slowly through the door and stood obediently by the chair. Grabbing a handful of the biscuits, Ned sank into the chair and began munching.

'Oh, thank you, these are delicious,' he said out loud.

'A pleasure, young sir,' said a voice beside him, making him jump with fright.

'Who said that?' he said backing away from the chair. 'Where are you? Are you a ghost or something?'

'I am quite clearly a table,' replied the voice.

Ned peered over the edge of the armchair and gaped as the table sprouted two delicate wooden arms and lifted the pot of tea and plate from its top. What Ned had originally thought was a deep crack in the table top broke into a friendly smile while a pair of knots in the wood blinked open and looked up at him. The face was complete when, with a squeaky 'pop', a small stump of a branch appeared in the middle.

'Hello, and who might you be?'

'I'm Ned. Ned Penhallow,' said Ned, grinning at the spectacle in front of him. 'Do you have a name?'

'Yes, I'm called Dennis. Table Dennis. It's his idea of a joke.'

'Mr Swanson's? He made you? And then called you Dennis?'

'Yes. Typical of him, really. Performs a marvellous piece of magic and caps it off with a silly joke,' said Dennis, and promptly dropped the teapot and plate back into place with an annoyed clatter.

Ned eyed Dennis carefully, not sure if he had just upset a piece of Mr Swanson's furniture or if this was normal behaviour for a talking table. Edging away, he continued eating his biscuit as he took in the rest of the study. Bookshelves covered nearly every spare inch of wall, and from one set of shelves hung a pair of flowery oven gloves.

'Oven gloves in Elgarolyn?' he said to himself, smiling at their curious presence.

'Swears by them,' said a voice by his knee, making him jump yet again.

'Crikey, Dennis, you nearly scared me to death,'

143

gasped Ned.

'Sorry, young sir, I've been enchanted to walk quietly so I can provide a nice hot cup of tea in bed without waking the master,' said Dennis. 'Now if young sir will follow me, I have something to show you which may be of interest.'

Ned turned and followed as Dennis turned and trotted nimbly from the room and into a short corridor, before stopping and opening a door.

'Here you are, young sir, I hope you find this to your liking,' said Dennis, bowing slightly.

A large bath stood in the centre of the room and as Ned approached, water gushed from ornate taps, filling the bath within seconds. Without any further ado, Ned stripped off his dusty garments and slipped into the bath, sighing blissfully as the water soaked away the aches and pains from the day's walking. After a deep soak (and even taking time to dig the grit from his ears), Ned stood up, looking for something to dry himself on. A large towel flapped its way from a nearby pile and wrapped itself around him as the now grimy bathwater drained away as rapidly as it had filled the bath. Towelling himself down, Ned stepped from the bath and found the clothes that he had discarded in an untidy heap had been neatly folded and were spotlessly clean.

'Oh wow, I wish my bedroom could do this,' he sighed.

The memory of his home reminded him painfully of Sam, and Ned suddenly felt very small, very alone and very, very far from home.

'Ned, are you ready to eat?' called Mr Swanson, knocking at the door to the chamber.

'Yes, just finished in the bath,' Ned called back, as he hurriedly pulled on the last of his clothes and wiped away the tears that had welled up. 'I wish my clothes could always clean and fold themselves – Mum would be delighted.'

'Very handy, some of these domestic spells, aren't they? Have you met Dennis yet? We had tremendous fun fitting our quarters out, we even put some practical jokes in, so keep an eye out!'

After they had finished eating a huge bowl of stew that Mr Swanson had cooked up from the provisions Bryn had given them, Ned found himself yawning and fighting to keep his eyes open.

'The long day is taking its toll on you, Ned, and I'm not surprised either – we've covered a good distance and you've not complained once – you're a credit to your mother. You'll find your reward through that door there,' said Mr Swanson, pointing across the circular hallway.

Barely able to stand, Ned hauled himself from his chair and with bleary eyes threatening to flutter shut, stumbled toward the room that Mr Swanson had pointed to. To his delight, the room held a huge four poster bed with the most comfortable mattress and quilt he had ever felt, and it was into this that he sank, falling instantly into a deep, deep sleep.

Chapter Twenty-Six

A Rude Awakening

A deep, thundering rumble shook Ned from his exhausted sleep. Somewhere nearby a man's voice bellowed words Ned had never heard before, words that made the air hiss and writhe around him. Another ground-shaking rumble followed, which was answered by a terrible roar that made Ned clap his hands over his ears. When the roar eventually stopped, Ned jumped from his bed and quickly pulled his clothes on, keeping a terrified eye firmly on the door to his room. He carefully inched the door open and peered through the gap. More shouts, another crash of thunder, and Ned flinched as daggers of light flickered across the ceiling and small blue sparks flashed up and down the spiral staircase. Again, a dreadful, primeval roar split the air sending him cringing back behind the door.

Slipping his hand into his pocket and curling a finger through the ring, Ned took a deep breath and, summoning up every ounce of his courage, charged from the room. The sounds of battle were coming from Bryn's old quarters next door and it was there that Ned sprinted, desperate to come to Mr Swanson's aid. Ned shouldered his way through Bryn's door and fell sprawling as his foot caught on the step. Ignoring the pain in his injured knees and elbows, he picked himself up from the floor and hobbled across the room to where battle raged. With the ring held out in front of him as if to ward off an attack, Ned burst through the only door he could see and froze in horror at the sight that met his eyes. One wall of the room had been torn away to reveal a huge cavern, and within the cavern swarmed what Ned could only describe as a horde of demons. Greenish foul-smelling smoke filled the air and, in the centre, armed only with his staff, he could see Mr Swanson locked in battle with several of the demons. Ned watched in awe as Mr Swanson moved and spun, ducking under slashing claws, neatly side-stepping pounding feet and somersaulting over sweeping tails, his staff a blur as he spun it in his hand before catching it in both and firing spells from one end and then the other, flashes of green, blue and red slamming into his attackers, sending them sprawling and howling with fury as they became entangled and bound in thick magical ropes.

As the last one fell, the floor of the cavern groaned and bulged upwards, a network of cracks shooting across the floor. A huge, brutal head began forcing its way through the floor, scattering lumps of rock before it and bringing a mountain of rubble crashing down from the ceiling, separating Ned from Mr Swanson. Stranded, Ned coughed and spluttered as he stumbled blindly through a heavy fog of dust and smoke until he bumped into something thick, scaly and horribly hot. Hardly daring to breathe, Ned slowly looked up and found himself staring directly into the flaming eyes of a monstrous jet-black demon that stood as tall as a tree and with terrible, wicked horns growing from its huge head - a demon that was now grinning hideously down at him, revealing a mouthful of razor-sharp teeth, thick, green poison dripping from between them. Ned slowly backed away until his shoulder blades came up against the wall behind, all the while the demon grinning and slobbering and cracking its knuckles loudly as it prepared to attack.

The first swipe split the air a whisker above Ned's head as he let out a terrified yell and ducked away. A smell of fireworks filled his nostrils as the demon's claws gouged huge scratches out of the rock where he had been standing moments before. The next swipe came low, giving him no room to duck. Instead he darted between the demon's legs and out behind, jumping over the thick, slithering tail that trailed behind the monster. As the demon spun round to face its nimble foe, the tail that Ned had jumped over whipped round and caught him hard across his lower legs, sweeping them away and sending him crashing to the ground with a bone-rattling thump that knocked the wind from him. His head pounding from the fall, Ned tried to crawl away, frantically scrabbling up the mound of fallen masonry. The demon roared with triumph and stamped a huge cloven foot on the ground, bringing more debris falling from the ceiling. Ned stopped crawling and rolled over, determined to face his attacker. Another roar and the demon raised both clawed hands high into the air and began to bring them smashing down upon Ned. In the final split second before the demon's claws dealt their deadly blow, a shout of "Aquaramificus" filled the chamber and deep blue streams of magic flew from the other side of the rubble and bound the demon, wrestling it to the ground where it writhed and strained against its bonds, the whole room shaking as it screamed with rage.

'Mr Swanson, what's happening? Are we being attacked?' yelled Ned as Mr Swanson climbed over the rubble.

'Morning Ned, did I wake you up? I really am sorry, I got quite carried away – it's been a while since I've been able to practise my battle spells, not much call for them in Weston Pewsey Primary School, although I'm sure some of the teachers might disagree!'

Ned stared back at Mr Swanson unsure of what to

make of his calm air. Mr Swanson, who was busy flicking pieces of masonry from his cloak, failed to notice Ned's stare.

'They really do smell quite awful, don't they?' he asked distractedly, as he shook dust from his hair. 'Sewage farm on a hot day crossed with rotten eggs, I'd say. Possibly with a hint of boiled spinach, wouldn't you say?'

'Who sent them to attack us?' asked Ned.

'What? Why, I did of course. Who else?' replied Mr Swanson, spinning his staff round one hand and then flicking it to the other.

'You sent them? Whatever for?' asked Ned incredulously.

'Hmm? Training. Practise. Blowing the cobwebs out of my poor old wizarding brain!'

'But we could have been killed! That one was going to tear me apart.'

'Not likely. I may be a bit rusty, but I can still hold my own,' replied Mr Swanson. With a flourish of his hand he said "Terminus," and the demons and the green smoke and the enormous, stinking cavern faded until they had all vanished leaving a small, empty room.

'You mean, that was all conjured up? Just so you could practise?'

'Yes. Marvellous spell, that one, simply marvellous.'

'I was absolutely terrified - that thing was going to kill me.'

'Admittedly they were quite frightening, but if you can cast a binding spell on a demon, then you can cast a binding spell on anything. It's one of the hardest spells to cast, I can tell you.'

'If you're so good, then why can't you just magic

us to Malverfuhren's castle and rescue Sam?'

'Alas, that's not possible,' Mr Swanson replied sadly. 'Malverfuhren would be aware of any sudden surge of magic and would be ready for us. Stealth is the only way to help Sam, I'm afraid.'

'So how can you use spells down here?'

'The temple has always had to serve not just as a place of learning and respite, but also a place of protection and safety. When Belastung and Malverfuhren began to grow in power, we placed a number of very powerful charms on the temple that would not only conceal it from the outside, but would also prevent any signs of magical activity from escaping. It's here that the Circle trained many of its mages in order to avoid bringing unwanted attention to itself.'

'Does this mean you can't use any magic outside of the temple without Malverfuhren knowing about it?'

'Only the simplest of spells and charms – the elemental ones – go unnoticed. You've seen me use elemental magic back in Weston Pewsey – the light when we met Great-Aunt Gail and the night we walked to the stone. The banishing spell I cast when Malverfuhren sent a vortex to take the ring from you was a bit more powerful. That would have been detected even if Malverfuhren hadn't been on the receiving end of it.'

'Oh, gosh, yes, I remember now – you shouted something that sounded really odd, and the light bulb shone really brightly and then blew up.'

'Yes, that's right. We nearly gave the game away pulling that one off. Especially with your father being there.'

'And Great-Aunt Gail,' said Ned.

'Hmm? Oh yes, and Great-Aunt Gail,' replied Mr Swanson, looking suddenly uncomfortable.

'But doesn't it matter if Malverfuhren detected you using magic back in my world?'

'No need to worry about that, Belastung and Malverfuhren are well aware that I live in Weston Pewsey – they wouldn't expect me to be anywhere else. After all that's where the ring was believed to have been lost.'

After a simple breakfast of bread and cheese, followed by tea and biscuits from Dennis, Mr Swanson and Ned stood upon the dais, Ned with his hands tightly clutching Mr Swanson's sleeve. With a final wave to a rather forlorn looking Dennis, followed by a crackle and the now familiar spinning sensation, Ned found himself shivering next to Mr Swanson on the rocky surface just as the sun began to lighten the horizon.

'It's freezing,' he gasped, as he gazed at the desert around them.

'Surprising, isn't it? The days are ferociously hot, but as soon as the sun goes down the temperature plummets. A man would die of exposure if he spent the night out in the open. As long as nothing else got him first, that is.'

'What's wrong?' Ned asked, as Mr Swanson suddenly knelt down and peered closely at the sand around them.

'Footprints – svartelf footprints. We've been followed,' came the tense reply.

'Are you sure they're svartelf footprints?' asked Ned.

'Yes – they're unmistakable. Look here – four points here made by their front claws and one large point here – that's their rear claw. They're small, too,' said Mr Swanson, as he traced his finger over the imprints.

'Where are they now?' asked Ned, looking in all

directions.

'They won't be around now – look over there – something large took one, probably a Sand Dragon,' said Mr Swanson, pointing to a sad patch of blood on the ground and a scrap of cloth nearby, 'and look how the footprints have scattered in all directions. Svartelves normally travel in single file.'

'What? Did you say "Sand Dragon"? You never told me there were dragons in this world!' said Ned, his eyes like saucers.

'Didn't I? Oh sorry, but fear not, Sand Dragons are purely nocturnal – they burrow deep down into the sand and away from the sun long before dawn.'

Mr Swanson, his brow furrowed, glanced warily around, scanning the miles and miles of desert that surrounded them.

'We must move quickly,' he said finally. 'Now that the svartelves are aware of us, they'll no doubt be wanting to enjoy our company.'

Chapter Twenty-Seven

Svartelves

As the blazing sun reached its highest point, Ned struggled to keep up with Mr Swanson's striding form. The last of the water had been drunk hours ago and the relentless dusty wind had scoured their skin with every step they took. A few hours after setting out from the temple, a huge sandstorm had engulfed them and for what seemed an eternity the two companions had sat side by side, huddled in their cloaks with the hoods pulled tight over their faces, as the hot, suffocating dust howled around them.

'You're looking exhausted. Today's hot even for springtime,' said Mr Swanson, as he waited patiently for Ned to catch up again.

Ned nodded wearily. A feeble cry escaping his parchment-dry throat as he flopped down next to Mr Swanson.

'Don't despair, Ned, you've marched like a trooper, and besides I think our luck may have changed for the better,' said Mr Swanson, pointing towards a large cluster of trees huddled around a rocky outcrop a short distance away. 'There'll be water there I shouldn't wonder,' he said, 'and it'll probably provide us with some shade. We can rest there a while and let the day cool a little. Here, I'll take your pack for you.'

'Thank you, but no. I'll carry it, I've carried it this far and I'm sure I can carry it a little further,' croaked Ned, as he struggled to his feet, a blister on his heel bursting and making him wince.

Mr Swanson said nothing, but smiled slightly and nodded his head before turning and leading them toward the trees.

Ned followed Mr Swanson closely now, a spring in his step at the thought of refuge from the sun and the wind, and if Mr Swanson was right, a cool drink of water. In the shade of the trees, Ned sank to the ground with a groan and unhitched his pack, sighing with relief as the weight fell from his shoulders. Unlacing his boots, he poured a pile of sand from each one and, carefully peeling each sock off, he wriggled his swollen toes in the cool air.

'These are desert oaks, Ned, we couldn't have found a better place to rest. They cool the air underneath them as though a clear mountain stream was running round their roots.'

Ned lay back, relishing the soft, springy ground that lay beneath the trees. High above, birds fluttered from branch to branch in the thick canopy, their twittering and birdsong accompanied by the steady hum of the insects they hunted.

'I'll have a look for water while you rest,' said Mr Swanson, as he, too, dropped his pack and, grasping his staff, began exploring their newly discovered haven.

As exhaustion washed over him, Ned's eyelids began to droop and, with the sound of the birds and the insects lulling him, he soon fell into a slumber.

'Ned. Ned, wake up, I've found water.'

Mr Swanson's voice broke into a confused dream of Sam being held in a cage and with a start he jerked fully awake.

'Here, drink some of this,' said Mr Swanson, holding a water bottle out to him.

Ned grabbed the bottle and gulped down several mouthfuls before Mr Swanson could stop him.

'Steady now, you'll give yourself an upset stomach if you do that.'

'I'm sorry, Mr Swanson, that was greedy of me. I was so thirsty,' spluttered Ned, wiping dribbles of water from his chin.

'I'm not surprised you're parched, you've marched like a grown man.' Mr Swanson smiled kindly. 'Have the rest of the bottle, but slowly, now – there's plenty more where that came from. Come, I'll show you. Bring your bottles with you.'

Ned pulled himself to his feet and, feeling refreshed, followed Mr Swanson as he led the way deeper into the trees until they reach a small jumble of rocks. Within the rocks lay a dark, narrow cleft that cut a channel straight down into the ground.

'If you listen carefully, you can hear running water,' said Mr Swanson, nodding toward the crack.

Ned placed his ear close to the opening and sure enough he could hear the faint murmur of water flowing deep underground.

'But how did you get down there?' asked Ned, looking at the cleft and then at Mr Swanson.

'I didn't – I asked the water to come to me,' replied Mr Swanson.

'Magic?' asked Ned. 'But what if we get noticed?'

'It's a risk I had to take. Without water we wouldn't get much further. Do you have all the water bottles ready? I'm going to summon the water up once more and you can fill them. But be swift.'

Ned fumbled the stoppers from their bottles and stood close to the cleft.

'"Aquam ducere,"' commanded Mr Swanson, holding the tip of his staff against the rock. Immediately the sound of running water grew louder and to Ned's astonishment, a fountain of crystal clear water sprang from the crack, soaking him to the skin before becoming a bubbling stream. Gasping for breath in the deliciously cold water, Ned plunged all the bottles into the stream. No sooner had he filled them all than the water disappeared, leaving the cleft dry once more and a few scattered pools on the rocky ground. After returning to their packs and stowing the newly filled water bottles, Mr Swanson led Ned to the very edge of the trees and pointed with his staff. Far behind them, birds that had flocked to what was left of the water suddenly burst up from the ground, their terrified cries echoing around the trees.

'In that direction lies Port Cadarn. We should reach it by nightfall, as long as we don't fall foul of our underground friends.'

Turning back to their packs, Ned and Mr Swanson found their way blocked by a line of very nasty-looking crossbows and, holding the crossbows were several of the ugliest creatures Ned had ever seen.

'Ah,' said Mr Swanson, 'a little too much magic, perhaps?'

'Any magic is too much magic if you ask me,' snarled the svartelf who was evidently the leader – larger, more heavily scarred and wearing a string of bird skulls as a badge of rank on its filthy leather tunic.

'And these, Ned, as you've probably guessed, are svartelves. Notice the particularly vile smell and foul manner,' said Mr Swanson.

Ned gulped loudly and took a step back, his face ashen.

'Shut up or I'll cut your tongue out for you, old man, or should I say, "wizard"?' spat the leader.

The svartelf eyed them with animal hatred and

with a guttural hiss commanded the others to spread out
in a semicircle, those on the ends reluctantly moving close
to the bright sunshine that dappled the ground at the edge
of the trees.

'Are they going to take us as slaves, Mr Swanson?'
whimpered Ned.

The leader walked up to Ned and, with its face
only inches away, cackled horribly.

'Oh, no, there's someone who wants to meet you.
Trust me when I say that being a slave would be far nicer
than where you're going.'

Ned recoiled, trying hard not to be sick as the
svartelf's rotten breath washed over him. Deep in his
pocket, the ring, which had been growing steadily colder,
now bit icily through the pocket and into his leg, making
him jump.

'We can pay you far more handsomely than
Atrabo can,' said Mr Swanson, leaning casually on his
staff. 'Gold, jewels, weapons that never miss their target,
swords that never break, you only have to name your
price.'

'Atrabo?' said Ned. 'I thought his name was
Malverfuhren?'

'Stupid old wizard, there's no one of that name.
We serve only Belastung and Malverfuhren,' snarled the
svartelf.

Behind the leader, the svartelves began to move
nervously, hissing and spitting with fright as the air
around them began to thicken and darken. Turning, Ned
felt his legs go weak as he saw that instead of bright
sunlight, a darkening, writhing mist was forming at the
edge of the trees, sending black tendrils of smoke snaking
through the trees.

'It looks as though your master doesn't quite trust

you to do his work for him,' said Mr Swanson, as the svartelves began to edge nervously away from the blackness that was deepening around them.

The leader, his eyes bulging, turned and with a scream of rage and fear ran back into the trees with the other svartelves running pell-mell after him.

'Come on, Mr Swanson, the Gravemen will take us,' squeaked Ned, pulling at Mr Swanson's sleeve. Mr Swanson ignored Ned's frantic pleas, and instead stood calmly watching the screaming svartelves as they scrambled over rocks and charged through bushes, pushing and shoving and trampling over one another in their bid to escape.

'No need, Ned, it's not the Gravemen,' replied Mr Swanson quietly.

'What is it then?' asked Ned, backing away from the pulsing pitch black that had halted mere inches from them.

'Do you recall me calling Malverfuhren by another name?' asked Mr Swanson.

'Yes, you called him "Atrabo" or something.'

'Correct, I did; however "Atrabo" is the incantation of a very handy spell that darkens everything around you. I couldn't say the incantation by itself, otherwise I'd have resembled a pin cushion before I'd finished.'

Mr Swanson stooped and, picking up Ned's pack, held it out to him.

'We'd best be on our way, Ned. The svartelves will even now be scurrying back to their master and after he's finished punishing them for their mistake they'll be even keener to find us. We'll travel through the darkness for a while. It'll help protect us.'

And with a light shining from his staff, Mr

Swanson shouldered his pack and led the way into the abyssal darkness that lay waiting.

Chapter Twenty-Eight

Port Cadarn

'There it is, Ned,' said Mr Swanson, as they crested yet another huge sand dune, 'our destination – Port Cadarn.'

Ned sank down beside Mr Swanson and gazed down upon the thriving city. The desert wasteland stopped short of the city, giving way to rocky scrubland that soon burst into verdant, lush grass covering the rolling hills that spread as far as he could see. In the gathering twilight the first stars could be seen shining in the heavens and a deep red moon was beginning to rise over the horizon.

Half the day had passed since Mr Swanson had dismissed the darkness that he had conjured, leaving them once again baking under the hot sun and with their water running dangerously low. Mr Swanson had urged Ned on, eventually shouldering Ned's pack as well as his own.

'It's huge,' croaked Ned, taking in the sprawling blanket of lights that twinkled on the rooftops. All at once the lights rose up as one and flew streaming and swooping over the city before returning to the rooftops.

'Those are one of Elgarolyn's most delightful creatures – lampwings,' said Mr Swanson, enjoying the look of marvel on Ned's tired face, 'tame nocturnal birds that have the most beautiful plumage, and wings that light up the dark.'

The two watched as the lampwings once again flew from their perches and began to surge and cascade high over Port Cadarn before forming an immense ball of light over the city. Ned laughed in wonder as the ball erupted and the lampwings dived helter-skelter back to their rooftop perches.

'Come, now, let's see if we can get in through one of the smaller gates. I have a feeling that the larger ones are being watched very closely.'

Stumbling with fatigue and wincing at the pain from their blistered, raw feet, Mr Swanson and Ned trudged down the dune and approached Port Cadarn. Picking their way between the melted and twisted rocks that lay scattered about them, they froze stock still when suddenly something ahead of them hissed and screeched and a furious quarrel broke out. Ahead of them hordes of small, dark figures swarmed around every possible entrance to Port Cadarn – svartelves.

'Oh, dear, things aren't looking too good for us, Ned,' murmured Mr Swanson, as the two of them crouched in the cover of a large rock.

'Can't we go to another port?' whispered Ned, as he joined Mr Swanson in peering over the edge of the rock.

'If only we could, but this one is nearest to the portal and the next one is another two to three days walk away. What makes things worse is that we need more supplies, as well as fresh water. There's nothing else for it, we need to get into the port, and we need to get in soon. The longer we're out here in the open, the greater the chance of being discovered by the svartelves.'

'So how can we get in?' asked Ned, eyeing the small, hissing figures that could be seen taunting the heavily armed city guards that manned every entrance to the city.

'Well, back in the old days when the Circle was complete, Port Cadarn had a thriving smuggling community,' said Mr Swanson.

'So we can be smuggled in?' asked Ned hopefully.

'Not quite. The smugglers had many tunnels in and out of the city, and if I recall correctly there was one that came out not too far from where we are now.'

Ned let out a groan and shuddered at the thought of sneaking through a suffocating tunnel with the cold earth pressing in from all sides.

'Are you sure there's no other way in?' he asked.

'No, I'm afraid not. Follow me, and keep close. If we get caught then our only option is for me to fight them while you escape and make your own way in to the port. If that does happen, try and make your way to one of the inns that are on the seafront and I'll meet you there.'

'But what if you don't? What then?'

'Well, let's just hope it doesn't come to that, eh?'

Mr Swanson set off stealthily across the barren land that lay between them and the tunnel entrance, keeping to the shadows cast by the red moon that hung over them like a crimson eye. Every so often he would pause to make sure they hadn't been spotted and at one point, just as they crawled on their bellies under the very noses of a group of svartelves, the lampwings again took flight and flew directly overhead, lighting up the ground all around them as though it were daylight. The svartelves, more interested in hiding from the sudden burst of light, didn't see their quarry lying motionless a mere metres away. After several more heart-thumping scares, Mr Swanson signalled a now utterly petrified Ned to stop and pointed toward the city.

'We're very close to the port now, Ned,' he murmured, 'and to add to the fun there's another svartelf patrol just over there by those rocks. A particularly ugly bunch, too, probably from the Eastern Reaches judging by their weapons – can you see their scimitars?'

Ned followed Mr Swanson's pointing finger and at first could see nothing until one of the svartelves moved slightly and picked something out if its ear. To Ned's disgust the svartelf held up whatever it had found and, after inspecting it closely popped it into its mouth and began chewing it with relish.

'How did you spot them? They're so well-camouflaged,' Ned whispered back, as he tried not to listen to the svartelf busily smacking its lips together as it enjoyed its snack.

'They always hide in obvious places and even if it was pitch black they'd steer clear of open ground if they could. We're going to have to be very, very careful looking for the smuggler's tunnel. Keep one eye on the svartelves and one eye out for a large flat rock that looks as though something has taken a bite out of it.'

Port Cadarn's Great Clocktower was just striking midnight when Ned finally beckoned Mr Swanson to the rock he had crouched behind as yet another svartelf patrol had slunk past.

'Could this be the one?' he whispered, pointing at a number of deep grooves that had been smoothed by years of harsh desert wind.

Mr Swanson crawled to Ned's side and ran his hands over the rock. He let out a low sigh of relief.

'Well done, yes, that's it,' he whispered.

'These teeth marks look so real,' said Ned, tracing the length of one furrow with an index finger.

'That's because they are,' replied Mr Swanson, as he watched the svartelves unfold themselves from the nearby rocks and scuttle away to keep watch from their hiding places.

'Really? What do you think did it?'

'Oh, I know what did it – a Granite Dragon. They're not native to this world – Belastung and Malverfuhren stole the eggs of one and brought them back to Elgarolyn to hatch them for their own purposes. They made the mistake of not realising just how intelligent and protective those beautiful creatures are.'

'It's huge though. How do we lift it?'

'It would take ten strong men to lift this,' said Mr Swanson, 'but if I touch it here, here and then here – ta da! It becomes as light as a feather.'

Mr Swanson lifted the rock with ease and motioned Ned down the dusty worn steps that it revealed. Following Ned down, Mr Swanson lowered the rock back in place and, tapping it once more, sealed the hole.

'I think we could use a little light, don't you?' asked Mr Swanson from the inky blackness of the tunnel.

Ned let out a frightened yell as the bright light that burst from Mr Swanson's staff revealed a narrow tunnel with curtains of cobwebs draped from the ceiling. Huge spiders scuttled across the webs, and dotted among the strands were the mummified remains of rats. A nest of pasty white scorpions erupted from a crack in the wall and skittered away from the light, screaming in high-pitched voices as they did so.

'I can't go near those things,' moaned Ned, his hands clapped over his ears, 'they're horrible. Look at them – they've got faces. They're screaming like Mum did when Sam got hit by the car.'

'It's OK, Ned,' said Mr Swanson, as he knelt down and pulled Ned's hands away from his ears, 'they're Frykt scorpions, they're harmless.'

'They don't look harmless to me; I saw Malverfuhren's face on some of them. And Sam's, I saw Sam's face and he was crying for me,' Ned screamed at

Mr Swanson, 'didn't you see them?'

'Ned, listen to me. Listen! To! Me!' commanded Mr Swanson, grabbing Ned by the shoulders and shaking him, 'this is how they work – they find the things that you're most scared of or that upset you the most and mimic them.'

'Why, though?' sobbed Ned.

'They think we're going to hurt them so they make us scared and make us fight among ourselves and while we're doing that, they escape,' said Mr Swanson. 'Look – they're gone.'

Ned looked gingerly past Mr Swanson's shoulder and let out a long shuddering sigh.

'I'm sorry I shouted at you, Mr Swanson,' he said, sniffing up his tears and wiping his nose on his sleeve.

'Don't be sorry, Ned,' said Mr Swanson, shaking his head, 'you're an eleven-year old boy far, far from home, in a world that is nothing like his own, looking for his brother's soul. Your courage is immense. Do you understand that? Immense.'

Ned nodded his head and sniffed once more.

'Mr Swanson,' he asked, 'what did you see? Did you hear a noise, too?'

'I did – I saw a world without teabags and I heard the sound of my teapot smashing on the floor – terrible. Absolutely terrible,' he said with a smile and a wink.

Ned grinned back and wiped the last of his tears away.

'Right, let's go and get Sam back,' he said, taking in a deep breath and standing up ramrod straight.

'That's the spirit, young man,' said Mr Swanson, and led them into the musty tunnel.

Chapter Twenty-Nine

The Lampwing's Feather

'We're right under the city now,' said Mr Swanson, much to Ned's relief, 'and here are the steps I told you about. The rest of the tunnel goes much further and branches out all over the place, but I think we've had quite enough of crawling through the earth for one day, don't you?'

The journey through the smugglers' tunnel had been long and exhausting. Several times they had had to stop to negotiate obstacles – huge spider's webs that clung to them, roof collapses, and at one point having to crawl through a section of tunnel that dipped down and was nearly full with stagnant water. Mr Swanson and Ned had had to crawl on their backs through this section, with only their mouths and noses above the water, so close to the tunnel roof was the water. Moving too quickly had made the foul water slop over their faces, causing them to choke and splutter. This had been particularly hard for Ned, who had hated water ever since falling into a deep pond as a small child and nearly drowning. It had been his father's frantic searching that had found him and pulled him out, stinking black mud and rotting weeds dripping from him.

Mr Swanson extinguished the light and the two companions pulled themselves wearily up the stone steps and squeezed through the tunnel exit. Collapsing against a rough stone wall, they breathed in huge gulps of fresh air and coughed out the dust and fetid air they'd endured for the last few hours.

'Whereabouts are we?' asked Ned, picking the last of the cobwebs from his hair and clothing.

'We're under a small bridge in the Smugglers' Quarter – there'll be no svartelves here but we may still encounter some unsavoury characters, so stay close,' replied Mr Swanson.

The two slipped from under the bridge and heaved themselves up into a deserted alley.

'This way, Ned,' said Mr Swanson, beckoning Ned toward a bustling street at the far end of the alley. Ned looked nervously at the mass of bodies that heaved and shoved its way along the thoroughfare and gripped the ring tightly, pushing it as far down into his coat pocket as he could. Joining the throng, Ned followed closely in Mr Swanson's wake as he forged his way along the crowded street, his staff earning several curious looks and comments as he did so. Slipping into a narrow street, Mr Swanson turned to Ned.

'We'll take a shortcut here. I think a visit to the Three Markets of Port Cadarn would be very welcome. Particularly the first one.'

The side street was well-lit from several lampwings that had perched along its length, casting their light far about them. As Ned gazed up at them, one of the birds, larger than all the others, left its perch and fluttered down to land just a few feet above their heads. Looking directly at Ned, the lampwing stretched its wings wide, and after carefully inspecting each wing, plucked a single feather from one. After taking another long look at Ned, it launched itself into the air, dropping the feather from its beak as it passed directly over him. The two companions watched as the sliver of starlight gracefully swooped and slipped through the air, before Ned reached out and caught the falling quill in his palm. Both Ned and Mr

Swanson stared, mesmerised, at the feather as its beautiful colours rolled in waves across its surface, lighting up their faces.

'You have indeed been blessed,' murmured Mr Swanson.

'I've never seen anything so beautiful,' breathed Ned.

'Lampwings never, never lose their wing feathers. Once they grow them, they have them for life. I've never seen nor heard of them plucking them out.'

'Why did it give it to me, though?'

'I'm not sure. Lampwings have always been a symbol of strength for those most in need, for the weak and the scared, bringing light and help even in the darkest of moments. Look how they light the way for the people of Port Cadarn.'

'I could have done with this when Malverfuhren tried to take the Ring from me.'

'You'd best hide it deep in your pocket. Many have sought the feathers of lampwings but none have ever succeeded.'

'But won't it crumple?'

'No. I've handled lampwings before. Their wing feathers last them a lifetime because they're incredibly strong.'

Nevertheless, Ned took great care in sliding the feather deep into his coat pocket and watched for a moment as its light shone on the ring that nestled there.

The side street led them onto a crowded market square bursting with food stalls, grocers and butchers trading their wares. Strange smells assailed Ned's nostrils – some mouth-watering and delicious, others eye-watering and foul. As they passed one stall, where huge skewers of meat were roasting over glowing coals, Ned's stomach made a loud growling sound, so loud in fact that the stall owner looked up in surprise and shouted to Mr Swanson.

'Hey, old man, your boy is starving – feed him at this fine stall of mine. Tell you what – he can have one of my specials for half the normal price. How's about that, eh?'

Mr Swanson turned and looked at the stallholder.

'What would you recommend the boy have?' he asked.

'Here, boy, you have this – I call it the Warrior's Feast,' said the man, offering a plate piled high with roasted meat and a tottering pile of outlandish looking vegetables. 'You look like a warrior to me!'

Ned grinned and thanked the man, and without any further encouragement, sat down at a nearby table and tucked into the food.

'I'll have the same, please, and could you be so kind as to fill these bottles for us?' asked Mr Swanson, as he joined Ned, who had already ploughed his way through half of his meal and didn't look as though he was going to have any trouble finishing.

'I'm sorry, I should have offered you some of mine. I've never been so hungry in my whole life,' said Ned shamefacedly, as he paused for breath.

'Don't you worry.' Mr Swanson laughed. 'I'd be concerned if you weren't hungry – you've endured two hard days across the wastelands, not to mention a brush with the svartelves and a rather long and unpleasant crawl through a tunnel.'

'Don't forget the Frykt scorpions,' said Ned, shuddering at the memory.

'That's an interesting staff you have there, old man; I haven't seen one of those since the days of the

Circle,' said the stallholder, placing a flagon of water on the table and a large plate of steaming food in front of Mr Swanson.

'Thank you; it's been handed down from father to son for generations. It's nothing fancy, just a reminder of those who came before us.'

'Did I hear you talking of svartelves?'

'Yes, you certainly did,' replied Mr Swanson, as he speared a piece of meat on his fork. 'We had a little trouble with them this morning.'

'Gah, filthy little things,' exclaimed the stallholder with a grimace, 'you were lucky they didn't whisk you off to one of their stinking caves.'

'Fortunately, if you can call it fortune, the Gravemen chose that moment to pass by. Scared them away as quick as you like,' replied Mr Swanson, catching Ned's eye.

'Well, you'll have no worries with svartelves around here,' said the stallholder. 'They may be swarming around the city gates and some parts of the city, but they'll not venture into this quarter – the Smugglers and Outcasts won't stand for anything or anyone who works for Malverfuhren.'

'That's reassuring to know,' said Mr Swanson.

'Well, enjoy your meal,' smiled the stallholder, 'and let me know if you want anything else.'

After several minutes of silence while he wolfed down the rest of his food, Ned sat back with a contented sigh and patted his bulging stomach.

'That has to be the best meal I have ever eaten – even better than Mum's roast dinners,' he said, grinning at Mr Swanson.

'The Market of Feasts is one of the wonders of

Elgarolyn. Not only that, but food tastes far better over here anyway. As does the air and the water. I've always said that,' said Mr Swanson, as he finished his last mouthful. 'There's far less pollution over here - no cars, no power stations, no chemical plants, and everything is so much cleaner for it.'

'By the stars, I'm sure there was a pattern on that when I put it in front of you, young man,' said the stallholder, as he picked up Ned's empty plate and peered at it in mock astonishment.

'That was the perfect meal for two weary travellers, but I'm afraid we shall have to take our leave now,' said Mr Swanson, as he too pushed his empty plate away. 'How much do I owe you for the food and water?'

'Water's free and it's a silver gillet for the food,' said the stallholder.

'A fair price – thank you. And thank you for the information, too,' said Mr Swanson, shouldering his pack as Ned did the same.

'A pleasure. Oh, one other thing – the svartelves daren't come into this quarter, but they have been sending gangs of Forest Ogres from the Far Eastern Reaches to do their kidnapping for them. They're particularly keen on taking Outcasts, for some reason.'

'Thank you again. We shall keep a keen eye open. Come, now, Ned, let's make our way to the Market of Healing. I think it would be wise to furnish ourselves with salves and medicines for the remainder of our journey.'

'Mr Swanson? The stall holder mentioned Outcasts. What are Outcasts?' asked Ned, after they had moved away from the stall.

'Outcasts are people just like you and I, but who were taken from their own world in their thousands by Belastung and forced to work on mining portal stones.'

'Why don't they return to their own world instead of living in Port Cadarn?' asked Ned.

'They would do, but Belastung and Malverfuhren destroyed the portal stones to stop them, and they've been marooned here ever since.'

'That's so sad. What about their families? They won't have seen them since they were kidnapped, will they?' said Ned, as he thought of his own brother lying unmoving in a hospital bed, his soul held hostage by Malverfuhren.

'Alas, they may never see them again. We believe that the Portal Map was destroyed too, so even if we made a portal we wouldn't know where to place it.'

'What's the Portal Map?' asked Ned.

'The Portal Map? Didn't I tell you about it?' said Mr Swanson, stopping in his tracks and frowning down at Ned.

Ned shook his head.

'Well, when we realised what the portal stones were capable of,' explained Mr Swanson, 'we decided it might be wise to keep track of where the portal stones were, and which world they connected to, and what that world was like.'

'Was it a paper map?' asked Ned, picturing a large Ordnance Survey map of Elgarolyn with all manner of strange symbols and warnings on it.

Mr Swanson sighed.

'No. Bryn made the most beautiful globe you could imagine and Sophos enchanted it. An exquisite piece of work, absolutely exquisite.'

'But what happened to it?' asked Ned.

'Stolen not long after Belastung - '

Without warning, a tide of people surged round a corner and came charging towards them, screaming and shouting in terror. Sounds of terrible destruction followed. Mr Swanson pulled Ned to one side and they ducked into a nearby doorway as the crowd sought to escape.

'What is it, Mr Swanson? Why are they running?' yelled Ned, as Mr Swanson stole a glance around the corner. 'Is it the Gravemen? Are the svartelves attacking?'

A merchant, blood pouring in streams from his head, staggered past them, propped up by his weeping wife.

'No,' said Mr Swanson, peering round the corner, 'but it looks like our friend was right about the ogres. There's a rather ugly group of them rampaging through the square and an Outcast has tried to stop them by the looks of things. Looks like he's bitten off more than he can chew.'

'Can't you stop them, Mr Swanson, please? We can't just stand by and watch,' Ned pleaded, flinching as a stall took a direct hit from something large and heavy.

'If I use magic we'll draw too much attention to ourselves,' replied Mr Swanson grimly. 'There's nothing we can do but wait until they've gone. Keep your head back, we mustn't let them catch sight of us.'

Ignoring Mr Swanson's warning, Ned joined him and poked his head carefully around the corner. Every stall in the market square had been demolished. Shards of glass and ornate pottery littered the cobbles and the gutters ran with spilled potions and medicines. A few feet away, scratching its stubbly head, stood the ugliest creature Ned had ever seen. Standing twice as tall as a man, its mottled green skin glistening with sweat and a crude iron club gripped in a fist the size of a dustbin lid, the ogre would have made a svartelf look handsome. Bending down, it rummaged amongst the debris of a stall and pulled free an intact cask. Frowning dimly at its find, the ogre pulled the bung free with its teeth and took a mighty swig.

'Blah! Yucky-yucky-yuck. Medicine taste like Grandma's cooking,' said the ogre, and flung the cask across the square, whereupon it smashed against the head of another ogre. The unfortunate ogre ignored the impact of the barrel and the shower of bright blue medicine and instead reached down and snatched something from the stricken figure that lay trussed at its feet.

'Look,' the ogre hooted, 'I've got the little Outy-casty's necklace. Outy-casty for svartelves. Pretty thing for me. Fair's fair.'

Ned pulled his head back and with a deep breath pushed away from the wall and dashed into the square. The nearest ogre, still complaining about the foul-tasting medicine, looked up with a startled grunt and swiped at Ned. The huge club missed by a whisker and left a crater in the cobbles. Legs pumping, Ned sprinted between two more ogres, ducking under their grasping hands and leaving them tangled and fighting, each blaming the other. Hurdling an overturned stall, he landed in a pool of spilled liniment and his feet shot out from underneath him. Sprawling on the cobbles, pain thudding from where his head had smacked against stone, Ned rolled frantically to one side, a boulder-sized foot whistling down and pounding the spot where he had fallen. Springing to his feet, Ned neatly sidestepped another flailing hand and charged toward the ogre that was still gloating over its loot. Mustering all his strength, Ned drew back his leg and kicked the ogre square in the ankle.

'Leave him alone!' he shouted at the top of his voice. The ogre stopped its inspection of the necklace and with a look of surprise finally arriving on its face, pulled free a piece of barrel that had become wedged in its ear.

Frowning dimly, the ogre turned around, searching for whatever had interrupted its fun.

'Did you throw something at me, little squeaky-mouse boy?'

It was Ned's turn to look confused.

'No, I kicked you. Just now. Now, let that man go.'

Reaching down and picking Ned up by the scruff of the neck, the ogre let out a howl of laughter and, gnashing its yellow, tombstone teeth, stuck its face close to Ned's.

The brute chortled as it examined him and smacked its lips loudly.

'Brave little squeaky-mouse for dinny-dinny din-dins. Outy-casty for svartelves.'

'Let him go, you big bully,' yelled Ned. 'You've nearly killed him.'

'Oh, not a dinner party – a rescue party!' teased the ogre as he swung Ned back and forth and poked a gigantic finger painfully into his ribs. 'Too skinny for food anyway. Too skinny – stick-bones, stick-bones, sticky, sticky, stick-bones. Nothing but stick-bones. Hey, look here, Outy-casty, your rescue party has arrived.'

The rest of the ogres laughed uproariously as Ned, his feet dangling uselessly above the ground, kicked and punched at his captor. The Outcast, blood darkening his long yellow hair, let out a groan of pain and struggled feebly against the thick ropes that bound him hand and foot.

Chapter Thirty

Amaldus

'You may wish to put the boy down now,' said Mr Swanson, his voice calm and polite, 'and while you're at it perhaps you'd also like to untie your unfortunate victim and let him be about his business.'

The gang of ogres turned as one and frowned stupidly at this new interruption. Ned was dumped painfully onto the hard cobbles as the ogre that had been swinging him back and forth doubled up, howling with coarse laughter.

'Oh, even better. An old man with a sticky stick, sti - .'

There was a thunderous boom and the ogre flew backward through the air and crashed against a nearby wall hard enough to leave behind an ogre-shaped dent before it slumped to the ground. A web of blue magical ropes coursed and weaved themselves tightly round its hulking frame as it bellowed and thrashed helplessly on the ground. The remaining ogres, their iron clubs held high, charged snarling and roaring at Mr Swanson, bowling Ned out of the way. The market square flashed, thundered and shook as Mr Swanson stood his ground and fired spell after spell at his attackers. Some, like their leader, were knocked flying, before crashing bound and struggling to the ground, while others toppled like felled trees as they were blasted senseless. Winded and gasping, Ned scrambled to his feet and, ducking under a flying ogre, limped to the Outcast, who lay fighting vainly against the crude bonds he had been trussed with.

'Wait,' said Ned, and using both hands he pulled a wickedly curved dagger from an unconscious ogre's belt and began to slice through the thick ropes until the Outcast was able to sit up.

'Here, drink some water,' said Ned, pulling a bottle from his pack and unstopping it. Doing his best to shield the man from yet another tumbling ogre and receiving a nasty wallop for his pains, Ned gently held the bottle to the Outcast's bloodied lips. After a long draught, the Outcast handed the bottle back to Ned and regarded him with a dazed look.

'Thank you, saviour, your bravery has saved me from a terrible fate,' slurred the Outcast, wiping blood and dirt from his face and revealing a mass of whirling tattoos.

'Here,' said Ned, picking something up that lay discarded on the cobbles, 'the ogre took this from you.'

For a moment, the Outcast's amber eyes struggled to focus on the object that Ned dangled in front of him.

'My warrior's talisman. Thank you. Thank you, my friend. To lose that would have brought so much shame upon my father,' said the Outcast, slipping the fine silk braid over his head and tucking the talisman inside the remains of his torn and bloodied jerkin.

'Ned, are you alright?' asked Mr Swanson, running to Ned who was now pressing a soaking cloth to the wounds on the Outcast's head.

'Yes, I'm fine,' replied Ned.

'That was foolish, Ned, you could have been seriously hurt,' said Mr Swanson, sharply pulling Ned round to face him.

'Hey, let go of my arm,' said Ned, startled. 'You're hurting me.'

'Do you realise just how stupid your heroic action was?' said Mr Swanson, his eyes blazing with fury.

'What? I couldn't just stand and watch, they were beating him even though he couldn't do anything,' said Ned, angrily twisting free of Mr Swanson's grip.

'Not only did you risk your own life unnecessarily, but by forcing me to use such powerful spells, you have now placed us in a peril greater than any we have so far encountered.'

'But you used those spells in the temple.'

'As I explained earlier, the temple is a guarded place. This, as I'm sure hasn't escaped your notice, is a very public place, and becoming more public by the second. Not only will Port Cadarn soon be buzzing with the news that a mage is in town, but we have just sent out a very clear signal to Malverfuhren as to our exact whereabouts.'

'I couldn't just watch. No way. Not in a million years,' said Ned.

'There are times, Ned, when you have to. No matter what you witness, no matter what you hear, no matter what or who you stand to lose, you will have to sacrifice a few to their fate in order to save the fate of many.'

'I can't do that, it's too horrible. It's wrong.'

'I know it's horrible, believe me, I know just how horrible it is. It is something that tears a strip from your soul and haunts you in the cold, dark hours of every morning. No matter how many lives it saves, the one or two that you sacrifice will haunt you forever.'

Ned glared at Mr Swanson, his nostrils flared and his mouth a thin white line.

'I'm sorry, Ned,' said Mr Swanson, his expression softening, 'your heart is true and courageous and no one can question that, but one day you will have to make a sacrifice. A terrible sacrifice that no man should ever have to make, and you have to be prepared for when that day comes.'

'I'll be ready, don't you worry. I'll do what it takes, but I still think it's wrong not to help people who need help,' said Ned, his face set grim and fierce. 'And if Malverfuhren knows where we are and comes looking for us, then all the better. There's a few things I want to say to him. I want my brother back.'

'Spoken like a trooper,' said Mr Swanson. 'Come. Now that we've rescued this poor fellow, we may as well tend to his needs.'

With Ned supporting one arm, and Mr Swanson the other, the Outcast rose unsteadily to his feet and blinked woozily down at them both.

'You're a mage,' said the Outcast, looking first at Mr Swanson's staff and then at the ogres, some struggling against their magical bonds, others lying crumpled and smoking on the cobbles.

'A mage? Aye, once upon a time I was,' replied Mr Swanson, looking around warily as the square now begin to fill with curious onlookers, who whispered and pointed at the trio.

'I've heard legends from when mages walked freely in all the reaches of Elgarolyn and served the kings and brought help to the needy, but I thought they had all been slain by Caryosus.'

'I was one of the lucky ones. All but a few were betrayed and murdered by Belastung. Now, unless you can point us to a very fast ship, then we will have to take our leave – it won't be long before this little incident reaches the wrong ears.'

'There is no need to take your leave, sire. I am the first mate of one of the fastest smuggling schooners ever to sail. So fast is it that some say it was charmed by none other than Elwyn Cygfilius himself.'

'Are you talking of *The Flying Lampwing*?' said Mr Swanson.

'You've heard of her?' said the Outcast, his eyebrows shooting upwards.

'In my day there weren't many who hadn't,' replied Mr Swanson.

'And why would you be wanting so fast a ship?' asked the Outcast, looking from one to the other.

'There is someone who is in desperate need of our help and the sooner we can come to his aid, the better. Not just for him but for countless millions, too.'

The Outcast nodded gravely.

'A serious undertaking for just two,' he said, 'but if it's help you want then I can take you to the Healer's Bowl – it's a smugglers' tavern on the seafront. You'll be able to lodge there tonight, and tomorrow at midday my captain will be there and, thanks to you two, so will I.'

'We're more than happy accept your help. This young chap is Ned, and my name is Charlie. Charlie Swanson,' said Mr Swanson extending his hand.

'Unusual names. My name is Amaldus. Amaldus Hagebak, and I am eternally in your debt.'

Chapter Thirty-One

The Healer's Bowl

From the outside, the inn looked run-down and in need of much repair. A grubby sign depicting a plain bowl hung above the door, grating rustily as the cold wind swung it back and forth. The thick timbers of the door did little to muffle the noise that came from within, and what windows there were had long ago been boarded up.

Huddling against the cold, Ned looked up at Mr Swanson, who merely shrugged. Amaldus laughed as he sensed their sudden unease.

'Don't be put off – this is probably one of the safest places in Port Cadarn, if not in the whole of the Northern Reaches.'

'Well, I suppose it can't be worse than the tunnel,' muttered Ned

'And I can guarantee there are no ogres inside,' said Amaldus. 'I'll meet you in here tomorrow at midday, and make sure you tell the barman that I sent you. Don't be put off by his manner – he's an old friend and he's as soft as butter if you're on his good side.'

'Thank you, Amaldus, I'm sure we'll be fine. Now, if you'll excuse us, Ned here is dead on his feet and starting to freeze,' said Mr Swanson, nodding at Ned who stood at his side swaying slightly.

'Until tomorrow, Charlie. Farewell, Ned – and thank you once again,' said Amaldus. With a wave, he limped off into the night.

Mr Swanson pushed the inn door open and ushered Ned inside. The rumble of voices stopped as the two threaded their way through a sea of people, many of whom had the same tattooed faces and amber eyes as Amaldus. Every eye in the inn fixed on them as Mr Swanson carefully picked his way through the broad figures, followed closely by Ned, who kept his eyes fixed firmly on the floor, half-wishing that they were still outside.

The barman, polishing a silver tankard, paused in his chore and glared down at them as they finally reached the bar.

'Could it be that you're in the wrong place, old man?' he growled, his huge black beard bristling and twitching as though something had made its nest in its curly depths.

Ned shrank even closer to Mr Swanson, looking up at the mountainous figure as his vivid green eyes regarded them with deep suspicion.

'And this is no place for a youngster,' he continued, turning his glare on Ned, who stood struck dumb, staring back with eyes as big as saucers, certain that they were both about to be picked up and thrown back out.

'Amaldus brought us here.'

The four words from Mr Swanson worked a magic of their own. Immediately, conversations and laughter resumed, and somewhere an accordion, halted mid-note, burst back into life with a lively tune.

'Well, why didn't you say so?' The barman beamed, revealing a mouthful of gold teeth. 'Hey, you lot over there, give up your seats for these two – this poor boy looks ready to drop.'

A group of Outcasts who had been playing cards by one of the several roaring fires that warmed the Healer's Bowl leapt up and motioned Ned and Mr

Swanson to sit down, helping them off with their packs as they collapsed into their seats.

'Gretta! Peggy! Come and see to these two, please! Grace! You can make them up a bed each, please.'

As the barman bellowed out his orders, three young girls appeared from a steaming, noisy kitchen, the youngest hiding shyly behind her elder sisters. Gretta and Peggy fussed and clucked around Ned, fetching him milk and Mr Swanson a large tankard of ale. As Ned finished his drink, the two girls reappeared bearing several plates of food.

'Here you are, a growing lad like you needs his food,' said Gretta mussing Ned's hair.

Despite having eaten at the stall in the market square earlier, Ned's stomach rumbled loudly as he eyed the pile of steaming food; with a word of thanks, he tucked ravenously into the food.

'My word, Mage's Respite – I haven't had this in years' Mr Swanson smiled as he wiped a line of foam from his upper lip. 'And I think you've got an admirer, Ned,' he continued, nodding his head toward the door that led into the kitchen.

Ned looked up just in time to see a mass of curly auburn hair disappear. He looked down and concentrated on his food, a red flush blooming over his face. After ploughing his way through the plate of food and two helpings of apple pie, both served by a smiling Gretta, Ned leaned back in his chair.

'Well, you've just eaten what would keep a grown man going for a week!'

The barman, now towering over their table, smiled down at Ned and Mr Swanson.

'I'm Magnus. Magnus Borthwick, barman of one of Port Cadarn's finest hostelries and father to three rather hot-headed girls.'

'I'm Charlie. Charlie Swanson, and the young man here is Ned.'

'Pleased to meet you both. Did you enjoy your meal, young Ned?'

'It was great, thank you very much. I'm fit to burst,' said Ned. 'I like your inn, by the way. Where did all those beams come from?'

'The ceiling joists? Some are rescued from old ships; some are from shipwrecks. Every beam in this inn tells a story, y'know. See that beam above the bar? You can just make out some of the old runes – carved into it for good luck. I guess they chose the wrong ones, though. Salvaged that one from the wreck of *The Burning Sword* and brought it back here myself.'

'What do the runes say?' asked Ned, peering at the figures.

'Not sure – can barely read them these days,' replied Magnus, sweeping their dishes and mugs into one hand and setting sail for the kitchen.

Ned peered through the smoky haze that had slowly filled the bar as Outcast and smuggler alike lit their long pipes. He could only make out a few of the stick-like figures spelling out a message in the scarred and smoke-blackened beam.

'Do you know what those runes say, Mr Swanson?' he asked.

'Hmm, I'm not too sure,' replied Mr Swanson, squinting at the beam. 'I think I can read the first few, but nothing after that.'

'What do they say?'

'My ... haven ... lies,' said Mr Swanson, slowly sounding the runes out.

'My haven lies?' echoed Ned. 'What does that

mean?'

'I expect it's a good luck charm that's meant to bring the ship home safely. Seems it didn't work too well, eh?' said Mr Swanson, as he stood and stretched.

'Come now, Ned. I think young Grace has finished making our rooms up – and you look as though you could sleep for a week.'

With an effort, Ned pulled himself up out of his chair and followed sleepily in Mr Swanson's wake, a furiously blushing Grace leading the way up the dark stairs, a lantern held high. The thump of his pack on the floor was the last thing Ned remembered before being woken by a gentle knocking at the door the following morning. Blinking at the bright sunlight that streamed through the curtains, Ned could see that Mr Swanson's bed was empty and that his staff, too, was missing.

'Good morning, young man, I trust you slept well. Your master sent this up for you,' said Peggy, as she came through the door bearing a tray piled high with food.

'Grace was too shy to bring it up, so I've done it myself before it grows cold.'

Ned thanked Peggy and, as he sat up in the embrace of a huge feather-filled quilt, he spied a small note perched amongst the plates.

"Good morning, Ned. I awoke early and didn't have the heart to wake you, too. I have gone for a stroll along the seafront to enjoy the fresh sea air. Enjoy your breakfast and I shall return soon. Mr Swanson."

After washing his breakfast down with several cups of milk, Ned quickly dressed and, after checking that the ring and the lampwing feather were still safe, carefully made his way downstairs.

'Well, that's very kind of you, Ned, very thoughtful indeed,' said Gretta, as she took the breakfast tray from him. 'Master Swanson asked me to look after you until he returns from his walk. Feel free to have a look round the inn – there's some interesting things to see, if you like the Old Tales.'

'What are the Old Tales?' asked Ned.

'Why, tales of the Circle of course – of how the Circle of Light tried to make this world and many others better places.'

'And about Belastung and Malverfuhren?' asked Ned.

Gretta scowled fiercely. 'Evil, they are. Pure evil. They still hold most of the Eastern Reaches. Completely taken over the Southern Reaches, too, thanks to their army of svartelves. The Gravemen have done plenty of damage, as well. Oh, the tales I've heard from folk who only just managed to escape with nothing but the shirts on their backs. Anyway, less of that – you have a look round. See if you can find anything to do with the Herald of Peace.'

'The Herald of Peace? Is that a ship?' asked Ned, already standing under one beam and tipping his head back.

'No, silly, the Herald of Peace is a harp that brings harmony to all who hear its song. At least that's what the legends say.'

Ned was in the middle of running his fingertips along an inscription carved into a fireplace when a familiar voice called out.

'Good morning, Ned. I trust that you have slept well and that you have made a dent in our host's larder?' said Mr Swanson brightly as he stepped into the inn.

'Hello, Mr Swanson. I've had a lovely breakfast, thank you, and I slept like a log.'

'Jolly good, jolly good.'

'Gretta told me to look around while you were

out. I'm trying to find the Herald of Peace,' said Ned.

'Oh, really? You'll have to look further afield than that I'm afraid.'

'What do you mean?' replied Ned.

Mr Swanson, however, wasn't listening, but had suddenly stopped in the middle of the room, his head cocked to one side as he looked back towards the door.

'I think now may be a good time to meet our captain,' he murmured.

'Pardon?' asked Ned, still peering closely at the inscription he had found and picking carefully at a flake of black paint that curled from its surface.

'Ned, go and fetch our packs. Make sure you have the ring and the feather with you.'

Ned stopped tracing the runes and looked at Mr Swanson.

'But wh – ' he began.

'Go now, and quickly,' barked Mr Swanson, his voice suddenly losing its gentle edge. 'There's something happening outside.'

As Ned sprinted up the stairs, he could hear shouts and the clash of weapons. Swiftly, he crammed their belongings into their packs and, checking once more that the ring and feather were safely tucked away, hurtled downstairs, the rickety wooden steps creaking loudly in protest.

'What's going on?' he shouted.

As if in reply, the Bowl's door crashed open and a formidable figure burst in.

'Stand to!' shouted Amaldus, as Ned and Mr Swanson spun round. 'There's an army of svartelves in the port. Ogres, too.'

The room shook as Magnus heard the news.

'Svartelves in the port? What times are these?

Stand to, my daughters, there's a battle to be fought!' he bellowed, bursting from behind the bar, a hefty cudgel in each hand.

Amaldus turned to Ned and Mr Swanson.

'I'll take you to *The Flying Lampwing* now – if our route hasn't been blocked, that is,' he said.

'Ned – stay between us, it's you they're after,' said Mr Swanson, hefting his staff in one hand, his eyes blazing.

More shouting, now much nearer, met their ears as they stepped into the street. As soon as they were spotted, the battle seemed to intensify, the svartelves throwing themselves bodily against the line of heavily armed Outcasts that held them at bay. Ned risked a glance over his shoulder as Mr Swanson urged him on. A short distance away he could see Outcasts locked in battle with a mass of ogres and svartelves who, to Ned's dismay, were beginning to gain the upper hand. As he watched, a squad of svartelves detached themselves from the main horde and swarmed its way up the front of a building before dropping down behind the line of embattled Outcasts. Once on the ground, the svartelves moved at a terrifying speed, crossbows and spears clutched menacingly in their hands. Turning on his heel, Mr Swanson drew his arm back and, as though throwing a cricket ball, flung his hand toward the svartelves. A line of flames leaped from the stone cobbles and twisted themselves into fiery snakes that charged at the approaching enemy, spitting balls of fire and flame. Screams of terror filled the air as svartelves ran, tripping and clambering over one another, the balls speeding after them, singeing their feet and setting light to their backsides. Despite his terror, Ned laughed with exhilaration as his pursuers scattered and fled.

'Gotcha!'

Ned's laughter died in his throat as a pair of meaty hands grabbed him from an alleyway.

'Looks as though your friend's a bit too busy to help you this time,' growled the ogre, who Ned had last seen writhing on the ground, trying to break free of Mr Swanson's spell.

Ned thrashed around, frantically trying to shake himself free of the ogre's grip.

The ogre leered at Ned, who lashed out with a kick.

'A wriggly little maggot, aren't you? Can't see what the svartelves want with y – .'

The ogre's piggy-eyes crossed as he sank gracefully to the ground, revealing the bulk of Amaldus behind him, hefting a wicked-looking cosh in one hand.

Amaldus grinned as he stepped over the unconscious form.

'Not the sharpest cutlass in the armoury is he?'

'Crikey, that was close. Thanks, Amaldus,' blurted Ned, picking himself up from the floor.

'Meeting up with old friends, Ned?' said Mr Swanson, running to join them.

'The ship isn't too far away now, but we're taking a slightly roundabout way to get on board, so follow me and don't ask questions.'

Ned and Charlie followed closely as Amaldus sprinted from cover, a swarm of crossbow bolts zipping past their heads as they ran. As the three rounded a corner they were greeted with the sight of dozens upon dozens of ships busy with crew hauling on ropes, heaving acres of canvas high into the air. Amaldus jumped onto the first one, *The Stirling Warrior*, and led Ned and Mr Swanson below.

'I thought we were going to *The Flying Lampwing*?' said Ned.

'Trust me,' came Amaldus' reply, as he led them deeper into the bowels of the ship.

'Quick. Through here,' he said, pushing open a porthole. Poking his head through, Ned could see the hull of another ship a few feet away, with a porthole already open and a sinewy arm reaching through.

'Come on,' urged the owner of the beckoning arm.

Ned grabbed the hand and was pulled roughly from the porthole into the second ship, where he was soon joined by Amaldus and Mr Swanson. Again and again Amaldus led them from ship to ship until Ned, scraped, exhausted and bruised, had lost count. At last Amaldus greeted a crewman with a hearty cry.

'Welcome aboard *The Flying Lampwing*,' he said, turning to the dishevelled pair.

'Why couldn't we come straight here?' panted Ned, rubbing a bruised elbow.

'And tell them which ship we were sailing on?' said Amaldus.

'But won't it be obvious? I mean we'll be the only one leaving port, won't we?' asked Ned.

'There's at least four dozen ships ready to sail at this very moment. The svartelves won't have a clue which one we're on,' said Amaldus.

'Four dozen? Really? Where are they sailing?'

'Anywhere their cargoes are needed, if you know what I mean. Now, if you follow me, I'll take you to meet the captain,' he said, and led them up several narrow flights of stairs until they stood outside a door beautifully veneered and decorated with a pair of ferocious looking dragons that reached from floor to ceiling. As the three approached, the dragons began to move and twist sinuously, lamplight reflecting off their deep red scales. Eyeing them suspiciously and baring their needle-sharp fangs, the twin dragons arched their backs and rattled their wings ominously.

'No need to worry,' said Amaldus, as Ned took a step back, 'The captain's in a good mood otherwise our feet would be feeling a little warmer by now.'

Ned looked at the floor, and sure enough the planks of wood beneath their feet bore a number of burn marks and on a nearby hook swung a bucket of sand.

'Are they real dragons?' whispered Ned.

'No, the doors are enchanted – nobody can pass unless they're allowed to do so. The captain had them fitted as a reminder of home during our first voyage to the Far Eastern Reaches.'

Ned watched in wonder as the two dragons suddenly flipped round and dived into the doors as though they were water.

'They're telling the captain that we've arrived and that we don't bear any malice,' explained Amaldus.

With a pop the dragons reappeared and the doors swung silently inward, revealing a darkened cabin. As Ned passed through the doors, one of the dragons moved slightly and aimed a mischievous puff of flame at his feet.

'That's quite enough of that, Ka Riu,' said a soft voice from the gloom. 'And what, may I ask, do you find so amusing, Han Riu?'

Chapter Thirty-Two

On Board The Flying Lampwing

'So you're the mage who's stirred up a hornet's nest, are you?' came the voice again, but this time from a different part of the cabin, the owner having slipped noiselessly from one side to the other.

'My attempts at keeping a low profile were somewhat thwarted by a gang of ogres attacking your first mate,' replied Mr Swanson, joining Ned in peering into the darkness.

'It came as a surprise, I must say – I thought that all the good mages had died out or been killed.'

'There are a few of us left, if you know where to look,' said Mr Swanson.

'I can't say I'd ever go looking for one – they're trouble if I've ever seen it.'

Amaldus shifted uncomfortably behind Mr Swanson and Ned.

'Captain Ruby, if I may say so – these two, Mr Swanson and young Ned, did save me from a lifetime of slavery under the svartelves. At great risk to themselves, too.'

'I'm well aware of that, and I am, of course, eternally in their debt. However, I have to remind you that I have a ship to run and an entire crew under my care, too,' said the voice.

'We can pay you handsomely, and not just with gold, either,' said Mr Swanson.

This time the voice came from the very back of the cabin.

'Ka Riu, would you be so kind as to provide some light for our guests, please?'

The dragon skittered excitedly and sent forth first one, and then a second sharp blast of flame. Lanterns on either side of the room flared with light.

Before them, only a few inches taller than Ned, stood a slight figure dressed in armour made from hundreds of small dark wooden plates laced together. A gauntleted hand rested lightly on the handle of the katana at her side as she studied Ned intently with her deep brown eyes. Light from the lanterns shone on the sleek black hair that framed the perfect white skin of her face.

'Will you be able to help us, though?' said Ned, beginning to feel uncomfortable under the unblinking stare.

Captain Ruby pulled her hair back into a ponytail and tied it in place with a short length of silk, her almond-shaped eyes never once leaving Ned's.

'Help deliver you to a gruesome end?' she said. 'If that's what you want, my heroic young Ned, then I can certainly get you very close.'

Ned frowned at Captain Ruby.

'But you haven't asked us where we want to go.'

'That's because I don't need to ask. Two strangers appear, one of whom just happens to be a talented, and possibly battle-hardened mage, and suddenly svartelves and ogres are daring to attack us in our stronghold in order to capture them. There's only one place you'll be travelling to – Malverfuhren's castle. I can understand why a mage would want to travel there, but why a young boy like you?'

Ned turned and looked helplessly at Mr Swanson. Mr Swanson looked at Ned and shrugged.

'I think our disguise as a travelling farmer and his

son may be a little see-through by now.'

Ned looked back at Captain Ruby and took a deep breath.

'I have to rescue my brother. Actually, it's his soul I have to rescue. He, sorry, it, his soul I mean, was taken by Malverfuhren. He's being held in Malverfuhren's castle. Do you know where it is? Can you take us there?'

'And throw my ship, my crew and myself into the jaws of death? No thank you, young man, but like I said, I can get you close enough – probably within a week's walk. If you can stomach it, that is.'

Ned opened his mouth in indignation, but before he could retort, a rapid thudding from behind interrupted as a crewman hurled himself down the steps and, earning himself a savage look from Ka and Han, ducked into the cabin.

'Begging your pardon, Captain,' he panted, 'all ships ready to sail and not a moment too soon – svartelves and ogres are nearly upon us.'

Captain Ruby's young features suddenly became fierce and warlike.

'Give the order to sail. Every spare hand is to stand by and repel boarders. I want archers in the rigging and the stern bristling with cutlasses.'

'Aye aye, Captain,' said the crewman, and sprinted back up onto the deck, yelling orders at the top of his voice.

'Amaldus, take our guests to one of the hidden holds – we're unlikely to be boarded, but let's not take any chances,' said Captain Ruby, tying on a battle-scarred helmet and hurrying to join her crew on deck.

'Very good, Captain,' said Amaldus and turning to Mr Swanson and Ned, beckoned them to follow him once again. After leading them back down into the bowels of the ship, Amaldus stopped and, grasping one of the lanterns that lined an innocent looking corridor, pulled down sharply. A small section of the corridor's floor creaked open, revealing steps that led down into the pitch black below.

'There's plenty of room in there, and the contraband is comfortable, too,' said Amaldus, as he ushered them into the hole.

'I can't risk giving you a lantern, but I'm sure you'll come up with something,' he added, nodding at Mr Swanson's staff.

Inky blackness engulfed them as Amaldus closed the hidden trapdoor above them, shutting out even the thinnest sliver of light.

'Mr Swanson, could we have some light, please?' asked Ned, a note of panic creeping into his voice. 'I think I can hear something moving down here. Lots of things, in actual fact.'

Mr Swanson's reply came in the form of a small but intense globe of light that grew from the tip of his staff. He gently lifted the globe from the staff and held it aloft. With a small pop, the globe burst into five smaller orbs that arranged themselves in a circle around the two companions. Ned blinked owlishly for a second or two as his eyes adjusted to the sudden brightness.

'Crikey, it's huge,' gasped Ned, as he looked around them.

The two companions were standing side-by-side on a wooden platform looking out over a warehouse that stretched as far as they could see.

'Impressive,' murmured Mr Swanson. 'A very good enchantment indeed.'

'Is it the same spell that was used in the temple? The Olusum spell?'

195

'Hmm, I think so. Our hosts have put it to good use, too.'

'What are they smuggling? It looks like one of those horrible carpet shops Mum takes us to,' said Ned.

'You're not far wrong – these are carpets, sure enough. Flying carpets, judging by the way that they're fidgeting.'

'Flying carpets? Really? Oh, wow, you never told me there were flying carpets over here.'

With the orbs bobbing about them, Mr Swanson inspected a nearby rack of carpets that had become even more restless as they had approached. Ned watched as Mr Swanson gently stroked one of the carpets, murmuring gently to it as he did so. After a few minutes he carefully pulled it from the rack and rolled it out at their feet.

'This one seems to have a nice nature – not as skittish as the others,' said Mr Swanson, giving the carpet a gentle rub.

'I'm sure I've seen a pattern like that before,' said Ned, as Mr Swanson walked carefully to the centre of the carpet and sat down. 'Was there one in the Healer's Bowl? Oh, wow. It's moving!'

Mr Swanson let out a laugh as the carpet rose and began to waft gently above the floor.

'Now, this could be very interesting or very embarrassing – I haven't flown one of these in years.'

Ned reached out and gingerly stroked the carpet.

'Well, don't just stand there, Ned, hop on!'

'Are you sure?'

'Quite sure; she's as steady as a rock. Very patient, too, I think, so she'll forgive us if we don't get things right.'

Ned stepped nervously onto the carpet and sat down behind Mr Swanson.

'How do they work?' he asked, clutching hold of Mr Swanson as the carpet moved slightly underneath them and lifted a little higher.

'Oh, it's quite easy – you just have to think,' replied Mr Swanson.

'Think what?'

'Well, if you want to go upwards, just think of rising up through the air,' replied Mr Swanson. 'Like so.'

The carpet rose a few more inches from the ground as Mr Swanson finished speaking.

'Oh, my word,' said Ned, carefully peeking over the side of the carpet.

The carpet moved gently forward and then banked to the right, taking them down another long aisle of carpets. Ned yelled with delight.

'This is fantastic! What a brilliant way to travel.'

'Well, I think it would be useful if you took control for a while.'

'Me? I can't fly a carpet, I'll crash,' cried Ned.

'Never be afraid to try something new, Ned. So what if you crash? Do you think you'll be the first person to crash one of these things? I can't tell you the number of times I had to be rescued from tree tops when I was your age,' said Mr Swanson. 'Now, swap places with me – the flyer sits in the centre here – only then will the carpet listen.'

Ned dutifully shuffled position until he sat where Mr Swanson was pointing.

'Right. First things first, we'll learn taking off and landing. Clear your mind and think of nothing else but rising through the air, please.'

Ned took a deep breath and pursed his lips, his brow crinkled with effort.

'Ouch! Perhaps that was a little too enthusiastic,'

said Mr Swanson, rubbing the top of his head.

'Sorry.' Ned winced, as the carpet dropped down from the ceiling. 'I was thinking of a buzzard circling up to the clouds.'

'Well, yes, that's a very good idea, but let's try again, shall we? Maybe this time think of a slow, old buzzard that doesn't like rushing around, perhaps?' said Mr Swanson patiently.

This time the carpet rose wobbling from the floor and bobbed gently two or three feet up in the air, then began to circle very gently above the spot they had just left.

'Much, much better – very good for a beginner,' said Mr Swanson. 'You obviously have a lot of natural talent.'

'Thanks. Oops, sorry,' said Ned, as the carpet bounced back to the floor with a thud.

'Don't worry, don't worry,' said Mr Swanson, picking himself up from the floor and rubbing his backside. 'It's just a matter of keeping one's concentration; it'll become second nature before too long.'

After a few more bumps, several close shaves with the ceiling and one or two rough landings, Ned spent the rest of the day flying around the hidden hold, exploring its depths, a light orb bobbing along in front of him.

'Wow, I'd love to take one of these home with me – they're awesome,' he yelled excitedly, as he returned to where Mr Swanson had been patiently waiting. 'I've flown for miles – this hold is huge. I thought it was going to go on for ever. It goes really high in some places – I couldn't find the ceiling. And I raced with the light orb.' He grinned breathlessly, his face flushed.

'You can certainly have some fun on them, can't you?'

'If I took one home I'd fly above Smugley and pelt him with eggs and rotten tomatoes!' said Ned exuberantly, zipping past Mr Swanson's head and making him duck.

'I'm sure there is a great temptation to do that, but you should pity the poor boy rather than seek revenge upon him,' said Mr Swanson, as Ned came to a halt beside him.

'Pity him? But why? He's mean to everyone in school, especially to me,' said Ned, stepping from the carpet and watching as it flew back to its rack and neatly rolled itself up.

'Pity him because he has nothing as valuable as you do.'

'But he's got everything – a tablet computer, a quad-bike, a laptop. Everything,' said Ned. 'And he goes on amazing holidays.'

'But he doesn't have what you have – a family who love him. Have you ever seen his parents not arguing with each other? That poor boy lives in a home where arguments and fights are commonplace, so much so that he never receives the love and affection from his parents that he should.'

'But what about all his toys? They're always buying him things.'

'Those gaudy trinkets will never be a substitute for affection – what that boy truly craves is a warm, loving home, as you have.'

'Dad's never nice to me, though.'

'Your father loves you no less than he loves Sam. He may be stricter and more brusque with you, but that is just his way.'

'I can't remember when we last spent time together – he's always so moody and grumpy.'

'It's true that a certain graveness has grown within him over the last few years. Sadly, your memories of him will be spoilt by it, but believe me, he once doted on you as he does on Sam today. Don't look so sad, Ned. Your father would stand between you and peril without a thought for his own safety.'

Ned shuffled his feet and looked away.

'I suppose you're right. It's just that I remember him from before he became so miserable. He used to make me laugh so much.'

'I know, I know.' Mr Swanson sighed, nodding. 'Now look, while you were playing Battle of Britain fighter pilot, and winning, I dare say, Amaldus brought some food down to us. It's a bit, er, different, should we say, but there's plenty of it. I get the impression that what the ship's cook lacks in culinary skills, he makes up for with an enthusiasm for experimentation,' said Mr Swanson opening one of several steaming cooking pots and handing Ned a plate.

'Honestly, I'm so hungry I could eat a horse,' said Ned. 'Thanks.'

Without any further ado, Ned dug into his food, pausing once in a while to savour, or perhaps grimace at, some of the riper flavours.

After the meal, as silence fell between them, Ned gazed sleepily into the light globe that bobbed and floated in front of them, dreamily watching waves of light flicker across its surface.

'I think that's enough excitement for one day, Ned' said Mr Swanson, clearing away the remains of their meal, but his words went unheard as Ned slumbered in his dreams.

Chapter Thirty-Three

Mr Swanson and The Gravemen

Night was falling rapidly as Ned gasped his way up the steep hill. Sam was already far ahead, bobbing from rock to rock, his cheeky laugh tinkling through the gathering darkness.

'Sam, wait for me!' Ned's lungs ached as he struggled to catch up with the tiny figure that appeared briefly on the summit, silhouetted against the last rays of the setting sun.

'No, no, no!' yelled Ned, now scrabbling over slopes of scree, grabbing onto sparse lumps of heather only to slide back every time he managed to crawl his way forward, his hands and knees now burning with the pain from so many cuts and grazes.

'Sam, where are you?' Ned yelled in panic, as he finally reached the summit.

A ghoulish voice laughed from the crowding darkness.

'Why, he's with me, of course!'

As Ned spun round, a figure capered out of the gloom and playfully tweaked Ned's nose, making him yell out in fright. The pale outline of a face, its features shadowy in the falling dusk, leered close to Ned's, making him take a step back and stumble over a jagged rock that stuck up from the ground.

Malverfuhren chortled, dancing and spinning around Ned, as he scrabbled back to his feet.

'Hello, my little friend. Have you had a pleasant trip? Pun intended, pun intended,' he cried, stopping briefly to punch Ned playfully on the shoulder before springing away and continuing his clowning.

'Where's Sam?' demanded Ned, feeling both angry and terrified.

'Tut, tut, tut, no need for such bad manners, my boy' said Malverfuhren, spinning to a stop in front of Ned and pinching his cheek.

'Where's Sam?' repeated Ned, slapping Malverfuhren's hand away in revulsion. 'I want him back.'

'Do you, now? Well there's a thing – we have something in common – you have something I want, and I have something you want.'

'You won't get the ring – Mr Swanson told me what you'll do with it,' shouted Ned.

'That old dreamer – he shouldn't have been such a fool when he held it.'

'Mr Swanson's not a fool – he's a mage, and a powerful one, too.'

'And so am I, child,' screamed Malverfuhren suddenly, spit flying from his mouth. 'Look!'

In the blink of an eye, Malverfuhren pulled an ugly, twisted wand from his cloak and fired spell after spell into the ground around them. From where the spells struck, huge scaly dragons erupted, splitting the night apart with their cries and burning the darkness away with their fiery breath. Ned cowered on the shuddering ground as leathery wings beat thunderously above his head, gusts of wind pummelling and battering him.

'Prepared to face worse than these to get him back, are you?' yelled Malverfuhren above the beating and the roaring of the dragons. Ned looked up as Malverfuhren thrust a small crystal orb in front of him, its brilliant pure white light bursting forth and making the

dragons rear and scream in alarm. Even above the
screams of the dragons, Ned could hear crying, the pitiful,
hitching sobs of a small terrified child. As he looked at the
orb, a tiny face pressed itself against the glass, weirdly
distorted but still instantly recognisable. Malverfuhren
tapped the orb with his wand and the glass flowed into
thin bars, imprisoning the light.

'Sam!' cried Ned, reaching for the cage, 'Sam, I'm
here, I've come to save you.'

Malverfuhren smirked and whisked the cage out
of Ned's reach, spitefully smacking his outstretched hand
with his wand.

'Not so fast, my little hero.'

'Please let him go, please, he's so scared.' Ned
wept as he begged Malverfuhren, clutching at the hem of
his cloak.

Malverfuhren grinned, enjoying Ned's pain.

'You know what I want from you, boy, and I
know you'll come to me. And, just to show that I'm not all
bad, I'll let you see little Sam one more time.'

Ned blinked his tears away as Malverfuhren
uncurled his fingers from around the cage and held it out
for Ned to see.

'Ned, Ned, please help me, I'm so scared. I don't
know where I am. Ned, I can see you! I can see you!
Please don't go.' Sam sobbed as his tiny face pressed
against the bars of the cage.

'Sam, I'm coming to find you. You have to be
brave. I'm coming to rescue you and I'm going to take
you home, just be brave. I love you, Sam.'

'So touching,' teased Malverfuhren, as he
whipped the cage away and hid it in the folds of his cloak,
muffling Sam's cries for his big brother.

Ned looked up at Malverfuhren as his cold,

snickering laughter filled the air.

'A little longer to think of your brother's suffering, perhaps? Now that you've seen just how miserable and scared he is, I'm sure that you'll be more than willing to hand the ring over when we meet again. Remember how he cried for you, Ned, remember with every breath you take. Remember how he wept and how he begged for you. He's so lonely and afraid, isn't he? And the longer he stays in that cage, the lonelier and more afraid he'll become.'

'I'm coming to get him,' shouted Ned, before looking round in surprise at a pure white cloud that appeared above them and gently folded itself around him.

'Ned. Ned, you're safe now, he's caught you in a dream spell.' Ned heard Mr Swanson's soothing voice as the cloud gently surrounded and then lifted him swiftly away from the awful scene below, Malverfuhren now screaming in rage.

Ned snapped awake and found himself staring into Mr Swanson's concerned face. Mr Swanson's right arm was glowing a beautiful, pearly white and he was holding Ned carefully by the elbow, as though guiding someone frail and elderly.

'I spoke to Sam – put me back into the dream – he had Sam. Please, Mr Swanson, Sam's so scared. Please put me back there.' Ned sobbed desperately.

'I can't, Ned, the dream has gone and with it the spell. I'm sorry, you poor boy, I'm so sorry.'

'What's happened to your arm?' said Ned, wiping tears away with his sleeve.

'Nothing to worry about, just a counter spell to Malverfuhren's.'

'How did you know he was in my dream?' asked Ned.

'Ice was forming on you – look,' said Mr Swanson, pointing at the shining crystals that had collected on Ned's arms and legs.

'It was horrible,' said Ned as he hurriedly brushed the dusting of frost from his clothes and hair. 'He had Sam in a little glass ball – you know the sort, like the ones fortune tellers use, and then he turned it into a cage.'

'A Soul Cage – things of dark mages. A dark mage can collect the souls of those poor bodies who have been rendered unconscious by injury or illness.'

'What? That's what happened in Sam's accident, isn't it? The car hit him and Malverfuhren was waiting for his soul.'

'Yes, Ned, but I fear it was no accident. The poor driver probably can't even remember why he was in Weston Pewsey on that day. And it was no freak gust of wind that blew the plane into the road. I fear Malverfuhren has become very adept at using the Winter's Grip curse – he can create anything from small, vicious storms that can be directed at someone, through to the gentlest of breezes.'

'Winter's Grip? I'm sure I heard you say that on the night Sam was hurt.'

'You did. Sadly, it's another good spell that has been warped into a curse.'

'What was it used for before it became a curse?'

'It was a farmer's friend – some areas of Elgarolyn, especially the Western Reaches, are prone to long droughts. Using the right spell we could bring rain and cool winds to even the most parched deserts.'

'Could you use it to fight Malverfuhren and rescue Sam?'

'I'd need a stronger curse than that, I'm afraid. Malverfuhren is an extremely adept wizard, he'd easily counter the curse.'

'So how can we get the soul cage from Malverfuhren?'

'Battling Malverfuhren will be hard. Getting Sam away from the castle and out of the soul cage will be harder.' Mr Swanson sighed.

'But we can get him out, can't we?' asked Ned.

'We can at least keep him safe from harm,' replied Mr Swanson.

'Will Malverfuhren attack me in my dreams again?'

'No, not while I'm here. I've put a protective charm about you that'll warn me if he tries again.'

Ned slept fitfully for the rest of the night, the thought of Sam forever trapped in a cage and Malverfuhren's gloating laughter haunting his dreams.

'Good morning, fellows,' came a familiar voice, as Amaldus dropped down through the hidden trapdoor. 'I trust you were comfortable,' he said, helping Mr Swanson to his feet.

Mr Swanson stretched and yawned, running a hand through his bushy hair.

'But for a few nightmares, we slept well, thank you,' he replied .

'I'm sorry about the accommodation, but the captain was wise to put you in here – none but a handful know how to open the trapdoor.'

'Oh, the lodgings were excellent indeed. Ned made good use of them – he's a promising carpet-flyer,' said Mr Swanson, smiling warmly at Ned.

Ned only returned the smile half-heartedly, his head muzzy from broken sleep. 'Are we at sea yet?' He yawned.

'Come up to the deck and see for yourself, and bring your things with you – we'll put you in a proper bunk now that we're safe,' said Amaldus, leading the two of them up the steps and out of the hold.

As soon as Ned stepped through the trapdoor, he could feel the lurch of the ship as it ploughed its way through the sea.

'Wow, we really are out to sea,' he yelled with delight, and ran to keep up with Amaldus.

Bright morning sunshine greeted Ned as he clambered up a flight of steps leading to the main deck.

'Oh my word – I've never seen so many ships,' he exclaimed, as he blinked in the sunlight. The bright emerald sea on either side of *The Flying Lampwing* was filled with dozens and dozens of ships, large galleons and faster, smaller schooners like the *Lampwing* herself.

'There are so many. It's amazing,' said Ned, as the wind whipped through his hair and sang through the ship's rigging.

'It'll sow confusion amongst our enemies – they won't know which ship you two have boarded.'

'You mean all of those ships are only here to help us escape?'

'Yes. In a few hours' time this fleet will disperse – most of them have voyages to travel, while a handful will return to Port Cadarn.'

'Where will we be going?' asked Ned.

'The captain has agreed to take you and Charlie as close as possible to Malverfuhren's castle without alerting him,' replied Amaldus.

'How close?' asked Ned

Amaldus smiled grimly.

'Close enough, don't you worry.'

After a breakfast in the ship's galley, Ned

returned to the deck to look for Amaldus.

'Sorry to bother you, Amaldus,' he said, 'but I couldn't help noticing that there aren't many crewmen – have we lost some?'

'No, we always travel with this number. What makes you think we should have more?'

'Well, it's just that I couldn't help noticing that there were hundreds of flying carpets in the hidden hold.'

'Yes, nearly a thousand,' replied Amaldus, looking puzzled.

'Well, won't it take a long time to unload them all at the other end?'

'Ah, I see now. No, don't worry about unloading them – we've got plenty of willing volunteers at our destination to help unload. Look now – see that blue flag being raised up the top of the main mast? That's the signal to disperse – we're on our own after this.'

As Ned watched, a crewman finished tugging on a lanyard and secured it to a cleat on the mast. Cheers rang from either side as the fleet began to disperse, smugglers standing high in the rigging of each ship waving *The Flying Lampwing* farewell.

As the last of the fleet disappeared over the horizon, a shout came from below.

'A stowaway, we have a stowaway!'

A trapdoor banged open and a crewman appeared from below with a small, furious bundle under one arm. The bundle spat, scratched and kicked with a terrible hissing noise.

'Is it a svartelf?' asked Ned, ducking behind Amaldus.

'A svartelf! How dare you!' the bundle squawked. 'Do I look like one?'

'You sound like one, young lady,' said the crewman, and promptly received another nasty kick to his already battered shins.

'Grace! What are you doing here?' Ned gaped, not sure if he'd have found a svartelf less frightening than the sudden appearance of a girl on the ship.

'Put me down,' squeaked Grace, kicking furiously and struggling against the crewman.

'Certainly.' Her captor obliged and promptly dropped the wriggling mass on the deck, bottom first.

'Ouch!'

'Grace, what are you doing on this ship?' repeated Ned in disbelief.

'Well, my dad always said I should go to sea,' came the angry reply as Grace picked herself up from the deck and brushed herself down. Tossing her hair back indignantly, she glared at the crewman who had discovered her.

'As a stowaway?' said Mr Swanson, joining the group on deck.

'Well, no, maybe not as a stowaway. But he didn't say that I couldn't.'

'This isn't any ordinary voyage, Grace. You're too young to face the dangers that we may face.'

'He's too young as well then, isn't he?' she replied crossly, waving her arm in Ned's direction.

'But I'm a boy and you're a girl.'

Amaldus caught Grace just as she launched herself at Ned, fists and feet flailing. Fortunately, none of the blows landed on Ned, who leaped backwards only to trip on a heap of coiled rope and land with a thud on the deck.

'Ha! Serves you right, boy!' shouted Grace, lunging once again at Ned.

'Not the wisest thing to say to an Outcast, young man.' Amaldus grunted as he held back the struggling mass of limbs and hair that was trying to attack Ned. 'Especially when her mother died in battle against Malverfuhren,' he continued, dodging a sharp elbow. 'Now,' he said, dropping Grace onto her feet and holding her firmly by the shoulder, 'I think it'd be wise if we kept you two apart while we decide what to do with our stowaway. Which one of you fancies climbing up to the crow's nest and taking over lookout duty for the next couple of hours?' he asked, looking first at Grace and then at Ned.

Ned craned his neck, peering up at a tiny platform high above them on the main mast, a pair of legs dangling casually over the side.

'Oh, dear, you sound like a frog when you gulp like that. Scared, are we?' Grace snorted, laughing at Ned. 'First Mate Hagebak,' she said, turning her back on Ned as he opened his mouth to speak, 'I'll be more than happy to take look out duty.'

'Very well, Acting-Crewman Grace, you can take the next two hours,' said Amaldus, with a nod of approval.

'If you'll excuse me, I have some rigging to climb. And I'm only a girl!' Grace snarled, as she spun round and pushed her way passed Ned.

'Well, I'm afraid that leaves you to help the cook – I hope you know how to peel potatoes, Ned.'

'Ha! – a spud basher! See you at dinner time, Captain Spud. Make sure you lay the table nicely and hang the cloths up after drying all the dishes.' Grace laughed and darted up the rigging, quickly disappearing out of sight.

'Come on, now, no need to look so sad,' said Mr

Swanson as a near tearful Ned looked down at his feet, his face burning.

'I was just worried about her, that's all,' he said quietly. 'I mean, she doesn't know where we're going or why we're here, does she?'

'Don't you worry – Outcasts have a near insatiable thirst for adventure. The more dangerous the better, as far as they're concerned. Besides, I'm sure Amaldus and Captain Ruby will make sure she's returned to Port Cadarn as soon as they've dropped us and their cargo off.'

'Well, if you ask me, I think you've got a friend there, Ned.' Amaldus grinned. 'Now, come on, I'll show you the galley – you can have the pleasure of meeting Elgarolyn's grumpiest cook.'

After peeling his way through a mountain of vegetables, interrupted either by a surly word from Trug the chef or the occasional shout of 'Scullery-boy' from Grace as she stuck her head through a porthole, Ned was more than glad to haul bucket after bucket of peelings up to the main deck and heave them over the side, where a shoal of silvery fish snapped them up as soon as they hit the water.

On the last bucket load, while he paused to chat to one of the crewmen, who was catching fish on a hand line, Ned looked back along their foaming wake. Far, far behind them he could see a mass of dark clouds building up.

'Amaldus, is that a storm coming?' he asked, as the first mate joined him.

'Looks as though it could be,' he replied, frowning. 'We do get sudden squalls in the summer but this is far too early for them. Mind you, it is building very quickly.'

As they watched, the boiling black clouds grew
rapidly nearer as though following the *Lampwing's* wake.
The temperature around them plummeted rapidly and
fierce gusts of wind began to slam into the *Lampwing*,
making her rock violently from side-to-side. Below them,
Trug bellowed with rage as he fought to keep his pots and
pans from sliding to the floor.

'That's not a storm,' muttered Mr Swanson, who
had come to see what it was that the two were watching.

'What is it, then?' asked Amaldus, looking at Mr
Swanson curiously.

'The Gravemen,' came Mr Swanson's tense reply.

'I'll tell the captain,' said Amaldus, and he raced
below shouting orders as he went.

'Are they coming this way?' asked Ned.

'It's us they're coming for,' said Mr Swanson, eyes
narrowing.

'Can we hide inside, like Bryn and I did?'

'That wouldn't help,' said Captain Ruby, as she
and Amaldus raced to the stern.

'But surely they can't get inside the ship?' said
Ned.

'And who would steer the ship? Who would reef
the sails when the winds pick up?' retorted Captain Ruby
sharply. 'All they would have to do is sit on us for a few
days until we founder on rocks somewhere and then
they'll be able to pick us off us at their leisure.'

'Any ideas, mage?' she said turning to Mr
Swanson.

'Only one,' said Mr Swanson, turning on his heel
and quickly making his way below.

Moments later, as the Gravemen began to block
the sun and the tortured, screaming faces towered above

them, Mr Swanson reappeared carrying something under his arm. Laying the carpet out on deck, he called Ned, Amaldus and Captain Ruby over.

'Whatever happens now, Ned, you must continue your quest,' he urged, shouting above the hissing of the Gravemen and the battering of the squalling winds, 'Malverfuhren will not stop until he has the ring, and Sam is the only way he can get to it. You must rescue Sam and return to your own world. There are others who can help you.'

'What are you going to do, Mr Swanson?' asked Ned.

Mr Swanson turned away and sat in the centre of the carpet.

'I'm about to find out if they remember me,' he replied, readying his staff under one arm as though he were a knight about to joust.

The carpet rose and darted up and away through the rigging, climbing higher and higher in the face of the oncoming wall of blackness. As Mr Swanson gained height, the Gravemen faltered in their pursuit of the ship and began to writhe furiously as he flew in close, taunting and blasting them with spell after spell before banking sharply and darting away out of reach. Bright flashes of coloured light burst upon the cloud and the tortured faces began to rage with frustration as their quarry slipped from their grasp time and time again. More and more faces began to appear, each one drawn into a silent scream and all reaching for Mr Swanson as though he were the cause of their suffering.

'He's drawing them away from us,' said Captain Ruby. 'Hoist every stitch of canvas we have.'

The crew raced into action, hauling on ropes and raising *The Flying Lampwing's* huge sails into the air.

'Come on, scullery boy, time to get some blisters on those dainty hands of yours,' yelled Grace, pushing Ned into action. Together they hauled on rope after rope until Ned thought his arms were on fire. *The Flying Lampwing* was now living up to her name and leaping across the sea at a frightening rate, huge plumes of spray crashing down on the deck as her bows forged through the waves.

'We're gaining headway. Look.' Grace panted beside him, giving him a sharp nudge.

Ned stopped and looked back. Miles behind them Mr Swanson was now a tiny speck of white against the shrinking cloud of Gravemen, bolts of magic still flying from his staff as he dodged and darted away from their clutches. The gunshot crack of his spells reached their ears as again and again he flew daringly close until with one last effort a ghostly arm rose from the Gravemen and snatched Mr Swanson out the air.

'No! They've caught him,' screamed Ned, running to the stern and watching with dread as the unvanquished Gravemen once more erupted high into the sky.

'Where are you going?' yelled Amaldus, as Ned turned away from the horror and began to race toward the hatch that lead down into the holds.

'I'm getting a carpet. I'm going to get them!' he shouted. 'They've got Mr Swanson! They'll turn him into a Husk.'

A pair of strong arms wrapped themselves around Ned and lifted him back out of the hatch.

'There's nothing you can do now, he's gone. You'll only be taken as well and all will be lost,' said Amaldus through gritted teeth, as Ned fought wildly against him.

'Let me go!' screamed Ned. 'Let me go, I'm going

to kill them!'

'He's sacrificed himself to save us. You can't waste his sacrifice,' said Captain Ruby.

'No, no, no,' sobbed Ned, as they stood and watched as, like lightning in a storm cloud, a last few bursts of light flashed in the depths of the Gravemen.

'Oh, Ned, I'm so sorry,' said Grace, wrapping her arms gently around Ned, holding him close as he wept. 'The Gravemen are leaving – look,' she said, wiping Ned's tears away.

Ned looked up and saw that the vast black cliff that had towered so menacingly over them was beginning to drift away, and as they watched, forlorn tatters of carpet fell from on high and wafted slowly down before being claimed by the sea.

Chapter Thirty-Four

The Outcasts' Hideout

Numb with grief at the loss of Mr Swanson, Ned was led below by Grace and Captain Ruby. The crew stood to one side, heads bowed, as Ned walked down into the galley. A few patted him on the shoulder and even Trug, the grumpy chef spoke his first kind words to Ned.

'Elgarolyn will be a darker place for his passing,' he said, as he sat down beside him.

'You'll have to be brave now, Ned, you must keep your spirit strong, you'll need it for what's ahead,' said Captain Ruby, as she too sat down at the table.

'What do you mean?' asked Grace, covering Ned's shoulders with a blanket that Amaldus had handed her.

'I promised Mr Swanson that no matter what happened, I would look after Ned as a crew member until we reached our destination. And afterwards, if need be,' said Captain Ruby.

'You'll not be in safer hands, young man,' piped up a crewman.

'Hear, hear,' rumbled the others.

'First mate Hagebak - the ship is in your hands. I need to have a word with Ned and Grace,' said Captain Ruby.

As Amaldus and the crew filed out of the galley and went about their duties, Captain Ruby stood and beckoned Ned and Grace to follow.

'Come with me – you can have my quarters for the rest of the journey. I'll bunk in the hold,' she said as she led them away.

Han and Ka, the dragons began to gambol with delight, appearing in one door before flicking to the other, all the while shooting bright orange smoke rings up the corridor as Captain Ruby approached.

'Settle down, my faithful guards, I have a special task for you both,' said Captain Ruby. 'You are to look after these two as though it were me you were looking after.'

Han and Ka leapt back to their own doors and reared up into a fighting posture, fangs bared and talons ready, the tiniest flickers of flame licking from their mouths as they glared fiercely about them.

'No need to look so worried, Grace, they won't harm a hair on your head. Heaven help anyone who tries,' said Captain Ruby, ushering the two of them in.

Closing the door behind her, Captain Ruby motioned for Grace and Ned to take a seat on the narrow cushioned bench that ran along one side of the cabin.

'As you're probably aware by now, we're smuggling flying carpets. We're also carrying a large consignment of weapons – bows and arrows mainly, as well as food. I understand that you, Ned, had a few flying lessons while you were in the hold?'

Grace looked at Ned in awe.

'You've flown a carpet?' she said, eyes widening as she stared at Ned.

'Er, yeah, I had a few bumps and scrapes, but once you get the hang of it, it's fairly easy,' he said, his face reddening under Grace's admiring gaze.

'What you probably don't realise, Ned, is that Belastung doesn't like the idea of people moving about too freely. As a result, flying carpets were outlawed and anyone found in possession of one was dealt with harshly. Very harshly. Not only that, the craftsfolk who could make flying carpets were hunted down and murdered by the svartelves. Murdered, not even enslaved, so dangerous were they considered to be. Only a handful escaped to carry on their trade, which is why not many people have ever seen a flying carpet, let alone flown one,' explained Captain Ruby.

'But there were hundreds down there,' said Ned.

'Nearly a thousand. It's taken decades to craft them. Many people have lost their lives just gathering the materials and taking them to the weavers. To say we have a precious cargo would be an understatement. Doubly precious, if what Mr Swanson told me is true.'

'What do you mean?' said Grace, looking from Captain Ruby to Ned.

'Ned can explain later, but I think it would be true to say that of the two cargoes on *The Flying Lampwing*, Belastung and Malverfuhren would be most interested in the one sitting in front of me.'

'Where are you taking the carpets?' asked Ned, carefully checking that the ring was still in his pocket.

'For years now there has been a secret army of Outcasts gathering in the Outer Isles of the Southern Reaches. The carpets and weapons are for them. What their "leader" intends to do with all of it is no business of mine.'

'I bet they're going to attack Belastung and Malverfuhren. Will they be able to help me rescue Sam?'

'I wouldn't pin your hopes on it. They've been carrying out raids for years, but have never managed to inflict any damage.'

'How come? Has Malverfuhren been too strong

for them?' asked Grace.

'Er, not quite. You'll have a better idea when we arrive at their hideout,' replied Captain Ruby.

Grace looked at Ned and shrugged.

'Now, if you'll excuse me, I'm due to take over from my first mate,' said Captain Ruby.

Ned and Grace talked long into the evening, until the night sky outside was awash with bright stars.

'Look,' said Grace pointing at one brilliant red star, 'that's the tip of the Spear, and over there is the Ship – see how those three stars line up – that's supposed to be the mast. My mum knew all of them.'

'Amaldus said something about your mum earlier. Did she fight Malverfuhren, too?'

'My mum was a thief,' said Grace, looking down into the water.

'Oh, dear. Really?' said Ned. 'What did she steal?'

'Oh, she wasn't a common thief, not a robber or anything like that. She was a King's Thief - they swear to work only for one king and help him become richer or more powerful by stealing things like secrets, or really powerful magic spells. Things like that. She became a King's Thief after the last one died. Hundreds tried the tests, some even got killed, but only my mum was good enough.'

'What happened to her?'

It was some time before Grace answered.

'She'd been asked by the Outcasts to help them steal a map from Malverfuhren. Nobody really knows what happened, but somehow she was caught. Some say she was betrayed. It was Amaldus who brought her body back. Dad says that I look just like her. Poor Dad, he didn't speak for a year after she died.'

'A map? What was it a map of? Buried treasure or something?'

'No, it was a map of the portals. The Outcasts want nothing more than to find the portal back to their own world, but no one knows where it is.'

'But Mr Swanson told me all the portals were destroyed,' said Ned.

'Maybe they have been, maybe Mr Swanson didn't know where they all were – it was Belastung who found the way to the Outcasts' world. At least, that's what I've heard them say in the Healer's Bowl. What's your world like, Ned? Do you have stars there too?'

Ned told Grace of the constellations in his world and how his favourite had been Orion's Belt, because it was the first one he and Sam had seen together.

'Is he the reason you're here?' asked Grace.

'Yes. Malverfuhren has stolen his soul and I'm going to get it back. I'm going to take him back to Mum and Dad,' said Ned.

'How?'

'I don't know to be honest.' Ned laughed shakily. 'I'm here on a ship smuggling carpets and weapons in the middle of an ocean in a different world and I have no idea at all how to rescue him.'

Ned slept fitfully that night, losing count of the number of times he jerked awake, heart hammering as the memory of Mr Swanson's demise stalked his dreams and quaking with fear at the unknown perils that lay ahead. At times a crushing, black loneliness fell upon on Ned, followed by waves of panic and despair that left him heaving in great lungfuls of air. Time and again he rose from his bunk meaning to search the ship for Captain Ruby and Amaldus and seek their help in finishing the quest. But each time he did so, he fell back weeping and curling himself into a tight ball, legs drawn up and his arms wrapped round his chest. It was not until the Ship and the Spear had finished their trek across the heavens and had begun to disappear over the horizon that Ned finally sank into a blessed, dreamless sleep.

A shout from high above woke Ned. Rubbing the sleep from his eyes and yawning hugely, he went to look for Grace.

'Hello, Ned, did you manage to sleep in the end?' she asked, as he joined her at the *Lampwing's* bow.

'Only a bit, I kept having bad dreams.' Ned yawned again and stretched. 'What was the shouting about?'

'See that dark line on the horizon?' asked Grace, pointing ahead.

'It's not the Gravemen again, is it?' exclaimed Ned, now fully awake.

'No, it's land,' said Grace, and then frowned. 'It means we're getting closer to Malverfuhren.'

Ned's heart began to hammer against his ribs and blood pounded in his ears.

'How long until we land? Is there a port there or something?' he asked, his face now set hard.

'There used to be back in the days of the Circle, but not anymore. Dad's told me hundreds of times about how it was destroyed by Belastung,' replied Grace. 'They only just managed to escape. I was born a few days after they left port.'

As the ship sailed steadily closer, a mixture of dread and excitement filled Ned. The weather, which had been fair when they'd first set eyes on land, began to steadily worsen. At first a thin, dismal layer of high cloud crept in, dropping a fine cold drizzle, a drizzle that leached everyone's spirits until even Amaldus grew short-tempered with the crew. The drizzle was soon followed by gloomy low clouds that crushed down on them, brushing the tips of the masts. Strange noises could be heard as huge beasts lurked unseen in the clouds, the clamour of their wings sending violent gusts of wind that rocked the *Lampwing* from side to side. Amaldus ordered the lookout down from the crow's nest, the unfortunate sailor nearly falling as he climbed down the rigging, so cold and so terrified was he.

'There's some terrible things up there,' he stuttered, teeth chattering as he was helped below, the ice in his hair slowly melting and falling to the deck. 'Why have we come to such a forsaken place? It's your fault, boy.' He glared at Ned.

'Take him below, and look after him,' ordered Amaldus, stepping between the crewman and Ned. 'Don't worry, Ned, it's his first time voyaging to these Reaches. It always has the same effect, but it's never as bad as the first time.'

Ned slid his hand into his pocket and grasped the ring tightly, its burning cold giving way to the warmth of a summer's day as he prayed that the cloud would lift and that they would make landfall safely. A weak, milky sunlight filtered its way through the cloud and fog, giving Ned a clear view of an immense cliff rising vertically from the sea, waves breaking against its base and sending bursts of spray high into the air. Even from half a mile away, the rock face loomed above them, filling the sky. Twin waterfalls fell from high on the cliff face, thundering into the water below, adding to the already churning sea. Ned peered through mist thrown up by the waves and the waterfall, searching for a dock, but still the *Lampwing* sailed swiftly toward the cliff, aiming at a point between the two waterfalls.

'Amaldus,' he shouted, shaking him by the arm, 'we're going to hit the rocks.'

He shook Amaldus harder, but the first mate merely stared straight ahead at the approaching doom. Ned ran from crewman to crewman, shaking them and shouting to be heard above the roar of the cascades and the thunder as they crashed into the sea on either side of the *Lampwing*. With only seconds to go before they smashed into the unyielding rock, Ned grabbed on to the railing and held on for dear life. A terrible grinding, splintering noise filled the air and the *Lampwing* lurched alarmingly. Ned watched, stunned, as a huge section of the cliff swung to one side, exposing a cave entrance. A glimpse of huge stony slabs sliding over one another and the *Lampwing* was sucked into the cave on a tide of water before the grinding noise once again deafened them and daylight was shut out. Apart from the gentle lapping of water against the ship's bows, the cave was eerily quiet.

Amaldus exhaled in a long whistle and congratulated the crew, who began shaking hands and clapping each other on the back. Burning lanterns were soon passed around until a ring of light shone from the *Lampwing*, allowing Captain Ruby to steer her ship through the narrow tunnel.

'Welcome to the Outcasts' Haven, Ned. It's a bit of a shock coming through the cliff – takes a lot of concentration even when you've done it as often as we have.'

'I honestly thought we were goners – everyone looked as though they were under a spell or something,' said Ned, a shaky laugh bursting from him.

As the *Lampwing* continued its course into the cave, huge beacons were lit on either side of the tunnel and greetings shouted across the water, as old friends hailed each other. Following a bend in the tunnel, the ship sailed gently into a bay lined with wooden houses and, with a shout from Amaldus, dropped anchor next to a long wooden pier thronging with Outcasts.

As soon as she was safely moored, a large, rolling figure laboured its way up the gangplank, accompanied by a rake thin, whey-faced Outcast.

'Hail and hello, Cap'n Ruby' the sweating figure boomed, 'you've made good time – we're nearly ready.' The figure struck a meaty fist into an equally meaty palm and beamed down at the Captain.

Amaldus and Captain Ruby exchanged a look, and stepped forward to greet their visitor as he ambled onto the deck.

'Withercliffe – a pleasure, as always. And Lucien – you're looking as healthy as ever,' said Captain Ruby shaking Withercliffe's hand and nodding at the figure hovering by Withercliffe's side.

'The pleasure is as always, mine,' boomed Withercliffe. 'And who are these two young imps? New crew, eh?' he said, turning to Ned and Grace, who were staring at the immense figure.

'This is Ned – he's our new galley hand,' said Amaldus, nodding at Ned, 'and this is Grace – a stowaway who's a dab hand in the rigging.'

'Ho, ho!! A stowaway – you young madam, you!'

'And you, young fella – come to join the fight, eh?'

'What fight?' asked Ned, wincing as porky fingers pinched his cheek.

'What fight? What fight, says the boy!' trumpeted Withercliffe. 'Why, the fight that will end the fetid rule of Belastung and Malverfuhren, of course! The fight that will bring us the Map of Portals and allow us to return to our own world!'

Silence greeted this declaration, and to Ned's surprise a number of Outcasts glared sullenly at Withercliffe while others looked down and shuffled their feet.

'Enough talk,' yelled Withercliffe, oblivious to the hostility, 'let us unload the battle gear!'

Ned and Grace stood and watched as hundreds of flying carpets and weapon bundles were unloaded from the *Lampwing* and passed down a human chain of Outcasts and into a storehouse. All the while Withercliffe and Lucien stood by, Withercliffe yelling encouragement and exclamations of how he would personally smite the enemy down, Lucien carefully counting the smuggled goods. At last the final carpet was unloaded and carried away to the storeroom by Withercliffe himself who, after placing his load carefully with the others, promptly fastened the door with a large padlock and slipped the key deep into his pocket.

'They won't know what's hit 'em,' he declared.

'There's one missing,' Lucien's reedy voice cut across Withercliffe's latest proclamation.

'What? One missing, you say? Captain Ruby! Come here immediately!' bellowed Withercliffe, puffing up his hairy cheeks.

Captain Ruby walked down the gangplank, a vein throbbing in her temple.

'Yes, Withercliffe, is there a problem?' she asked through gritted teeth.

'I should say there is, my little friend!' boomed Withercliffe, looming over her. 'You've tried to pull a fast one, haven't you?'

'I have done no such thing, Withercliffe,' replied Captain Ruby icily, staring Withercliffe steadily in the eye.

'Lucien has counted – never gets it wrong, do you, lad?' said Withercliffe, clapping Lucien on the back and sending a thick cloud of dandruff into the air.

'Never,' came Lucien's arrogant reply, as he flicked his lank hair back into place.

'We can't have any missing, y'know. I need every man jack there is if we're to carry this plan off. What am I going to tell my troops, eh? That we can't go to battle because our only link to the outside world tried to pull a fast one on us?'

'I'm not saying his counting is incorrect,' said Captain Ruby, her gauntleted fingers tapping lightly on the handle of her katana. 'Quite the opposite, he has correctly spotted that there is one carpet missing.'

'Ah, oh, see – so you, er, did try to outwit me, eh?' said Withercliffe, nervously eyeing Captain Ruby's tapping fingers.

'The carpet in question lies in tatters a day's sailing from here,' said Captain Ruby, taking a step closer.

'Too many rats on the ship, I expect,' drawled Lucien, looking pointedly at Ned and Grace.

'Rats! How dare you!' Ned yelled furiously. 'That carpet was lost in battle. Battle against the Gravemen, and by one man, too!'

Lucien sneered at this.

'One man? Really?'

'Yes, really. We were almost taken by the Gravemen. If it hadn't been for the courage of this boy's companion then you'd have nothing,' said Amaldus, stepping between Ned and Lucien and staring the latter squarely in the eye.

'No one could take on the Gravemen, only the Great Mage Cygfilius could have done something like that,' said Lucien, staring straight back.

Withercliffe began to bluff and bluster and elbowed Lucien hard in the ribs.

'Oh, well, um, lost in battle, eh? Against the Gravemen, you say? Such a noble cause. I can only beg your forgiveness, Captain. I'm sure we'll be able to cobble something together and keep to our plan.'

'I'm sure we will,' said Captain Ruby.

'Worry not, my troops, the plan is safe. The enemy had better not be sleeping easy,' boomed Withercliffe, turning to the assembled Outcasts.

To Ned's amazement, some of the Outcasts rolled their eyes at this and shook their heads, muttering to each other.

'Right then, let us not tarry here any longer – let us feast and celebrate your safe arrival, Captain Ruby,' said Withercliffe, draping a flabby arm across Captain Ruby's shoulders and leading the group toward the largest of the buildings that filled the Outcasts' Hideout.

'I don't think much of Lucien,' whispered Ned to Grace, as they tagged along.

'Odd, isn't he? Have you seen that burn scar on his neck? He keeps trying to cover it with his horrible hair,' she replied.

'No,' said Ned, 'I wonder how he got it.'

'And as for Withercliffe – he's bit of an empty barrel, isn't he?' replied Grace.

'What do you mean by that?' asked Ned.

'It's a something my dad says a lot – "it's an empty barrel that makes the most noise",' replied Grace. 'We'll have to ask Amaldus what he knows about them. Try and get him alone after the feast. I don't think Withercliffe is all that he makes out to be.'

'Hmm, but he must be a pretty good leader,' said Ned. 'I mean, look what he's done here. It's an amazing place, isn't it? Look how high this cave is. They've even got a flock of lampwings, and look over there, on the far side of the bay – they've got ships.'

'Hmm, I saw those ships when we came in. I wouldn't trust them to get me across a puddle, let alone across the sea,' said Grace, glancing back at the two hulks that floated listlessly in the distance.

'Come along you two, no dawdling, please.' Lucien smiled greasily as he stood waiting for them to catch up.

Ned and Grace jumped guiltily and hurried after Amaldus, and Captain Ruby, who had by now shrugged Withercliffe's arm from her shoulders. Withercliffe was in full flow.

'Changed it a bit since your last visit, what, what, eh, Captain?' he trumpeted, waving a hand at the wooden buildings that lined the colossal cave. 'No more tents and we've cut new lodgings into the rock up there,' he said, pointing high up above their heads. 'Perfect for the reinforcements when they arrive,' he continued, as the group stopped and stared up at the hundreds of small caves that lined the rock face.

'You have reinforcements coming?' asked Captain Ruby, looking at Withercliffe with surprise.

'Why, yes, of course,' boomed Withercliffe, shifting uneasily. 'Well,' he said after a pause, 'I dispatched some of my most trusted men to seek them and sign them up to the cause.'

'But no actual reinforcements as yet?' asked Amaldus.

'Well, ah, no, er, you see, my men have had to travel far and wide. And they can't do it openly, y'know – all very secret and hush, hush. Can't just turn up and shout about our secret army – wouldn't be very secret for very long, now, would it?'

Amaldus and Captain Ruby stared at Withercliffe.

'I think the feast awaits us, sir.' Lucien interrupted the awkward silence and ushered the group into the feasting hall.

The feast itself was a dismal affair of pickled fish, leathery seaweed salads and iron-hard bread. Only Trug tucked into his food with any gusto, and even helped himself to second, and then third, helpings.

'Baked it myself!' Withercliffe had proclaimed, as a plate of the bread was dropped in front of Ned and Grace with a thud.

'Looks like it's been chiselled out of rock,' Ned whispered to Grace, who tried desperately to hide a fit of giggles behind a forkful of seaweed, 'tastes like it, too.'

'I'm not sure if you're supposed to eat that or make a pair of boots from it,' said Ned, nodding at the seaweed that Grace was trying to chew through.

'Oh, nice manners, Grace. Do you want these pieces back?' he teased, as Grace, snorting with laughter, sent lumps of half-chewed seaweed spraying across the table.

'If you two have finished, I'll show you to your lodgings,' said Lucien, who had sidled up behind them unnoticed.

'Oh, yes. Thank you. Couldn't eat another thing.' Grace smiled brightly and pushed her plate away.

'You certainly have enjoyed our leader's great generosity, haven't you?' said Lucien, eyeing them both with a cold smile.

'Hmm, yes, delightful,' replied Ned, trying to hide the half-eaten meal on his plate under his knife and fork.

'Good; then follow me, if you please.' Without waiting for a reply, Lucien turned on his heel and strode from the feasting hall.

Ned looked desperately over his shoulder, trying to attract Amaldus's attention as he and Grace followed Lucien. Amaldus, however, was deep in conversation with one of the Outcasts, laughing uproariously at something the Outcast had just told him.

'Up here,' Lucien called over his shoulder, making his way towards a flight of steps that had been hewn into the rock.

'Er, where do these go?' asked Ned, craning his neck and trying to follow the steps as they wound their way up the cliff face.

'To the reinforcement's caves – the very highest ones,' Lucien replied menacingly.

'But what if the reinforcements arrive?' asked Grace sweetly, causing Lucien to stumble slightly.

'They'll arrive soon enough, my girl, don't you worry, and when they do I'm sure we'll find somewhere else for you to sleep. If you're still with us, that is,' replied Lucien, shrugging his cloak back into place. He fixed Grace with a hard stare. 'I know you from somewhere, don't I? Where have we met before?' he said, 'I never forget a face. Never. And yours has been bothering me from the moment you landed.'

By the time they had arrived at the highest of the caves, Ned and Grace were both panting heavily. Not only had the climb been steep, but the path had at times narrowed so much that they'd caught dizzying glimpses of the Outcasts' harbour, hundreds of feet below.

'Here we are,' declared Lucien, turning abruptly to face Ned and Grace. The two friends peered round

Lucien, trying to catch a glimpse of their new home.

'But before we go in, a few questions I'd like to ask of you, boy,' said Lucien quietly, taking a step toward Ned.

Ned took a step back, glancing nervously over his shoulder at the edge of the path that hid a precipitous drop to the harbour below.

'Yes, you should be careful of these paths – we lost a few men when we built them. Usually the ones who were causing us a little trouble, but that was pure coincidence, of course. Now, it'd be a terrible shame if you two suffered a similar fate, wouldn't it?' Lucien smiled nastily and stepped even closer. 'Now tell me, boy, who are you, and why are you here? Who was your companion? How did he fight the Gravemen?'

Ned desperately searched for an answer.

'He's my grandfather. Was, I mean. Er, we're farmers,' he blurted. 'I'm a farmer's apprentice. My grandfather was taken by the Gravemen. We were travelling the world. To, er, see more of it. More of Elgarolyn, that is.'

'Your "grandfather" fought the Gravemen from a flying carpet, you fool. There's not a farmer in this world who could fly one without years of instruction, imbeciles that they are. Now, I'll ask you again – who are you, and what are you doing here?' he snarled, grabbing both Ned and Grace by the front of their clothes and holding them teetering on the very edge of the path. Pebbles crumbled from the edge and fell rattling and tumbling down the precipice, the sound of their splashing following seconds later.

'I wouldn't do that if I were you,' came a silkily dangerous voice, as several inches of razor-sharp steel stroked Lucien's throat.

Lucien gulped and carefully stepped back, hauling Ned and Grace to safety. He winced as the blade pressed against his neck, drawing a thin trickle of blood.

'Now, I don't think it would be to anybody's advantage if I ran this sword through your scrawny throat, so be off, and don't let me see you anywhere near these children again,' said Captain Ruby.

Lucien nodded frantically, eyes bulging as he backed away from the captain and fled down the steps, almost falling over the edge in his terror.

Captain Ruby sheathed her sword and smiled cheerfully at Ned and Grace.

'Right, then, shall we see what our lodgings are like? Bags I get the top bunk.'

Ned and Grace blinked as a bright flash lit the cave. Captain Ruby grated her flint and steel together again and after several more rasping strikes coaxed a lantern into life. Light flickered around the cave. At the far end stood a number of bunk beds, and between the entrance of the cave and the bunks stood a table and chairs and a small stove.

'Very nice,' murmured Captain Ruby.

'It must have taken them a long time to make these caves – look how smooth the walls are,' said Ned, running a hand over polished rock.

'I think you've hit the nail right on the head there,' said Captain Ruby.

'What do you mean?' asked Grace, as she, too, inspected their living quarters.

'Well, I get the feeling that Withercliffe and Lucien have had to keep their men busy for a very long time,' replied Captain Ruby.

'But why? And why did Lucien nearly push us off

the path?'

'Withercliffe likes playing King of the Castle –
he's no intention of leading his men into battle,' said
Captain Ruby, kindling the stove with a handful of dried
seaweed.

'But what about the Map of Portals? I thought
they all wanted to find the portal back to their own world,'
said Grace.

'And if he does find it and leads his men home,
then he'll no longer be king – he'll just be another ordinary
man in his world, whereas here he has managed to make
himself an empire – and he doesn't want anyone
disturbing it. That's why he tasked Lucien to bring you
here.'

'But it's pretty miserable here. Why would he
want to spend his life in a grotty cave rather than
somewhere nice?' said Grace.

'Some people prefer to have their little empires, no
matter how miserable it makes other people,' said Captain
Ruby, 'even if it does mean living in a place like this.'

'Withercliffe told Lucien to threaten us? But he
seemed so friendly,' said Ned.

'That is his way – on the outside he plays the
hearty hero, on the inside he's a scheming coward,' said
Captain Ruby.

'So why don't his men leave?' asked Grace, as
though this was the most obvious thing in the world.

'How many ships do you see in the harbour?'
asked Captain Ruby.

'Two,' replied Ned promptly.

'But they could only carry half the Outcasts here,
and besides, they didn't look seaworthy to me,' replied
Grace. 'For a start the rigging was in a terrible state – did
you see all those tangles?'

Captain Ruby laughed and looked at Grace.

'You're definitely a girl of the sea, Grace. Yes, indeed, those two ships down there in the harbour probably wouldn't get as far as the hideout entrance. I doubt that Marganth would even bother raising her tail.'

'Marganth? Who's Marganth?' asked Ned and Grace.

'Marganth is the Granite Dragon who hides the entrance to the hideout with her tail – didn't you see her?'

'Oh, my gosh – no, well, yes, I saw something – huge slabs of rock moving. I thought it was an avalanche or something. I didn't see a dragon, though. I thought we were going to crash,' said Ned.

'I thought Granite Dragons were a myth,' said Grace.

'As far as I know Marganth is the only Granite Dragon on this world,' said Captain Ruby.

'Did she come through a portal?' asked Ned.

'Yes, just before Cygfilius destroyed them all,' said Captain Ruby.

'Cygfilius destroyed the portals?' asked Ned, looking at Captain Ruby oddly.

'He had no choice – Belastung and Malverfuhren were close to taking complete control of them, so they had to be destroyed, and that's how Marganth came to be trapped in this world.'

'But why did she come here in the first place?' said Grace.

'Belastung wanted to form an army of dragons – Granite Dragons are impervious to attack from practically everything but the most powerful of curses, and so Belastung and Malverfuhren stole her eggs and brought them back here and tried to raise them.'

'And Marganth followed them?' said Grace.

'There is nothing that a mother dragon will stop at to protect her eggs or her young.'

'And did they create their dragon army?' asked Ned. 'Will they be guarding the castle?'

'No. There's one thing they didn't know, and that is that a dragon egg will only hatch if it's been incubated in the fiery breath of its mother.'

'Does she still search for them?' asked Ned.

'She can't,' replied Captain Ruby.

'Why not?'

'I'll show you in the morning – what you will witness will tell you a lot about Withercliffe and Lucien.'

Chapter Thirty-Five

Marganth

'Not far now,' called Captain Ruby over her shoulder, as she led Ned and Grace puffing and panting through another narrow tunnel. Amaldus, lantern in hand, squeezed in behind them, pausing every so often to check that they weren't being followed.

'I'm sure she said that ages ago,' muttered Ned, as he banged his head on a particularly low part of the tunnel's roof.

'Mind your head, there's a low bit,' Captain Ruby called.

'I know,' grumbled Ned, 'I just found it.'

'Good show,' said Captain Ruby.

Grace giggled behind Ned and poked him in the back.

'Come on, slowcoach, anybody would think you don't like scrabbling about underground with tons of rock above your head.'

'Don't say that,' moaned Ned, 'please don't say that. Where's Amaldus got to?'

'Do you want me to hold your hand for you?'

Even in the pitch black, Ned could tell Grace was grinning at his fear.

'I hope there aren't any scorpions in here,' she whispered.

At last, after yet more scrapes and bangs, Captain Ruby, Ned, Grace and Amaldus stood in a large, dimly lit cave. What light there was filtered in through large cracks that ran down one wall of the cave. A warm wind washed over them, reminding Ned of his dusty trek through the wastelands, and somewhere nearby a waterfall could be heard falling and splashing. Amaldus held the lantern high and its bright glow chased the gloom away.

'Oh, my word!' breathed Grace, clutching Ned's arm as hard as she could.

Ned and Grace stopped dead in their tracks, not daring to move a muscle, and stared at the sleeping dragon's head that filled the end of the cave, its snout resting on the floor. A large pool of water lay on either side of the dragon's head, each with a stream running away and out over the lip of the cave's mouth. As Amaldus lifted his lantern higher, Ned could see that water fell from the dragon's eyes and collected in the pools.

'Even in her dreams she weeps for her lost children,' murmured Captain Ruby.

'The waterfalls that we passed between – ' said Ned.

'Are dragon's tears,' finished Amaldus.

'Why does she have that horrible ring through her nose?' whispered Grace.

'To keep control of her – look, there's a chain attached to it,' said Ned, pointing to a heap of coiled steel links, each the size of a car. 'They do the same to bulls in my world, I think it's horribly cruel.'

'Look – the chains run up to those pulleys. That wheel over there must be for pulling on them,' said Grace.

As Grace spoke, a loud grating sound filled the cave. Ned and Grace clutched each other and took several steps backwards as the huge head stirred and eyes as bright as moonlight blinked open.

'Who is it that disturbs me?' came a voice forlorn

and lost. 'Amaldus. Captain Ruby. And two new ones that I don't recognise.'

'Hello, Marganth,' said Captain Ruby, moving forward and resting her cheek affectionately against the dragon's snout.

'You've been gone a long time, Captain Ruby, your company is always a joy, my friend.' rumbled Marganth, the tears slowing.

'Ned and Grace are your new visitors.'

'Hello, Ned. Hello, Grace. You are both children, yes? Why so far from home? You especially, Ned – your scent is very strange to me, not of this world at all.'

'Hu-hullo, Marganth. I come from a different world. We call it Earth – I came through a portal. I've come to rescue my brother,' blurted Ned.

'There is another scent about you, though, of a friend who came with you, yes? A scent from my most ancient memories.'

'I came through with Mr Swanson, Charlie Swanson. He's the caretaker of my school, but he's a wizard really.'

'The name is a new one. Swanson? A son of a swan? I never knew a Swanson, but wizards I have known, and that scent is the scent of a good man and it is the scent of a man I know,' rumbled Marganth, sniffing the air deeply.

'Captain Ruby told me that you're from a different world, too,' said Ned, feeling brave enough to take a step closer.

'Alas, yes, I came seeking the evil that took my children from me,' said Marganth, letting out a desert-hot sigh that rippled their clothes.

'But you seek them no longer?' asked Ned.

'I would, but for these chains that bind me here.'

'But who bound you like this?' asked Grace. 'It's so cruel.'

'Who else but Withercliffe and his toady, Lucien,' said Amaldus, spitting onto the dusty floor.

At the mention of the two names, Marganth bared her teeth, each one taller than a man.

'They lured me here with promises of help and trapped me instead, and while I lay deep in sleep they bound me with this collar and then pierced me with this ring.'

As she turned her head slightly, Ned and Grace could see a huge metal collar clamped around Marganth's neck.

'And now I spend my days clinging to this cliff, lifting my tail when Withercliffe commands it,' she said bitterly.

'Do you mind if I have a close look at the collar?' asked Grace, peering thoughtfully up at Marganth's neck.

'Be my guest. You can climb up the cracks in my cheek – don't worry, I won't bite.'

Grace scrambled effortlessly up Marganth's face while Ned followed tentatively behind, arriving between Marganth's ears out of breath and shaking.

'Oh, sorry, I forgot. You're scared of heights, aren't you?' Grace grinned mischievously.

'No, not all,' panted Ned, clinging to a handhold.

'Come and stand here and look over the edge then,' teased Grace, leaning out over the long drop to the floor.

'What did you want to see anyway?' said Ned, eager to change the subject.

'I want to see what the lock looks like,' replied Grace, skipping her way lightly along Marganth's long neck, arms spread out on either side.

Ned gulped and followed, crawling along and clutching every possible crack and spine on Marganth's neck, and freezing in terror when Marganth shifted slightly underneath them.

'Come on, will you.' Grace urged, as he finally caught up. 'I need a hand getting onto this thing.'

With a heave, and a yelp of pain as Grace stepped on his head, Ned helped Grace clamber onto the lock that joined the two ends of the collar.

'Hmm, interesting,' said Grace, getting down on all fours and peering closely at one part of the lock before crawling on hands and knees and running her fingertips expertly over another.

'What is?' said Ned, from where he hung on to a spine.

'The lock hasn't been welded together by magic or anything like that,' she said, jumping back to her feet and looking down at Ned.

'So?' said Ned, wishing that Grace would stop standing on the very edge of the lock.

'Well, come up and look at this bit here,' said Grace.

'Er, can't you just describe it to me?' said Ned.

'Oh, Ned, really,' said Grace, stamping her foot and planting her hands on her hips.

'Please?'

'OK,' said Grace letting out a deep breath, 'There are – '

'Quick, there's someone coming,' hissed Amaldus from below.

Ned and Grace slithered and bumped down from Marganth as quickly as they could and ran toward Amaldus, who stood beckoning them from beside a large rock that lay against the cave wall. Taking great care,

Marganth rolled the rock away, exposing a narrow crack that plunged deep into the earth. With the lamp held in front of him, Amaldus squeezed his broad frame into the crack and wriggled out of sight.

'Oh no, not another tunnel,' moaned Ned. 'Can't we just hide?'

'Too late for that,' said Captain Ruby, as she and Grace pushed Ned after Amaldus.

'You know what to do, Marganth,' whispered Captain Ruby, crouching down at the opening.

When all were crammed inside, Marganth once again rolled the rock back into place. With the grinding of the rock still in their ears, a muffled voice could be heard outside.

'Had visitors, have we?' came a sneering taunt.

The voice was unmistakable even through the thick rock.

'What makes you think that?' said Marganth.

'The footprints I followed here, you foolish beast,' said Lucien.

'There are no footprints here.'

'No, but there is a fresh layer of dust over everything – one of your favourite tricks,' spat Lucien.

'I'm sorry, I have no idea what you're talking about,' said Marganth.

'Well, then, let me assist you with your memory.'

There followed a clanking sound as the huge wheel began to turn and then a thunderous bellow of pain.

'Come, you don't want to hear this,' urged Captain Ruby, pushing Ned and Grace further into the crack.

'But he's torturing her,' exclaimed Ned furiously, as he tried to push back past Grace, but only succeeding in banging his head against hard rock.

'We can't do anything about it,' said Captain Ruby. 'Marganth won't betray us.'

'But can't we get back into the cave and stop him?' begged Ned.

'Marganth won't move the stone, she's too loyal. I'm sorry, the only thing that we can do is return to our cave,' said Amaldus, shaking his head.

With the roars of pain echoing through the rock, the four companions crawled and squeezed through the tunnel, Ned weeping silently at the cruelty behind them.

'Try not to worry about Marganth,' said Amaldus kindly, placing two steaming mugs in front of Grace and Ned. 'She's tough, really tough, even for a dragon.'

'But Lucien was torturing her for the fun of it – he knew we'd been there, it would have been obvious,' said Grace.

The four of them had returned to their cave dusty, exhausted and covered in scrapes and bruises. Amaldus had set about fixing a meagre evening meal of pickled fish and bread taken from the *Lampwing's* stores, while Captain Ruby had set about dressing the worst of Grace's and Ned's grazes.

'This drink is lovely. What is it?' asked Ned, wafting the bright yellow steam that rose from his mug.

'It's called "fahrus" – it's a herb that only grows in high mountains. It's supposed to help you sleep,' said Grace.

'How did you know that?' said Captain Ruby.

'My mother had to find some once for a customer,' replied Grace innocently.

'You mean she stole some.' Amaldus grinned.

'Well, yes, but she did have to find some first of all,' explained Grace.

'And just how much did she find?' asked Amaldus.

'Oh, I think Dad said it was two bales.'

'Two bales? That's more than a man could drink in a lifetime. It would have been worth a fortune.'

'Hmm,' said Grace frowning.

'Hmm what?' said Ned.

'Talking of my mother has reminded me of Marganth's collar,' said Grace.

'What do you mean?' asked Ned dreamily, sipping his drink.

'It was something she once told me about locks, one of the last things she told me, in actual fact,' said Grace, fiddling with her mug.

'What? What did she tell you?' said Ned, sitting up abruptly, his drink forgotten.

'That's the problem – I can't remember,' said Grace, her frown becoming an angry scowl.

'Oh dear, that's no good,' groaned Ned, slumping in his chair.

'Well, I am sorry, Mr Smarty Pants! I suppose you've remembered everything your mother ever told you,' snapped Grace, fixing Ned with a fiery glare.

'Er, well –' began Ned.

'Er, well, no, you haven't,' finished Grace for him.

Ned stared into his mug, avoiding Grace's angry look.

'If Grace did manage to free her, do you think she would help us?' asked Ned quietly.

'I should say so,' said Amaldus, swilling the last of his drink around.

'You've got to remember that Malverfuhren and Belastung stole her eggs – she'd pursue them to the very ends of Elgarolyn to get her revenge,' said Captain Ruby, who had been sitting at the mouth of their cave deep in thought.

'When do you think it'll be safe to go back?' asked Ned.

'Wait a few days. Amaldus and I'll have to come up with some way of distracting Lucien and Withercliffe, so that you can spend more time with her.'

Chapter Thirty-Six

A Delicate Matter

'Now that didn't come as a total surprise.'

Ned looked up as Captain Ruby and Amaldus stepped into their cave.

'What didn't?' said Grace, who had been teaching Ned how to read runes.

'Withercliffe asked me to join him to discuss a rather delicate matter,' Captain Ruby replied, joining them at the table.

'What delicate matter?' asked Ned.

'They took some of the flying carpets out today to give them a try out,' said Captain Ruby.

'And? What happened? Did they work alright?' said Ned.

'There was no problem with the carpets. The problem was with the flyers – Withercliffe failed to mention that none of his Outcasts have ever flown a carpet before.'

'So why did he ask you to smuggle them to him? What about all the risks that were taken to make them and bring them to Port Cadarn? All those poor people. Why doesn't somebody do something about Withercliffe and Lucien?' said Grace.

Captain Ruby glanced sharply at Amaldus and imperceptibly shook her head.

'Withercliffe's way – look to be doing something impressive to keep everyone fooled,' replied Captain Ruby.

'To be honest, I think he was surprised that we

managed to get them to him,' said Amaldus. 'I rather believe that he was hoping we'd fail.'

'So who's going to teach the Outcasts to fly carpets?' asked Grace.

'Captain Ruby and myself volunteered to do it – we've, er, both had some experience flying carpets,' replied Amaldus, smiling his best innocent smile.

'I bet Withercliffe was pleased to hear that, wasn't he?' said Ned

'Not in the slightest – he was quite taken aback when I told him that we could do it.' Captain Ruby smiled. 'Started to bluff and bluster about all sorts of things, but I was insistent.'

'But what was he going to do if you and Amaldus couldn't help?' said Ned.

'He asked me to go and find him someone who could teach them – gave me a name and everything. Told me I could find him in Port Nespere in the Western Reaches.'

'I bet he made the name up,' said Ned.

'And you'd be right, too,' replied Captain Ruby, 'but not only that, the Western Reaches are very much under Belastung's rule – we'd never have made it back.'

'Withercliffe would have blamed Belastung for that, wouldn't he? And it'd give him another excuse for not attacking,' said Ned quietly.

'Correct – you're beginning to understand how Withercliffe works,' said Captain Ruby.

'So when do you start training them?' asked Grace.

'Tomorrow morning – it's going to be a long process, the Outcasts have not only got to learn to handle a carpet, but they've got to be able to fire arrows at the same time,' said Captain Ruby.

'But will Withercliffe let you? Surely, he'll find some way of stopping you,' said Grace.

'We'll have to see. Now, I believe it is time for you two to sleep; you're going to be busy over the next few days,' said Amaldus.

'Doing what? Helping to train the Outcasts?' asked Ned.

'No. At least not yet, anyway. I think it would be a perfect opportunity for you and Grace to spend more time with Marganth,' said Amaldus, with a sly grin.

Chapter Thirty-Seven

Marganth's Fury

The portal's crackling alerted Ned that someone was coming through. Terror gripped him as familiar, snickering laughter filled the clearing and a dark shadow stepped triumphantly from the portal. With a flick of his arm, Malverfuhren swept the thorny bushes aside and strode into the night. Ned crept after him, watching the shadow flit between the trees of the Dell and climb up the steep bank that marked its edge. In the distance, Ned could see the outline of home, a night light burning in Sam's window, his own empty and black. Malverfuhren paused in his advance, looking up at the house and smiling. Ned winced as gravel crunched under his foot as he crept along the path that Mr Swanson and he had so long ago walked after Ned had first discovered the portal stone. Malverfuhren swept through as the gate at the end of the path swung open with a flick of his wand. The front door to Ned's house, too, swung open at Malverfuhren's command, and the shadow swept up the stairs.

'Please don't hurt them,' begged Ned, running into the hallway, but Malverfuhren continued to climb the stairs, striking the wall with his wand at every step, each strike ringing out as loud as thunder.

Ned was now climbing the stairs, each step sucking at his feet, draining the energy from his legs, evil twisted faces leering from the wall where Malverfuhren's wand had struck. Staggering along the landing he could see the dark figure entering his parents' bedroom.

'Hurry, hurry, Ned, you don't want to miss the

248

fun, do you?' Malverfuhren grinned horribly as he turned to Ned for the first time since passing through the portal.

'Don't hurt them, please don't hurt them,' beseeched Ned, tugging at Malverfuhren's cloak.

Malverfuhren cackled, and pointing his wand at Ned, froze him on the spot.

'Now watch,' he instructed Ned.

Malverfuhren spun and lashed his wand across the sleeping forms, uttering the words 'Ostulo purio'.'

Ned's parents woke up screaming in agony as vicious red welts bubbled and hissed across their faces and arms. Again and again Malverfuhren lashed his wand to and fro, each time screaming 'Ostulo purio,' Ned's parents writhing in their bed unable to flee the assault, and Ned could do nothing but look on, paralysed by Malverfuhren's spell.

'Do you see how easy it is for me to do this, Ned?' asked Malverfuhren.

Ned willed his mouth to move, but only a groan escaped his lips.

'Don't mumble, boy, I can't hear you,' Malverfuhren cackled as Ned struggled. With a flick, Malverfuhren released Ned, who collapsed to the floor.

'You know what to give me, boy, don't dawdle, don't delay – bring me the ring!' said Malverfuhren, and pointing his wand at Ned, he spoke one last time – 'Ostulo purio.'

Ned woke clutching at his chest where Malverfuhren's curse had lashed him. Grace, Amaldus and Captain Ruby were bent over him, concern etched on their faces.

'Ned. Ned, wake up now. You're having a nightmare,' said Captain Ruby, shaking Ned by the shoulder.

'He was torturing my parents. He's travelled to my world now. He's not afraid of using the portal. He's got passed Bryn,' said Ned, struggling to sit upright.

'You're covered in ice!' said Grace.

'Malverfuhren came into my dream – he did it before, but Mr Swanson stopped him,' said Ned, wincing as pain shot across his chest.

'What's wrong?' asked Amaldus, 'have you hurt yourself?'

'No, Malverfuhren used the same curse on me as he used on my parents – it feels like I've been burned.'

'Let's have a look,' said Captain Ruby, gently pulling Ned's shirt apart.

'My word, that is bad,' exclaimed Amaldus. 'I'll make a poultice up for you – another use of fahrus, should you ever need to know.'

'What happened in your dream, Ned?' said Captain Ruby, as Amaldus busied himself boiling water and adding a few leaves of the herb.

'Malverfuhren went through a portal to my world. He knew where I lived and he tortured my parents. He told me to hurry up and bring the ring to him. What can I do?' implored Ned looking at Captain Ruby.

'You have to remember it was a dream, Ned – he was blackmailing you,' said Captain Ruby.

'This isn't a dream, though, is it?' said Ned, pointing at the livid weal that ran across his chest. 'What about my parents, how do I know that he's not tortured them for real?'

'Ned, there's nothing we can do other than prepare the Outcasts for an attack and for you and Grace to try and free Marganth – she'll prove a useful ally,' said Amaldus, carefully pressing the poultice to Ned's wounds.

'And how long is that going to take?' said Ned.

'I'll be honest with you, Ned – I have no idea. We may only get half a dozen Outcasts who can fly and fire a bow at the same time.'

'That's if Withercliffe lets you,' said Ned gloomily.

'Don't worry about Withercliffe and Lucien – Amaldus came up with an idea while you slept,' said Captain Ruby.

The following evening, Grace and Ned returned triumphantly to the cave to find Captain Ruby and Amaldus already waiting for them.

'Well, you two look pleased with yourselves,' said Amaldus, looking up from the stove.

Ned and Grace grinned despite their fatigue.

'Grace has been brilliant,' said Ned. 'She managed to pick the lock that held Marganth's nose ring in place.'

'Well, that's a pretty good start,' said Amaldus, clapping Grace on the shoulder.

Grace blushed and shrugged her shoulders.

'It wasn't too difficult once I worked out what to do,' she said.

'Not too difficult? You've spent most of the day cooped up inside Marganth's nose. I've lost count of the number of times Marganth sneezed you out!' said Ned.

'It was worth it, though. I only had to think of Lucien torturing her. That made all my bumps and bruises seem like nothing and now Lucien and Withercliffe can't harm her.'

'I don't think they'll be doing much of anything for a while,' said Captain Ruby.

'Why not?' said Grace, carefully cleaning one of

her many scrapes.

'Amaldus's plan worked perfectly – he took them on a flight around the cave, but unfortunately had to make a sudden turn when Elgarolyn's grumpiest chef lumbered into their path just as they were coming into land.'

'Trug? What happened?' asked Grace and Ned at the same time.

'Well, let's just say that hitting the ground from even a low flying carpet can be painful – a broken leg for Withercliffe and two broken arms for Lucien. Oh, and a broken nose, too, you'll be glad to know. But that might have been from Trug when he rushed over to help.'

'That'll serve them right.' Grace clapped gleefully. 'You should see Marganth's wounds from that horrible nose ring.'

'And you say that Trug just happened to get in the way?' said Ned

'Yes, odd, isn't it? I wonder what the chances of that happening were?' said Amaldus, shrugging innocently.

'Where are they now?'

'They're in the hospital wing receiving some rather unsympathetic care,' said Captain Ruby.

'How long will they be there?' said Grace.

'Several weeks I should think and what's more it seems that the Outcast's healer has lost both pairs of cutters. There's no telling how they'll get the plaster off once their bones have healed,' said Captain Ruby, smiling as she laid what looked like a huge pair of scissors on the table.

'So that'll give us plenty of time to train the Outcasts and for you to free Marganth,' replied Amaldus, as he laid an identical pair of scissors on the table.

'I'm not sure we can wait weeks, though,' said

Ned, remembering his dream as Grace hugged him and bounced around their cave, hooting with joy.

'I know, but we can't dash in ill-prepared. Even if we waited a week, only a handful of Outcasts would make it as far as the castle,' said Amaldus, shaking his head.

'We need to prepare for this battle, and prepare well. The men down there are more than willing to fight Malverfuhren, and I intend to make sure they have every chance of surviving,' said Captain Ruby grimly.

Ned and Grace were back in Marganth's cave as they had been every day since freeing Marganth from the nose ring weeks before.

'Marganth. Marganth, it's us, Ned and Grace,' called Ned, leading them into the cave.

The now familiar rumbling snore faltered and then ceased as Marganth blinked awake and yawned, sending a puff of warm dust over the two children.

'Most sorry, my children. It's been wonderful sleeping without that awful ring waking me up every few minutes,' said Marganth, breaking into another yawn. 'Bless you both.'

This time Ned and Grace stepped aside, avoiding another dusting. As had become habit, Grace scampered up onto Marganth's neck, a rucksack of tools clanking on her back.

'What are you going to try today?' asked Marganth.

'Amaldus has given me some marlin spikes and an old cutlass to use,' replied Grace, as she clambered up a ladder they'd taken from the *Lampwing* and onto the lock.

'I've asked one of the Outcasts to make me some dragon-sized lock picks. They've got a smelter and a pretty decent forge down there in the harbour, but I'll have to make do with these for now.'

Setting out her tools, Grace began another long day of picking at the lock that held Marganth captive. Back down on the floor, Ned picked up a large broom that Trug had given him, and took to scrubbing Marganth behind the ears. A deep purring sound soon filled the cave as Marganth began to snooze.

'I'm sure my mum would have been able to do this in minutes,' muttered Grace hours later, as the lock failed to budge. Sliding down Marganth's face, Grace landed with a thump next to Ned, who had been midway through telling Marganth about his world and how he'd come to be in Elgarolyn.

'What? No dragons at all?' said Marganth.

'Well, Dad says that Great-Aunt Gail can be a bit of a dragon at times, but I don't think he means it literally,' said Ned.

'Your dad should get his facts right,' snapped Grace, snatching the bottle of water that Ned had offered her. 'Dragons are incredibly wise, loyal and brave – I'd quite happily be called a dragon.'

Wiping her mouth with the back of her hand, Grace sat down next to Ned and let out a loud groan.

'What's for lunch? I'm starving.'

'Trug's really pushed the boat out today,' said Ned brightly, but then stopped as he caught Grace's look.

'Sorry, it's stew again. Extra seaweed, by the looks of it.'

After they'd polished off the last of the slop, Ned looked warily across at Grace, hoping that the food would have improved her mood.

'My Great-Aunt Gail took me to the museum in London once. It had an exhibition about Houdini,' said

Ned.

'Really? And who's he?' snapped Grace.

'An escape artist,' said Ned, packing their bowls away.

'I'm not an escape artist – I'm a lock-pick,' said Grace, picking at a large blister on her hand.

'No, but he had to pick locks, too,' said Ned.

'And?' said Grace.

'Well, it's just that he used to use trick handcuffs that looked real, but could be undone without a key.'

'How did he unlock them, then?'

'That was the clever bit. He used to make them himself and use a false rivet as part of the lock, so the lock would always look like a lock, but it was actually the rivet that undid it,' said Ned.

Grace let out a loud screech, making both Ned and Marganth jump.

'That's it!'

'That's it,' she said again, leaping to her feet and pulling Ned up, 'that's what Mum told me – a lock may not always be a lock! You marvel, Ned,' she screamed, and gave the rather startled Ned a hug before scrambling once again up to Marganth's collar.

'Ned,' she called shortly, 'I'm not sure that any of these rivets are false.'

Trying not to look down, Ned scaled Marganth's stony face and joined Grace where she stood on the lock. Four huge rivets held the hasp of the lock together, one in each corner.

'You don't look as though you've done much to the lock,' said Ned.

'What do you mean?' asked Grace, frowning.

'Well, I thought maybe you'd have bent some of the metal out of the way – you've not even scratched the lock.'

'That's because I'm a lock-pick and not a ham-fisted idiot with a hammer and chisel,' said Grace, glaring at Ned.

Ned was about to point out that Bryn used a hammer and chisel and was by no means ham-fisted, but after seeing the look on Grace's face, decided not to.

'A good lock-pick doesn't leave a trace, Ned Penhallow,' said Grace, stamping her foot hard in anger.

The moment Grace's foot stamped down on the lock, there was a series of loud clunks followed by a several clicks, and then a whirring sound from deep within the hasp. As they watched, a rivet in one corner slowly unscrewed itself and grew from the metal, quickly followed by the second, third and then fourth rivet.

'Quick, Ned, get off the lock,' yelled Grace, jumping down onto Marganth's neck.

Ned quickly followed, and as the final rivet unscrewed itself the whirring noise stopped, and with a loud snap, the lock sprung open, sending the huge collar crashing to the ground.

'You've done it,' yelled Ned, as Marganth gingerly flexed her neck.

'You two had better come down now,' said Marganth, 'I have a few aches and pains to straighten out.'

Scrambling and slithering down Marganth's face, Ned and Grace stood clear as the ancient dragon reared her head high up into the roof of the cave where she had been captive for so long. With a deafening crack, Marganth turned her neck one way and then the next, groaning with pleasure as her stiff neck could at last move.

'You marvellous children. I never thought I would be free again. Thank you, thank you, thank you,' rumbled

Marganth, as she continued to flex her neck and rustle her mighty wings.

'Now stand aside, there is something I must do,' she said, and with a sweep of her claws she tore the levers and pulleys from the wall and stamped them into the dust.

'What do we do now?' shouted Grace above the noise.

'Quick, we'd better go and tell the others,' said Ned, as Marganth continued to flex her aching, cramped limbs.

'Marganth, where are you going?' yelled Grace.

'I have some unfinished business with Malverfuhren,' roared Marganth, as she began to pull herself backward out of the cave. 'I'm going to smash his castle into dust and him with it.'

'No, no, wait, you can't go,' shouted Ned, 'Sam's in there, too.'

Ned raced forward and scrambled onto Marganth's face as she continued to free herself from the cave that had been her prison.

'What are you doing?' thundered Marganth. 'Get off me, child.'

'You're not going without me – I'm here to rescue Sam. You can't destroy the castle, you'll kill him if you do,' yelled Ned desperately.

'I have waited too long for this. It's time for me to avenge the death of my children,' she roared, her eyes blazing a savage red.

With a final heave that sent an avalanche of rock crashing into the sea, Marganth freed herself from the cave and, with Ned clinging to her with all his might, took flight, leaving a huge gaping wound in the cliff face.

Chapter Thirty-Eight

A Dragon's Word

A horrified yell escaped Ned's lips as the sea fell away below them with each beat of Marganth's wings. For a moment he thought that he could hear Grace shouting his name above the howling of the wind in his ears. Ned began to shudder with cold and terror as Marganth circled over the Outcasts' hideout, quickly gaining height. Bursting through the thick grey clouds and into bright sunlight, Ned gasped as the wind began to freeze his rain-soaked clothes.

'Marganth,' Ned yelled at the top of his lungs, 'Marganth, please, I can't feel my hands any more - I can't hold on!'

Marganth's wing beats ceased and she began to glide, dipping once more through the clouds and back down into the dull grey mist that hugged the world below them.

'Marganth, you have to go back to the hideout. We have to get the others.'

'Return to my prison? Never!'

'Where are we going? You can't attack Malverfuhren's castle. Sam's still in there. Please stop.'

'The mist is clearing. Look. Look below now,' commanded Marganth, beating her wings in a hover.

Ned gulped, tightened his grip and peered carefully over the edge of Marganth's snout. Through wisps of mist he spied the ground far, far below.

'Do you see the river?' said Marganth.

'Y-yes,' said Ned, pulling back from the edge and

wiping his streaming eyes.

'Look again and follow it back to the mountains. What do you see?'

Ned let out a low moan. Leaning forward again he picked out the river snaking its way through miles of pitiless, snow-blasted mountains. At its very source stood a bleak, icy fang of rock that towered over the surrounding mountains.

'That's his castle, isn't it? That's where Sam's being held!' said Ned, rage filling his heart at the sight of the monstrous castle that stood atop the frozen crag.

'Do you see the landslide?' said Marganth.

'Yes – all those rocks in the valley below the castle?' said Ned.

'That's where I finally confronted Belastung and Malverfuhren in a battle that lasted days, and was nearly defeated, too,' said Marganth. 'With the last of my strength, I tried to tear the mountain down on top of them. And now I shall finish them.'

'No! Please, Marganth, no! You can't. Sam's in there.'

Marganth's rage thundered through the clouds that swirled around them.

'I can and I will. I've waited so long for this. Chained and tortured I have counted the years. You cannot stop me now. They stole my children. I cannot let one child stand in the way of my revenge.'

'Please, Marganth! We freed you. Please listen to me! You are not the only mother who grieves. My mother grieves for her baby, too. Every day she becomes more and more empty. Every day her pain becomes greater. Please don't destroy Sam. She loves him so much. Please don't destroy my mum. Please don't destroy my dad. I want my family back. All of them. Please.'

For a moment they hung there, Marganth's eyes fixed on Malverfuhren's castle far below them. Then, with a roar of fury, Marganth folded her wings, and with a stomach churning dive, plummeted down into the depths of the ravine through which the river thundered. The ground barely trembled as Marganth landed with the lightness of a butterfly.

'You may get down now,' said Marganth placing her head close to the ground. Ned didn't move.

Marganth sighed, nearly uprooting a clump of trees that stood by the river.

'You have my word, the word of a dragon, that I will not attack the castle.'

Ned slid down Marganth's face and collapsed onto the soft grass as his shaking legs finally gave way.

'Marganth, I know Belastung and Malverfuhren stole your eggs, but I must try and rescue Sam before you attack them,' said Ned, walking round to face Marganth. 'Please try and understand.'

'Oh, I understand, my dear friend. I understand as only one mother can understand another mother's sorrow. Please forgive my rage. For so long I believed that I would be held captive until my dying day. To taste freedom again and the chance of destroying my old enemies was too much.'

Marganth sighed again and looked down at Ned.

'You and I both left the safety of our own worlds and faced many dangers to come to the aid of the ones we love and, just as I did, you must be prepared to make a terrible choice when you face Malverfuhren,' she said.

'What do you mean?' asked Ned.

'When I discovered that Malverfuhren and Belastung had escaped the avalanche, I was terribly injured and close to death. One more curse and I would have been slain.'

A long shuddering cry escaped Marganth.

'I had no choice but to destroy my children. They were ready to hatch. I could hear them calling to me from inside their eggs. My heart has wept for them ever since that day, but I had to do it to stop them from becoming slaves.'

'You destroyed your own eggs? I didn't know that – Captain Ruby said that they'd been stolen from you to become battle dragons.'

'That was Belastung's intention. But would you let someone you love suffer so much? I had no choice but to destroy them.'

A thin drizzle began to fall from the dismal sky, chilling Ned even further. From somewhere close by the pitiful cry of a small animal rent the air before being cut dead by a savage growl and grisly sounds of chewing.

Ned looked imploringly up at Marganth.

'Can you help me? Can you fly me to the castle?'

'I can go no nearer the castle without alerting Malverfuhren and, if he knows of my presence, there will be no telling what he'll do to Sam. You will have to face him alone. It is what he is expecting.'

A cry of disbelief escaped Ned's lips.

'Alone? I can't face him alone. I'm an eleven-year old boy with nothing and he's a sorcerer with some really horrible spells. And he's got the Gravemen. And an army of svartelves. I've got nothing.'

'You have three things, Ned – the ring, a lampwing feather and above all, an unbreakable love for your brother that you will never lose. You may have to make a terrible choice, Ned, but in the end your true nature and your courage will be key to defeating Malverfuhren and stopping him from gaining power again,' said Marganth.

Ned shook his head wearily and began to sob.

'I can't do this. Not by myself. I just want my brother back, that's all. I don't want to fight Malverfuhren. I just want Sam back.'

'You may not need to fight him.'

'What do you mean?'

'Use your wits. Use your courage. You can turn Malverfuhren's anger against himself. He wants that ring and will not yield until he possesses it. Remember what happened to those boys. His desire for that ring, his greed for its power will cloud his judgement and fuel his anger. That is his weakness.'

'What about you? What will you do? What if I can't defeat him?'

'Malverfuhren's castle is a day's walk from here. I've waited this long and I will wait another day, but at midday tomorrow I will descend on Malverfuhren's castle and I will reduce it to dust, no matter what.'

'But how will I know when midday is?' said Ned.

'Listen for the call of the Mittag Ravens – they only call when the sun is at its highest point, whether they can see it or not,' said Marganth.

Ned sighed and looked over at the tumbling river.

'All I have to do is follow the river, isn't it?' he asked.

Chapter Thirty-Nine

Ned Alone

The chill that had clung to Ned soon began to relinquish its grip as he clambered over boulders that littered the steeply rising ground of the ravine. Stopping to take a drink of water from a pool at the base of a churning waterfall, Ned could see Marganth far below leisurely rubbing her back against a rocky outcrop. Shortly after leaving the pool, the trees surrounding the river began to thicken, and as they did so, the air became gloomy and thick with cobwebs that clung to Ned until he had to stop time and time again to clear them from his hair and feet. To his right, the river continued to thunder, sending its spray high into the air before it fell as a light drizzle onto the trees, from where it dripped and soaked the ground into a foot-sucking mulch. Cracks and snaps, followed by the rapid thudding of running feet, terrified Ned every time he strayed too far from the river.

After several gruelling hours trudging up through the steep forest, the trees began to thin out and Ned's panting breath hung in pale clouds around him. Picking his way wearily through the thinning trees, Ned came out onto a high valley and shuddered as a desolate wind sawed at his face as it bowled down from the crags above. High up on one side of the valley lay the huge gash where Marganth had battled to rescue her eggs, and between Ned and the final ascent to Malverfuhren's castle lay a barrier of avalanche debris spreading from one side of the valley to the other. The valley grew gloomier as the sun began to set behind the brooding clouds, and with the forest behind him echoing with howls and screams, Ned began to search for shelter amongst the jumble of rocks. Eventually, as full darkness pressed in around him, he came to the foot of a particularly large rock and spied a thin ledge high on its face that led into a deep gouge. Twice slipping and tumbling from the rock face, he finally managed to haul himself onto the shelf of rock and wedge himself as far as he could into the gouge, the unforgiving rock freezing him where it touched his exhausted body.

Sleep didn't come to Ned, as the temperature plummeted even further and the icy wind whistled into his meagre cave. The valley floor was now alive with animal cries and wretched groans of pain and misery. Glowing eyes lit up the forest and the surrounding rocks as nocturnal beasts began their nightly hunt. A cloud of bats billowed forth from the castle and filled the air in the valley with their high-pitched screams. As his fear and misery deepened, Ned reached deep into his pocket and curled his hand around the ring and the feather cocooned in his jacket. As he did so, warmth began to spread through his tired, aching limbs and his thoughts turned to those who he held dear, and he began to whisper their names.

'Mum, Dad, Mr Swanson, Bryn, Grace, Great-Aunt Gail.'

A smile flickered across his face as he remembered others.

'Amaldus, Captain Ruby, Marganth.'

And then, 'Sam. Sam, I'm so close now. I love you, Sam. I'm so sorry, it's been all my fault. I'll be with you tomorrow, I promise.'

At the thought of Sam and his cheeky grin whenever he was caught doing something naughty, Ned began to laugh. He laughed and laughed until tears ran down his face as memory after memory rolled over him. Memories of Sam as a toddler waving goodbye to him at the school gate. Of his delighted face when the school day finished and big brother was walking across the playground to him. Memories of Christmas when Sam had fallen asleep in a pile of wrapping paper. Then the memory of this Christmas. The leaden grief, the cold empty hours, and the silent house that should have been ringing with excited screams. And as this memory cut through his joy, the pain and anguish and terror that had grown in him since the accident reared up and crashed over him, turning his laughter into pitiful, fearful sobs.

The morning grey drained all life from the world around Ned as he awoke and stretched his tired, cramped limbs. A shuffling, grunting from below made Ned peer cautiously over the lip of his hideout. Below, at the base of the rock, a figure lurched and stumbled in the pale dawn, drawn to what looked like a pile of filthy rags. The shambling figure fell greedily on the corpse, stripping the rags for itself before scuttling away into the mist and leaving the twisted remains staring into the grey heavens.

'An Outcast,' gasped Ned, looking at the tattoos that stood out in stark contrast to the corpse's white skin.

By the time he had slithered and slipped to the ground the mist had lifted, allowing Ned to clearly see the end of the valley and the path that wound its perilous way to Malverfuhren's castle. Littered between the avalanche debris and the beginning of the path were hundreds of clusters of smaller grey boulders. Keeping a wary eye out for the figure that had robbed the corpse, Ned threaded his way between rocks and boulders, steadily drawing nearer to the path that led to his brother. Stepping around one particularly large boulder, Ned stopped dead in his tracks. Sitting in a huddle a few feet from him, filthy unkempt rags dripping from their emaciated frames and straggles of greasy hair falling to their shoulders, was a group of figures. As Ned carefully backed away from the huddle, he froze, as he heard the same grunting and shuffling that had alerted him earlier. Hardly daring to turn his head, Ned watched from the corner of his eye as the figure lurched past, brushing against him as it did so. The thing barely acknowledged Ned, turning only to glance disinterestedly at his frozen features. Everything about the pathetic figure, from its filthy rags to its air of utter misery, filled Ned with despair, but it wasn't until he looked into the figure's slack face and the dull, vacant eyes that he realised what he was looking at.

'Gravemen – they're victims of the Gravemen. Husks,' he whispered.

Ned waved his hand in front of the Husk's eyes, but the poor thing showed no response and merely continued on its way and joined the other Husks as they sat in their pathetic group. Dread filled Ned as he drew closer to the huddle and saw a lock of filthy white hair slip from below a dirt-stiffened hat. The hand that clumsily shoved it back into place had once been slender and beautiful, a woman's hand.

Ned scrambled to the top of the nearest rock and surveyed the boulder field that lay between him and the path. To his horror, he could now see that the clusters of small boulders he had seen earlier were instead hundreds upon hundreds of Husks, all clad in the same filthy grey rags, some rocking back and forth but most sitting motionless and pathetic in the dirt, and every one of them clutching a faded keepsake.

Waves of wretchedness and dejection crashed over him as he began to pick his way through the forlorn huddles and soon each step became harder and harder until Ned barely had the will to lift his feet. Desperately, he raised his eyes to the heavens and fixed his eyes on the castle looming high above. Picturing the Soul Cage that held Sam, Ned began to surge forward, keeping his eyes set grimly on the castle until, finally, the sanctuary of the path lay before him. Dragging himself onto its flat surface, he collapsed in a heap and sobbed with exhaustion. Wiping his tears with his sleeve, Ned picked himself up and, looking high above, traced the route of the path as it snaked its way up the cliff above him. With fear and desperation in his heart, Ned began the final dreadful ascent to Malverfuhren's castle.

Chapter Forty

Malverfuhren's Castle

The last few hundred metres of the path were mantled in thick snow and ice. The bitter cold gnawed through Ned's meagre boots and into his aching feet, making his climb an agonising hobble. Needles of ice stung his face as he battled against the tugging arctic wind that whipped around the castle so ferociously that at times it threatened to lift him off completely and send him spinning and tumbling to the valley floor far below. Above him towered the castle's gatehouse, a portcullis biting its way through the drifts of frozen snow. As he clambered through the drifts, the portcullis began to rise, its creaking and rumbling sending a flock of large black birds wheeling and tumbling through the skies.

'And you must be the Mittag Ravens,' muttered Ned. 'When will you start to call?'

As the portcullis finished its ascent the doors it protected swung silently open, revealing the castle's courtyard beyond. With shaking legs, Ned took first one step, then another, and after peering out mouse-like from the huge doorway he stepped out into the courtyard. As soon as he was clear of the doors there was a mighty rumble and the portcullis slammed down, sending a blast of snow and ice over Ned. Again and again the portcullis rose and fell, each time sending shards of ice whirring past Ned, some striking him hard enough to make him cry out in pain. Ned scrambled away from the crashing fangs and into the desolate courtyard, sprawling flat and winding himself as he slipped on a patch of ice. The portcullis

thundered down one final time, and as the booming
echoes that had rolled around the walls began to fade, the
doors swung silently shut. Standing up and brushing the
snow and splinters of ice from his clothing, Ned spun
round startled as a low grinding rumble replaced the
thunder of the portcullis. It wasn't until he looked up at
the battlements that Ned saw what was making the noise.
All along the high wall the stone seethed and boiled until
from deep within dozens of struggling figures fought their
way free of the liquid stone. Ned clapped his hands over
his ears as, one by one, gargoyles perched upon the
battlements and filled the air with their eerie shrieks. As
one, the gargoyles stopped their shrieking and began to
beat their wings together, slowly at first but then faster
and faster until the courtyard rang with the cannon-fire
crash of stone against stone. With a cry, the gargoyles
leaped from their perches and swooped down toward
Ned, passing within inches of his head, their piercing
screams mimicking the screech of brakes. Cowering on the
ground and desperately looking for somewhere to hide,
Ned spied a pair of huge wooden doors at the far end of
the courtyard and, set to one side almost hidden in the
shadows, a small stone doorway. Mustering every ounce
of his courage he leaped to his feet and sprinted for the
small doorway, ducking and dodging the screaming
gargoyles as they continued to mob him, their flint-tipped
talons slashing the air around him. With a shove, the thick
wooden door flew open, and with one gargoyle still
slashing at him through the doorway, Ned slammed the
door as hard as he could. The gargoyle shrieked in pain
and rage as the heavy timber bit down on its leg and,
slashing wildly, the gargoyle snagged Ned's arm, cutting
it deeply. Suddenly furious, Ned hauled the door open
and once more slammed it against the flailing leg. A shout

of rage punctuating each slam, he beat the edge of the door against the leg until with a loud crack the leg snapped off and fell to the floor. Scattering the shattered fragments with an angry kick, Ned strode into the hall he had found, his footsteps echoing round into the vaulted ceiling high above. Stopping in his tracks, Ned gazed in awe. The hall, in its heyday, would have held thousands of people. Along the centre and running into the far distance stood the longest table Ned had ever seen. Underneath the thick layer of dust and cobwebs that coated everything in the hall, Ned could see the entire table had been laid in preparation for a feast. Here and there, candlesticks festooned in webs rose from the dust like the rigging of phantom ships. Goblets and tankards stood as silent monuments to times of joy and laughter. Walking slowly down on side of the table, sneezing on the dust that his feet kicked up, the back of Ned's neck began to tickle. Whirling round, he was sure one of the many suits of armour he had walked by had moved ever so slightly, a fine avalanche of dust falling from its helm. Standing stock still and watching the armour closely, daring it to move again, his heart leapt into his mouth as a loud, jarring clatter from behind him reverberated up and down the hall. Leaping behind a nearby chair, he peered over the top and saw that one of the hundreds of rotting tapestries that hung from walls had finally torn free and had fallen, knocking several suits of armour to the floor. Breathing a sigh of relief, Ned stood up and stepped out from his flimsy hiding place. A portrait of a nobleman on the opposite wall seemed to stare down at him, mocking his panic.

'I'm here,' he yelled, his words sounding flat and deadened by the cloud of dust that the falling tapestry had thrown up, 'I've come for my brother.'

There was no reply other than the howl of wind outside and the occasional thud as a gargoyle threw itself against the door behind him.

'Show yourself. I know who you are. Show yourself, Malverfuhren.'

From under the fallen tapestry came a metallic clunk as a piece of armour finished toppling over.

'So what do I do now?' he muttered to himself, looking round for a clue.

Ignoring the throbbing wound in his arm, Ned peered into the distance and could just make out another large door hiding in the gloom at the far end of the hall. Stepping round the tangle of torn tapestry and scattered armour, Ned froze as his foot snagged on a fallen lance, making a nearby jumble of metal rattle loudly. A sudden image flickered into his mind, that of his dad standing over him after he'd tripped on the garden path and had howled in pain as blood ran from both knees. 'Clumsy fool,' his dad had muttered as he'd picked him up by the scruff of his neck and hauled him to his feet.

'I might be clumsy but I'm here,' said Ned, giving a metal gauntlet that had rolled free a hefty kick that sent it spinning and clattering against the wall. Ned stared as the gauntlet came to rest on its back, like a stranded crab on the beach, and was just about to walk on when one of the fingers twitched. His breath caught in his throat as, one by one, the other fingers began to twitch, at first slowly as though waking from a long sleep, and then faster and faster until with a spring, the gauntlet flipped itself into the air and scuttled back toward him. Ned leapt out of the way with a yell of disgust as the gauntlet scurried past and back under the tapestry. Backing away from the fallen armour, Ned let out a loud gulp as more of the scattered pieces slowly twitched into life and began to drag themselves together, aided by a swarm of gauntlets. Before he had taken more than a dozen steps, several suits of armour had risen to their feet and were reaching for their fallen weapons. Steel scraped harshly on bare stone as swords, battleaxes, war hammers and lances were gathered up and held menacingly at the ready. A moment's pause and then, as though listening to a silent command, the suits of armour marched at Ned. Darting away, Ned pulled chair after chair away from the table and hurled them into the path of the oncoming wall of metal, only to see them reduced to splinters under their pounding feet.

Picking up speed, the suits of armour started to gain on Ned, who with a flash of inspiration, leapt onto the table and off the other side. Ned's triumphant laugh died in his throat as his pursuers took one look at the barrier and began to hack through it, swords and axes blurring. By the time they had hewn halfway through the table, Ned had made the most of his head start and was hurtling down the hall, the sounds of destruction falling behind him. Running past the end of the table, Ned skidded to a terrifying, teetering halt at the very edge of a deep, rocky chasm that had suddenly belched open, a narrow stone bridge his only way across to the far door.

Throwing himself back from the crumbling edge, Ned watched as wreaths of smoke began to rise up from the black depths below, twisting and curling in on themselves until they floated above the bridge. With a sudden swirl, the smoke formed itself into words.

'Keep moving, best foot forward!' read Ned aloud.

Looking behind, Ned could see that he had little choice – the suits of armour had finished mauling their way through the table and were moving at speed as they continued to hunt him down. Facing the chasm again, the smoke had reshaped itself and before him floated a picture of his family – Mum, Dad, Sam and himself – and as he watched each face faded away, leaving only his own, which then, too, slowly disappeared.

The bridge was barely wide enough for his feet and so, crouching down, Ned prepared to cross on all fours. The instant he did so, the bridge began to writhe and heave under his hands, forcing him to scramble back onto safe ground where his shaking legs nearly gave way. The pounding of steel boots shook the stone floor around him, sending a slew of pebbles tumbling into the chasm. Once again Ned crouched down and placed his hands on the stones and once again the bridge heaved sinuously, forcing him to take a step back. Looking behind him, Ned could see that the nightmarish figures were almost upon him and so, with a trembling foot, he gingerly stepped out and onto the bridge. This time the bridge remained solid and, stretching his arms out wide to steady himself, Ned crept his other foot onto the bridge and began to inch his way slowly across the chasm. To his horror, as he reached the middle, the far end of the bridge crumbled and fell crashing into the darkness below. Shuffling round to retrace his steps, and nearly tumbling as he did so, he watched as the other end of the bridge, too, crumbled and fell, leaving the decaying bridge floating unsteadily in mid-air.

Hardly daring to look downward, Ned could see the blackness below rolling away to reveal a fiery orange inferno, plumes of lava and flame leaping upwards as they tried to pluck him from the bridge. The small span of bridge that remained suddenly began to drop, almost causing Ned to fall. Ignoring its writhing, Ned fell to his knees and clutched what was left of the bridge for all he

was worth. The remains of the bridge now began to
plummet even faster, the heat becoming unbearable as it
fell closer and closer toward the furnace. A jolt almost
threw Ned as the bridge came to a sudden halt and began
to drift towards a narrow, pitch black crack in the sheer
rock of the chasm's side. As the bridge nudged against the
opening Ned peered in trying to make out what lay
within. As he warily reached his hand as far into the crack
as he could, the bridge began to crumble again, this time
more rapidly than before. Taking a deep breath, Ned
launched himself into the opening just as the last of the
bridge collapsed. Flames licking at his feet and scraping
his belly painfully against its jagged lip, Ned pulled
himself into the tunnel.

Squirming deeper into the suffocating darkness,
Ned paused to catch his breath and pressed his scorched
face against the blessedly cold rock. As he rested there in
the dark something hard and unyielding squeezed his
burnt feet, making him cry out in pain and surprise. As
suddenly as it started the squeezing stopped, and released
Ned, allowing him to wriggle a little further, all the while
trying to peer down the length of his body to see what was
attacking him. As soon as he stopped the squeezing
returned, biting painfully into his calves until it again
released him. Forced to crawl ever deeper into the
terrifying darkness, and with his shins now an agony of
cuts and bruises, Ned stopped only when exhausted. But
every time he paused, the walls of the tunnel would again
bite down on his legs, chasing him further and further and
faster and faster until, his breathing a desperate and
ragged sob, he slithered down a sudden plunging drop in
the tunnel and fell from the ceiling of a small, brightly lit
cave and landed with a bone crunching thud. A loud
grinding filled the air as the tunnel sealed itself shut

behind him. Blinking painfully against the light, Ned
rolled onto his back and sat up, nursing his injuries.

'Well, at least I'm warm and dry now,' he said to
himself, fingering the scorch marks on his boots.

As if in reply, a sandy hissing sound began to fill
the cave. Standing up and backing away from the centre
of the cave, Ned watched as a small whirlpool appeared in
the floor and began to spin rapidly, turning the floor to
sand, the hissing swelling to a roar as the whirlpool grew.
Once half the floor had been sucked away, the roaring was
replaced with a gurgling as crystal clear water bubbled up
from below and lapped at the edges of the hole. Suddenly
aware of his raging thirst, Ned dropped to his knees and
drank deeply. Surprisingly, the water was delicious and
cold as snow melt, a shiver running through him as it
settled in his stomach. Looking down into the clear pool,
Ned could see that the whirlpool had formed a broad
funnel that sloped sharply down to a wide hole, through
which the clear water flowed. With his thirst quenched,
Ned sat back and saw that while he had been drinking, a
number of small holes had appeared in the wall of the
cave. From each hole came the same chilling sound that
Ned had heard in the darkened hall and as he watched,
rock exploded into the cave, as without warning the edges
of the holes were savagely chewed away. With a cry of
terror, Ned backed away, as crawling out the holes came
the largest scorpions he had ever seen, their pincers
snapping as they advanced and bright yellow venom
dripping from their quivering stings.

Helplessly, Ned looked round for a way out of the
cave, as the holes through which the scorpions had
appeared sealed themselves one after the other. The only
hole that didn't disappear was the one in the centre of the
cave, the one filled to the brim with water. Ned let out a

yell as one of the scorpions sidled up behind him and snapped viciously at the back of his leg, its pincer biting deep into his calf. Whirling around he kicked out frantically, sending the beast tumbling backwards across the floor, its shriek of fury filling the cave. Immediately righting itself, the scorpion divided itself into two identical scorpions, both of which darted back towards Ned, stings lashing wildly and thick drops of venom sending plumes of smoke into the air as they landed sizzling on the floor.

Now sobbing with terror, Ned looked at his only means of escape and, taking a deep breath, plunged into the icy water and wriggled desperately downward, scorpions snapping at his calves and feet. The sides of the tunnel pressed in on Ned as he pulled himself along, his lungs bursting and his body already starting to go numb as the freezing cold sent fingers of ice lancing through him. Frantically clawing up a slight rise in the tunnel floor, Ned pulled himself into a small air pocket and, by shuffling onto his back, found that he could rest there, his face just clear of the water. Drawing in deep, gasping lungfuls of air, Ned could make out a message scrawled in fiery letters on the roof of the air pocket.

'Keep going, my dear boy, you're doing so well. Unless of course, you wish to hand the ring over now? You only have to ask! M.'

The taunting message broke up and swirled around before forming another.

'No rest for the wicked; time to get moving.'

The water level began to rise as Ned read the

message and he had to push his face hard against the roof
as he dragged in a last deep breath and, biting back the
plea on his lips, he began to crawl and wriggle his way
through the tunnel. Time and time again, just as his lungs
felt as though they were about to burst, a small pocket
would appear with just enough air to allow Ned to draw
breath before the water rose, forcing him to continue his
dreadful journey.

Exhausted and wracked with cold, Ned finally
pulled himself sobbing from the nightmarish tunnel and
flopped onto the floor of a roughly hewn cave. Crying and
retching, he curled himself into a ball and, hugging his
knees to his chest, rocked back and forth in the pool of
water that dripped from him. A deep rumbling sound
brought Ned to his senses as the walls of the cave began to
slowly close in on him. Scrambling to his feet, he dashed
to the mouth of the cave only to find himself looking out
over a deep chasm. Hunting for an escape on the sheer
rock faces on either side, Ned spied handholds leading up
to a narrow ledge that ran across the face of the rock.
Wincing as the feeling returned to his scratched and
bleeding hands, Ned grabbed on to the handholds and,
hauling himself up, belly flopped onto the ledge. There
was barely enough room for him to crouch, but by
standing up and wedging his fingers into cracks in the
rock, Ned shuffled slowly sideways along the shelf of
rock, which in some places became so narrow that only the
tips of his toes were touching and in others sloped away so
sharply that it threatened to throw him from the face and
into the chasm. Time and time again chunks of the ledge
crashed away as he passed them, leaving Ned with no
way of retreating, but instead forcing him ever onward.

Pausing momentarily to rest his straining arms
and to wipe away the sweat, Ned risked a glance over his

shoulder. Far below him, the darkness of the chasm had given way to a boiling fire of molten rock, which was bubbling slowly toward him. Desperate for escape, Ned began to move sideways again, gritting his teeth in pain as his fingertips were rubbed raw by the rough rock. Creeping perilously round a leaning corner, he could see salvation ahead. A solid looking bridge spanned the chasm and led to a flight of steps that spiralled upwards into the heart of the Keep. But as Ned made his next move, a tongue of flame belched up from the lava and seared his legs. The flare of pain made Ned scream out loud and as he did so his left hand, slick with blood and sweat, slipped from its precious purchase leaving him dangling precariously by one hand. The stench of the fires below was now making Ned cough and retch, and as he choked on the horrible fumes, and as his torn and bloodied fingers slowly slipped from the rock, an image popped into his mind, that of buses lined up to collect queues of waiting passengers.

Chapter Forty-One

Silence From the Ravens

'Terminus.'

The moment the single frantic word burst from his lips, Ned felt himself drop and crumple on to a cold, solid floor. Sobbing and laughing with relief, he lifted his ringing head and, propping himself up on one elbow, looked around. There was no sign of the rock face, the treacherous ledge had disappeared and the grasping flames were nowhere to be seen. There was nothing except the huge, dusty hall, echoing with Ned's laughter. A new sound joined the echoes, one familiar from his nightmares, a cold voice that slithered through the air.

'Well, you are quite a tough one to break, aren't you?' said Malverfuhren, standing triumphantly over Ned's exhausted body. 'All you had to do was beg pitifully and I would have made all the nasty things go away.'

'Beg you for help? I don't think so,' said Ned, as he dragged himself unsteadily to his feet and for the first time stood face-to-face with his tormentor.

This is the man who hurt Sam, Ned thought taking in the hooded figure that mocked him. A draught rippled the jet-black cloak that draped over Malverfuhren's thin frame, its hem brushing the floor. Thin, white hands, the fingers long and tipped with pointed, blackened nails, flicked from the sleeves and slowly drew the hood back. A web of thick blue veins squirmed and pulsed like worms under the translucent skin of the face that appeared. A mouth like a crimson wound cut across a twisting livid scar that covered Malverfuhren's jaw and neck, and plunged down into the depths of his tunic.

Malverfuhren grinned at Ned's revulsion, his wild yellow eyes glittering with malice.

'Even more handsome in real life, aren't I?'

'I've come for my brother. I've come for Sam,' he said, flinching back from Malverfuhren and gagging as the stench of putrid meat washed over him.

'Yes, yes, yes, all in good time,' said Malverfuhren airily, his wet, red lips drawn into a gloating smile. 'Let me enjoy the moment.'

Malverfuhren closed his eyes and, steepling his fingertips together, drew in a deep breath as though savouring the scent of spring flowers.

'Ah, yes,' he breathed, 'finally, after all this time. To have the ring so close to me. Exquisite. I can feel its call. So much power. So much power awaits me. I can feel it calling to its true mast – '

'That's a nasty looking scar you've got there. Who gave that to you? Mr Swanson?' interrupted Ned.

Malverfuhren recoiled as though Ned had slapped him.

'What? Never mind me, look at you! You really are a mess, aren't you, boy?' Malverfuhren snapped, looking Ned up and down. 'Filthy, absolutely filthy, what would your mother say, hmm?'

'I don't know what she would say about me, but I've a pretty good idea what she'd say about you,' said Ned, taking a step toward Malverfuhren.

'Oh, very good, but I'm afraid she won't be able to help you very much, she's still in quite a lot of pain I would imagine, ostulo purio, and all that,' grinned Malverfuhren nastily as he and Ned circled one another.

'That was just a dream – you didn't really torture my mum and dad.'

'Maybe it was a dream. Maybe it wasn't,' he jeered, pushing his face close to Ned's. 'Maybe I did torture them. Maybe I didn't. Or did I? Didn't I? Did I? Can't remember. Did. Didn't.'

Malverfuhren began to scream theatrically, imitating the agony Ned had seen in his dreams.

Ned took another step closer and jabbed Malverfuhren hard in the chest with his finger. To his surprise, Malverfuhren stopped his revolting pantomime and took a step backwards.

'I want Sam. Where is he? You've got him in a Soul Cage, haven't you?' Ned demanded.

'Got to keep him somewhere,' said Malverfuhren, with a smirk that reminded Ned of Smugley.

'Where is he?' said Ned, looking round the empty hall.

'Patience, patience, all in good time, my little dragon,' chided Malverfuhren, 'you know the deal, the ring for your darling little brother's soul.'

'I want to see Sam first. Where is he?'

'Very well, come this way,' said Malverfuhren, turning and walking briskly toward a small doorway that led from the hall. Ned followed, all the time listening carefully but hearing only the howling wind that whipped around the castle's battlements.

'Do you live here all alone?' he asked.

Malverfuhren stopped so abruptly that Ned almost walked into him.

'What do you mean by that?' he snarled, the whirl of his cloak cracking through the air like a whiplash.

'Well, I couldn't help noticing that you're the only person here and it's such a big castle. I thought you'd at least have servants or something.'

'Servants? What would I need servants for? I'm a sorcerer,' spat Malverfuhren.

'Wouldn't you rather live somewhere else?' asked Ned. 'I mean, it's so desolate and cold here.'

'Belastung gave me this castle as a gift. An expression of gratitude for my service,' said Malverfuhren, straightening up and looking down his long nose at Ned, a vein in his forehead pulsing angrily.

'Don't you ever get bored of listening to the wind? There's not even birdsong to listen to, is there?' Ned asked tentatively.

'What would I want to listen to birds for? I have the Mittag Ravens at my beck and call. The song of my loyal servants is enough.'

'Those big black birds? I didn't hear them singing,' said Ned.

'They call when the day is halfway done and not a moment before.'

'I look forward to it,' said Ned, eyeing Malverfuhren hopefully.

'You'll have to be patient. Mid-morning has only just passed, and besides, I believe we have some business to attend to?'

Ned's heart sank as Malverfuhren's words sank in.

'Not much of a thank you, is it?' said Ned, looking around.

'I beg your pardon?'

'Not much of a thank you, is it?' repeated Ned. 'You said it was a gift of gratitude?'

'And indeed it is,' replied Malverfuhren.

'But look at it – cold, empty, desolate and lonely, with a bunch of oversized crows for company. Are you sure Belastung was grateful?'

Malverfuhren's hand flickered and Ned found himself staring at the tip of a twisted and evil-looking wand.

'Be careful, boy, be very careful with that tongue of yours or I shall burn it out,' said Malverfuhren, his voice low and menacingly soft. 'Now follow me, it's time to make a deal.'

Malverfuhren's cloak cracked again as he spun round and continued his brisk walk. Ned followed slowly, listening intently for any noise outside other than the wind, which had continued to rise in strength, howling and screaming through the turrets that towered over the castle.

'Here we are,' announced Malverfuhren, as they passed through the door and into a much smaller chamber.

Ned stepped in and looked around. In the very centre of the room lay a flat disc of stone from which a writhing cord of magic snaked, its branches crackling and spitting into the ceiling high above. A little above the stone the cord bulged slightly, as though knotted. Over the crackling of magic an occasional sob could be heard.

'Sam!' shouted Ned, pushing past Malverfuhren and running toward the stone. A snake's tongue of magic flickered out and lashed at Ned, followed by another and another as Ned, ignoring the pain, reached out for Sam.

'Ned, Ned,' the tiny voice cried, 'I can hear you, I can hear you. We're not in a dream, are we? Where are you?'

Flickers of magic continued to whip at Ned, leaving a rash of welts across his hands and face as he struggled to get closer. The lashing ceased with a flick from Malverfuhren's wand and Ned ran to his brother.

Chapter Forty-Two

A Moment in Another World

In a world far away, connected to Elgarolyn by a slim pillar of magical stone, a small unconscious figure moved in his bed and a beautiful smile of joy played across his lips. His father, who had been reading out loud to him, had looked up moments before as the boy's bedroom had been bathed in a bright flash of purest white, lighting up the collection of toy aeroplanes that lined the bookshelf.

'Alice,' shouted Ned's father hoarsely, 'Alice, come quickly, Sam moved, I swear it, and he's smiling. Look!'

Chapter Forty-Three

A Reunion

'Sam, I'm sorry. I'm so, so sorry. I've been so long coming for you,' said Ned, gazing upon his brother's face as it pressed against the bars of the Soul Cage.

'Are we going home now? Will you make the bad man go away?' said Sam.

'Boo! No, still here, I'm afraid,' said Malverfuhren, jumping up from behind Ned.

The figure in the Soul Cage flinched away from the bars with a cry.

'Stay away from him!' yelled Ned, and shoved his elbow hard into Malverfuhren's belly.

'Oof! I'll make you sorry for that, you nasty little boy.' He groaned, clutching his stomach.

'You've scared him enough. Now leave him alone!'

Malverfuhren gave Ned a sour glare and then smiled horribly.

'Don't worry, I'll release him as soon as you give me the ring. Willingly, of course; I know how the ring works. And to help you make your mind up, perhaps you should look above you.'

Looking up along the length of the cord, Ned could see not one but two more bulges, both much bigger than the one made by the Soul Cage. With a word of command from Malverfuhren, the twisting cord slowly dropped towards the ground, its untidy coils still sparking and flaring until it faded like smoke, leaving two limp figures lying on the stone next to the Soul Cage.

'Charlie! Bryn!' Ned cried, as the two figures stirred slightly.

'Quite a touching reunion, I must say,' chirped Malverfuhren, patting Ned on the shoulder. 'Now, how's about that, eh? Three for the price of one. Rescue one, get two for free – grab it while you can. The offer only lasts while I'm in a good mood, which is never for very long, so hurry, hurry, hurry!'

Ned spun round and glared at Malverfuhren.

'What have you done to them?!'

'Me? Nothing – well, I told the svartelves to rough the big one up a bit if he looked like he was going to put up a fight. Which he did. So they roughed him up. A bit.'

'Bryn. His name is Bryn.'

'Yes, yes. I know who he is, don't interrupt. Did I mention svartelves? Oh, yes, I did, didn't I? Svartelves as we speak are in possession of the portal that you came through and are poised to swarm into your world at a moment's notice,' said Malverfuhren. 'It'd be lovely to bring Mum and Dad along to liven things up, wouldn't it?'

'What have the Gravemen done to Mr Swanson?'

'Oh, they were quite restrained, to be honest, which given their feelings towards "Mr Swanson" was quite decent of them, I thought. And look, they even brought me something to remember him by,' said Malverfuhren, flourishing an ancient, timeworn staff.

'Will he become a Husk like those poor souls in the valley?' said Ned.

'Not yet, but he will in time – in fact, you will all become Husks if I don't get what I want,' said Malverfuhren, stepping toward Ned with his hand extended.

'And if I don't hand the ring over?'

'If you don't hand the ring over?' spluttered Malverfuhren. 'Weren't you listening, you stupid boy? If you don't give me the ring, I'll let the Gravemen feed upon these two and when they've done they'll have your parents, your brother and you, too.'

For a moment Ned stared at Malverfuhren, whose last sentence had been punctuated by a muffled roar of thunder from the rising storm outside.

'If I give you the ring, I know what you'll do with it. You and Belastung will bring misery and suffering to countless millions on countless worlds. Look at what you've done to the Outcasts. Look at what you've done to those poor souls in the valley. Look at what you've done to my little brother. You'll do the same, time and time again, and I can't let you do that.'

'Oh, don't give me that weak-minded drivel. You sound like that fool and his Circle of Light,' shouted Malverfuhren, waving his hand dismissively at the barely conscious figure that lay sprawled next to the Soul Cage.

'He's no fool - he helped you and he trusted you. He let you join the Circle and you betrayed them all. You're the one who's weak-minded – you were too jealous and stupid to see what the Circle was doing,' said Ned.

'Don't you dare call me stupid. Don't you dare! I was as good as any in the Circle. Better, even. Yes, that's right, boy, better than those fools and their foolish spells and their foolish dreams of saving the weak and helpless. They had so much power and they wasted it on the pathetic and the feeble. Belastung knew we could bring peace to all worlds if we ruled them.'

'Peace? The only way you would have brought peace was by using the Gravemen to turn everybody into Husks,' said Ned.

Malverfuhren drew himself up tall and glared at

Ned, his whole body shaking with fury.

'Give me the ring,' shrieked Malverfuhren, flecks of spit flying from his mouth, 'Give me the ring now, or I'll blast these into tiny pieces.'

'Touch them, and I'll destroy the ring. Mr Swanson told me how to,' shouted Ned, pushing Malverfuhren's wand aside.

Malverfuhren's reply was drowned out as the thunder outside once more rumbled, shaking the entire castle.

Shoving Ned away, Malverfuhren took careful aim with his wand and blasted Mr Swanson, flinging him across the room. Ned screamed and dashed to Mr Swanson's side, guarding him from Malverfuhren. Shaking him roughly, he shouted his name over and over again.

'Hello, Ned,' murmured Mr Swanson, as his bleary eyes finally fixed upon him.

'Mr Swanson, have the Gravemen hurt you? Don't become a Husk, please don't become a Husk,' begged Ned.

'Oh, don't you worry, my dear boy,' murmured Mr Swanson, 'I'm more valuable to Malverfuhren as I am. At least, I like to think that's the case.'

Turning to plead with Malverfuhren, Ned was knocked flying by Bryn, who crashed to the floor next to Mr Swanson. Winded and dazed, Ned staggered to his feet as Malverfuhren trained his wand on the Soul Cage.

'Let's see how much we love little brother, shall we?'

'No, please don't,' screamed Ned, lurching to the stone and placing himself between Malverfuhren and Sam.

'You little fool. You stupid, interfering little fool.

How dare you try and stop me? Give me the ring! Give me the ring, now!'

'No. Never!' yelled Ned, bracing himself as he stared at the unwavering wand tip.

'Then perhaps a taste of what your parents had will help you change your mind,' said Malverfuhren, and as he raised his wand, his livid red mouth formed the start of the scalding curse, 'O – '

Chapter Forty-Four

Battle

'Oh, no you don't, laddie,' said a voice, followed by an earth-shaking boom as a flash of crimson light struck Malverfuhren square in the back and sent him hurtling across the room, his cloak smoking slightly where the spell had struck him.

'Great-Aunt Gail, what are you doing here!' Ned gaped at his Great-Aunt as she blasted Malverfuhren every time he tried to get to his feet. Standing over the stricken Malverfuhren, her battered old bamboo chopstick pointed unswervingly between his eyes, Great-Aunt Gail called over her shoulder.

'Are you in one piece, Ned? Have you got Sam?'

'Mairwen,' groaned Malverfuhren, flinching as Great-Aunt Gail jabbed her wand at him. 'But you died.'

'Evidently not,' replied Great-Aunt Gail, 'but I came very close, thanks to you and that awful creature you serve.'

'Mairwen? What? I don't understand. Why did he call you "Mairwen"?' said Ned, staring open-mouthed at his great-aunt, 'And anyway, how did you get here?'

'Carpet, mostly. Haven't had so much fun in years – just like delivering Mosquitoes during the war. Came in so low over the waves, there was sea spray all over the underside of Mr Swanson's carpet. Simply marvellous. Now, Ned, gather Sam and the others. We have to leave quickly. Very quickly.'

'Why?' said Ned.

The castle shuddered as something massive

smashed into the walls, sending Great-Aunt Gail staggering as the force of the blow rippled through the floor. Seizing his chance, Malverfuhren scrabbled for his fallen wand and, rolling to his feet, sent a curse flaming toward Great-Aunt Gail, narrowly missing her. A snaking rope of white light hit Malverfuhren square in the chest and sent him toppling as it bound itself around him.

'You should have destroyed my staff while you had the chance,' said Mr Swanson. 'Mairwen, could you help Bryn, here? He's not coming round.'

Another thunderous crash and this time Marganth's entire head thrust its way through the Keep wall, masonry scattering as she bit chunks from the walls. Kneeling beside Bryn, Great-Aunt Gail carefully passed her wand over his heart, murmuring an incantation. With a groan and a flicker of his eyes, Bryn slowly sat up and, looking at Ned, gave him a thumbs up before climbing unsteadily to his feet.

'Mairwen, so good to see you. You really should pop over for a cup of tea sometime,' he slurred, tottering slightly and leaning against the wall for support. 'I think I've still got some Yorkshire teabags, if Charlie hasn't had them all.'

Ned flinched as something split the air a hair's breadth from his face. A black crossbow bolt stuck, juddering, in the stone wall inches from where Bryn rested.

'Svartelves,' Ned yelled, as several more bolts whistled past and spattered the wall around him. A salvo of blasts from Great-Aunt Gail and Mr Swanson sent the creatures squealing for cover, but more and more surged through the trapdoor that had been slyly opened as they had tended to Bryn.

'Mairwen,' shouted Mr Swanson, as Marganth

tore down another section of the wall, 'take Ned and Sam and head for the portal.'

'Malverfuhren said that svartelves are at the portal. We can't go there,' said Ned.

'Trust me, there weren't many left by the time I'd finished sending their filthy hides scurrying back into their holes,' replied Great-Aunt Gail with a grim smile. 'Come, now, Ned, I think it's high time we took Sam home.'

Dodging crossbow bolts, Ned scrambled for the stone and grabbed the Soul Cage. Clutching it close to his chest, he ran from the chamber and into the hall, Great-Aunt Gail, seemingly impervious to the hail of bolts that flew around them, striding alongside, blasting the swarming svartelves aside as they tried to block their escape. Ahead of them Marganth smashed her way through the roof of the Hall, and through the gaping hole flew carpet after carpet, each carrying a pair of bellowing Outcasts. The air darkened as arrows rained down from the carpet flyers, felling swathes of svartelves, who in turn unleashed their crossbows, bringing several Outcasts crashing down.

'There they are,' came a cry from above, and a flight of Outcasts detached itself from the others and spiralled down, landing around Ned and Great-Aunt Gail. Heavily-armed figures leapt from the carpets and formed a solid wall around the two of them, sending volley after volley of arrows at the charging enemy. A familiar figure appeared beside Ned and Great-Aunt Gail, his calm voice cutting through the chaos of battle that raged all around them.

'Come on, you two, we have to go now; things are starting to look a little dark outside.'

'Amaldus!' yelled Ned, hugging the first mate and grinning despite his ominous words. 'Where's Captain

Ruby?'

'Right here,' said a voice from behind Amaldus, as Captain Ruby notched another arrow and dropped a particularly large svartelf that had charged, raging and screaming, toward them.

'What about Gra – ,' began Ned, before a small figure topped by fiery auburn hair burst between Captain Ruby and Amaldus and grabbed Ned in a rib-crushing hug.

'You did it, Ned, you did it,' yelled Grace, jumping up and down.

'We're not home and dry yet,' said Captain Ruby, 'Amaldus is right, it is getting dark outside.'

Looking through the gaping hole that Marganth had torn, Ned could see an all too familiar boiling black cloud heading toward the castle, with such menace in the ghostly faces that even Marganth stopped in her destruction to turn and face the approaching malevolence.

'You see,' yelled a voice triumphantly, 'you're too weak for me! You're outnumbered! You're surrounded! My Gravemen are here and they'll consume you all, one by snivelling one until I have the ring. Mark my words - before this day is out, you will all live in the valley below and the last of the Circle will have been destroyed.'

The companions turned to see Malverfuhren dodging a curse from Charlie and returning one of his own, which narrowly missed and blasted a suit of armour into hundreds of jagged pieces.

'My Gravemen have come for you again, Elwyn, and they won't be so kind this time,' he shrieked gleefully, before Mr Swanson's next curse wrapped itself around Malverfuhren's legs and sent him crashing to the ground. Marganth began to back into the hall, blasting the Gravemen with her fiery breath, but for all her valiant efforts, the black cloud rolled closer and closer. Helpless, the companions could only turn and watch as the first black tendrils crept through the gaping hole in the castle's wall and the air around them began to freeze.

Chapter Forty-Five

Lampwings and Dragon Flight

'Ned, no!' shouted Great-Aunt Gail, as Ned pushed his way through his bodyguard and reached into his pocket. Walking to where Malverfuhren stood waiting, Ned looked sorrowfully back at his friends.

'That's right, my boy, bring me the ring. Save your friends, save your family, save your world! I promise you safe passage back to your home. I promise,' said Malverfuhren gleefully. Around him the stinking mass of svartelves, some of them feeding on their dead and wounded, cackled in glee and screamed taunts at the besieged Outcasts, who stood bloodied and defiant, their bows raised and arrows notched.

'Silence!' bellowed Malverfuhren, lashing the svartelves with a blast from his wand.

Ned looked at Mr Swanson and held his gaze for a moment.

'I'm so sorry,' he said, in a voice that could barely be heard above the moaning wind.

Mr Swanson slumped and leaned his head wearily against his staff, his eyes closed in despair.

'I'm sorry, but I'm not giving you the ring,' said Ned, switching his gaze to Malverfuhren.

Malverfuhren's gloating smile faltered and contorted into a look of disbelief and then horror as Ned, with a flourish, pulled his hand from his pocket and held the lampwing's feather high above him.

In a silent explosion, everything from the darkest corners to the highest rafters of the ruined hall was bathed in a blazing silver-white light and, as the svartelves screamed and cowered away from the beauty before them, the single feather that had been dropped into Ned's hands so long ago began to blossom into a pulsing globe of flaming light that grew and grew until it floated from Ned's hand and hung silently, filling the air above them. When the globe reached its brightest, it burst with a single pure, beautiful note that silenced the chorus of screams and sent thousands of tiny crystals of light floating gently down, and as they fell slowly through the air, each crystal grew and shifted and folded, taking on a new shape until the hall was filled with swirling, flying, singing light.

'Lampwings!' cried Grace, her joyous face bathed in scintillating light. 'So many lampwings.'

And as the companions and Outcasts watched open-mouthed, the flock of lampwings billowed up and down the length of the hall as one huge pulsing, cascading cloud and then, as though listening to a silent command, the glittering birds flew one behind the other and began to circle the Gravemen until the black maelstrom was held in a net of fluttering light. Ned flinched as curse after curse split the air and bounced harmlessly off the flock as Malverfuhren fought to free the Gravemen. With a triumphant roar, the Outcasts unleashed a torrent of arrows at the svartelves, scattering their ranks and sending them fleeing from the hall, their weapons abandoned in their desperate flight from the Outcasts' assault. The air about them crackled with renewed battle as Mr Swanson and Malverfuhren locked curses, lightning forks of magic spitting and snarling as spells tangled and ricocheted in all directions, some whirring perilously close to friend and foe alike.

'Go! Go now,' commanded Captain Ruby, shouting to make herself heard above the salvo of spells and clamour of fleeing svartelves.

Great-Aunt Gail grabbed Ned and together they ran from the hall, clambering and hauling themselves over the piles of masonry that had once been the castle wall. Above them the grey clouds burnt away as the glowing ball of lampwings flew gracefully away, the subdued Gravemen still held captive within. Jumping down from the rubble, Ned let out a yell.

'Look out, there's – '

A swift blast from Great-Aunt Gail's wand destroyed a pair of gargoyles that had survived Marganth's assault and were stalking the two as they climbed their way free of the ruins.

'Nasty looking brutes,' declared Great-Aunt Gail, as though she'd done nothing more than shoo a pair of dogs away.

'Great-Aunt Gail, how are we going to get to the portal?'

'Follow me; we hid Charlie's carpet by the gatehouse. With a following wind, we'll get there before nightfall,' replied Great-Aunt Gail.

'It's faster by dragon,' yelled a voice from high above them.

'Ned, Mairwen, hop on next to Grace, you'll have some shelter there,' said Marganth, lowering her head and allowing Ned and Great-Aunt Gail to clamber on to her neck and wedge themselves next to a ferocious-looking Grace, still armed with her bow and now nearly empty quiver of arrows.

'Hold on tight,' said Marganth, 'Grace has told me to fly low. We don't want my precious cargo getting cold, now, do we?'

With a clap of her wings, Marganth leapt from the crag and, in a dive that left her passengers breathless, swooped down into the now sunlit valley that Ned had toiled up earlier that day. Grace whooped with delight as Marganth pulled out of the dive, her wings clipping the tops of the trees that marked the start of the ravine. Closely hugging each twist and turn of the river, Marganth soon reached the sea and at a height that earned a whoop of approval from Great-Aunt Gail, flashed above its surface. In what seemed like only a few beats of her wings, Port Cadarn came into view.

'I don't think we should fly at roof top height – wouldn't want to upset the lampwings, would we?' Marganth called, her words whipping away in her slipstream. Tilting her wings, she rocketed into the air, vapour trails falling from her wing tips. Ned, his knuckles already stiff and tired from gripping her hide, turned marble white.

'I can see the Healer's Bowl,' yelled Ned, trying not to sound terrified as Elgarolyn fell away below them.

'There's Dad! I can see my sisters, too,' screamed Grace, bouncing up and down with delight. 'They'll be so jealous.'

Ned gulped and clung even harder.

'Oh, please sit down, Grace, please.'

'Ha! Ned, your face has turned the same colour as the sea,' said Grace, giving him a poke in the ribs with her elbow. 'You're not going to be sick, are you?'

Port Cadarn passed by in a blink and, folding her wings in, Marganth dropped into a near vertical dive, only pulling out at the very last possible second. At a speed that cracked the air, two days of dusty, burning desert blurred past underneath.

'There, Marganth, down there – the circle of trees,' shouted Ned.

Whisking the ground with a wing tip, Marganth

banked sharply round the twenty trees in a turn that left her passengers giddy and, with a flare that barely disturbed the tall grass around them, landed with the poise of a gymnast. Laying her head on the ground, Marganth let Grace, Ned and Great-Aunt Gail scramble down.

'Well, I must say that really was quite exhilarating,' said Great-Aunt Gail, adjusting her bun. 'Ugh, how did that get there? Here, a souvenir for you, Grace.'

Grace took the black crossbow bolt from Great-Aunt Gail and held it between two fingers, her nose wrinkling in disgust.

'Marvellous bit of flying, Marganth, and such a soft landing, too. You really must teach me how to bank like that.'

'It will be an honour and a pleasure, Mairwen' replied Marganth, bowing her head.

'Great-Aunt Gail, why does everyone keep calling you "Mairwen"?' asked Ned.

'Not enough time to answer that, I'm afraid, my dear boy,' she said, before turning to Grace and Marganth.

'Marganth, I shall have to impose upon your kind nature once more, I'm afraid, and ask you that once we've gone through the portal, you return this lovely young lady to her family – I'm sure they're desperate for news of her, and she, no doubt, is simply dying to tell them about the wonders of dragon-flight.'

'But I want to return to Malverfuhren's Castle, to the battle,' said Grace, stamping her foot.

'My girl, you are so like your mother, you really are,' said Great-Aunt Gail with a soft smile, 'but I really think your father will be wanting to know where you are.

Besides, the battle will more than likely be over by now and the others will be arriving back in Port Cadarn before too long. I dare say there will be wounded to tend to.'

Ned stepped back as Grace let out an angry, 'Humph,' and turned on him.

'Well, you'd better come back and see us all soon, Ned Penhallow, that's all I can say,' she said, before leaping nimbly back onto Marganth and poking her tongue at Great-Aunt Gail.

Slipping and sliding down to the portal, Ned lifted the Soul Cage from his pocket.

'Great-Aunt Gail's with us now, Sam. We're going home now. We're going back to Mum and Dad.'

'Will it still be Christmas when we get back?' came Sam's voice from within the cage.

Ned laughed.

'It will be for Mum and Dad. And me, too, hopefully.'

'Ready, Ned?' asked Great-Aunt Gail.

'Ready,' said Ned, turning to wave one last time at Grace and Marganth, who were watching from the lip of the crater.

A crackle, a sharp tug of the shoulders, a clutching cold, and Ned gasped as the frosty cold night of the Dell embraced him.

'We're nearly home now, Sam,' said Ned, prying at the bars of the Soul Cage. 'Great-Aunt Gail, I can't open it,' he cried.

'That's hardly surprising – it is a Soul Cage, after all. Only the mage who created it can open it,' said Great-Aunt Gail.

'But that was Malverfuhren – he made it.' Ned groaned.

'Malverfuhren always was a fool,' declared Great-

301

Aunt Gail, taking the Soul Cage from Ned.

'What do you mean?'

'While it's true that the cage can only be opened by the maker, it doesn't mean that what's inside can't be freed,' she said, and with a tap of her bamboo wand, the white light that filled the cage began to swirl and fold and from it was formed a beautiful pure white butterfly that slipped between the bars of the Soul Cage and fluttered to Ned's outstretched hand.

'Well, let's not dawdle, this isn't the weather for butterflies,' said Great-Aunt Gail.

The bushes at the edge of the clearing leapt aside as Great-Aunt Gail strode toward them, Ned trotting alongside, his warm hands carefully cupped around the butterfly. A light burst from Great-Aunt Gail's wand as they climbed out of the Dell and followed the same path that Ned and Mr Swanson had walked along that moonlit night so many weeks before.

'There's a light on in Sam's room,' said Ned, as they walked down the path that Smugly had pursued him along and clanged through the iron gate.

'Your parents brought Sam home some time ago. I expect they'll be sitting with him,' said Great-Aunt Gail, as she pushed open the garden gate and tapped the lock of the front door with her wand.

'Ned, where have you been?!' his mum exclaimed, as they burst into Sam's room.

'No time to explain, Alice,' said Great-Aunt Gail, as she hurriedly poked her wand back into her hair.

'What? What's going on?' said Ned's dad, rising from his seat.

'Stand aside, William. Let Sam go now, Ned.'

Ned carefully opened his hands and the butterfly stretched and fluttered its wings, and to gasps of wonder

flew around the room before alighting on Sam's forehead.
After a moment or two, the butterfly shone brilliantly and,
as a ball of pure white light, sank slowly out of sight. A
flutter of eyelids and Sam's words broke the silence.

'You beat the bad man, didn't you, Ned?'

Chapter Forty-Six

A Return to Elgarolyn

'But I want to go with Ned,' said Sam, trying his best to detach himself from Great-Aunt Gail's firm grip.

'Now then, Sam, just be patient and wait a second,' said Great-Aunt Gail, sealing the thicket behind them with a flick of her bamboo chopstick. 'Oh, you're just like your father used to be – impatient, fiery and unstoppable. The doctor said you wouldn't be up and around for another few weeks and just look at you!'

Ahead of them, Ned and Mr Swanson stood by the portal stone, the last of the winter's snow still lingering at its base. A gentle buzz filled the warming air as the first of spring's bees flew sleepily among the snowdrops that blanketed the clearing. Mr Swanson, his hands shoved deep into his pockets, looked deep in thought as Ned fiddled with the strap of his rucksack.

'Is Bryn getting better?' said Ned, waving an inquisitive bumblebee away.

'He's still very weak. Mairwen, sorry, Great-Aunt Gail, I mean, pulled four crossbow bolts from him. She thinks they were tipped with poison,' said Mr Swanson, plucking the deerstalker from his head and rolling it tightly between his hands.

'Will he be alright, though?'

'Oh, yes, don't worry. He's as tough as they come.'

Ned gazed around the clearing.

'He'd love it here, wouldn't he? All these flowers.'

'They're quite something, aren't they? Have you

seen the crocuses over there?' said Mr Swanson, pointing with his staff at a patch of flowers. 'I'm sure they grow better here than anywhere else. Must be something to do with being so close to Elgarolyn.'

Before Ned could answer, Sam arrived, towing Great-Aunt Gail behind him.

'I want to go with you, Ned,' he said, grabbing his big brother's hand. 'If the bad man's there, we're going to bash him, aren't we?'

Mr Swanson laughed.

'Don't you worry, Sam, I'm sure I would have been warned if he was waiting, but all the same, we'll stick to the plan. I'll go through first and if I don't return within ten seconds then Great-Aunt Gail is to seal the portal.'

Ned and Sam nodded solemnly.

'Stand back, Sam, this will make you jump,' said Ned, placing a protective arm around his little brother's shoulders and pulling him close.

A crackle, a flash of blue light that left them all blinking, and Mr Swanson disappeared into the stone.

'Wow. That's awesome!' gasped Sam, stepping toward the stone. 'Is it our turn now?'

'Wait. You heard what Mr Swanson said. Hold my hand,' said Ned, grabbing his charging brother.

Another crackle and Mr Swanson appeared before them.

'All good. Beautiful day. Couldn't have wished for a better one. Who wants to go first?'

Sam squealed, jumping up and down in front of Mr Swanson with his arm raised.

'I'm going with Ned. Come on, Ned, I want to go now. Now.'

Mr Swanson smiled at Ned and Great-Aunt Gail and shrugged.

'Doesn't seem too badly affected by his ordeal, does he?'

'These two are a tough brace, there's no denying it,' said Great-Aunt Gail proudly.

'OK, Sam, I'll take you through,' said Ned, exasperated by his brother's tugging.

'Awesome. Come on, then!' yelled Sam.

'Hold onto my sleeve. Both hands. Tightly now. Tighter.'

Sam squeaked with excitement as Ned reached out and touched the portal stone.

'Wow! It's beautiful here. What kind of birds are those up there?'

'Those are springfinches. Wait, come here. Wait for the others,' said Ned, grabbing Sam by the scruff of the neck.

'Oh, it's always good to come home,' said Great-Aunt Gail, stepping clear of the portal. 'So clean. So unpolluted. David Attenborough would be delighted to come here, I'm sure.'

Ned and Sam looked at each other and grinned.

'All through safe and sound?' said Mr Swanson, as the portal crackled for the last time. 'Good, good, then let us enjoy the company of our wounded hero.'

The flock of springfinches leapt into flight as the four companions stepped out of the crater and gazed out from the cool shade of the trees.

'There's somebody walking around. It doesn't look like Bryn. Is everything alright?' said Ned, squinting toward Bryn's homestead.

'It'll be Peggy or Gretta. They've been taking turns to look after Bryn while he recuperates,' said Mr Swanson, striding out into the grass that grew lush and tall under Elgarolyn's sun.

'Really? They've walked all the way from Port Cadarn?'

'Flown, actually. Defeating Malverfuhren and the Gravemen has made some things a little easier, travelling by flying carpet is one of them. Port Cadarn is but a few hours away now.'

Halfway across the open ground that separated Bryn's house from the trees, Ned stopped and turned to Great-Aunt Gail and Sam.

'This is where I saw the Gravemen for the first time,' he said. 'They started billowing up over the fores – Look out!'

All four instinctively ducked as something whipped past their heads at a terrific speed.

'Ned! These really are good fun, aren't they?' yelled a familiar voice.

'Grace! You nearly took my head off.' Ned laughed delightedly as Grace, with great expertise, banked sharply and brought the carpet to a hover next to them. Ned winced as she leapt from the carpet and flung her arms around his neck and squeezed with all her might.

'Oh, Ned, it's so good to see you again. I've missed you so much,' she said, giving him one more big squeeze before releasing him. 'Hello. You must be Sam. My name's Grace. Oh, you're so sweet, come here. Look at those gorgeous chubby cheeks. Hello, Mr Swanson. Hello, Mairwen.'

'Is that a real flying carpet?' said Sam, his eyes goggling.

'It looks just like the one I flew when we were on *The Flying Lampwing*,' said Ned, watching Grace leap on.

'Come on, Sam, hop aboard and I'll take you for a spin,' said Grace, sitting down and patting the carpet in front of her.

'Are you sure? Do be careful, won't you?' said Ned, heaving his ecstatic brother up onto the carpet.

'Stop worrying, Ned. I'll fly slowly and I won't go any higher than the top of the grass. Well, not much higher. I promise.'

The clear air rang with squeals of excitement as they skimmed the top of the grass, Ned jogging alongside.

'Not too fast, not too fast,' he panted.

'Faster, faster! Be a P-51 Mustang – the Cadillac of the skies,' yelled Sam, hooting with laughter.

Ned sighed with relief as they reached Bryn's yard.

'Can we go again? Pleeease, can we go again?'

'Haven't you had enough flying for one day, Grace?' said Peggy, stepping out to meet them. 'Hello, Ned. We were wondering when you'd be back. You must be Sam. What an absolute sweet pudding he is. He's lovely! Come here and give me a hug.'

'My brother fought the bad man,' said Sam, puffing up his chest as Peggy whisked him from the carpet and bounced him on her hip.

'Did he? What a brave big brother you have. Oh, you are soooo adorable. Look at those gorgeous freckles,' cooed Peggy, planting a big kiss on Sam's cheek. Grinning, Ned rolled his eyes.

'How's the invalid?' said Great-Aunt Gail, as she and Mr Swanson arrived.

'Much better after your last visit. Up and walking around when he should be resting, but you know what he's like. Come on, come and see for yourself, he's in the back garden enjoying the sun.'

As the group walked round to the back of Bryn's house, passing under the oak tree that Bryn, Mr Swanson and Ned had so long ago sat beneath, a great cheer erupted.

'Ned! Mairwen! Mr Swanson!'

Ned blinked with surprise as Captain Ruby strode up and hugged him tightly.

'Ned, well done. You were so, so brave to face so much peril on your own. You are braver than any man or woman I have ever met, and believe me, I've met some of the bravest.'

'Thank you, Captain Ruby,' said Ned, his eyes welling. 'Thank you for coming to help me.'

'She wouldn't have missed a battle like that for the world,' said Amaldus, clapping Ned on the shoulder. 'Well done, Ned, you were magnificent. If I ever have children, I'm going to name them all Ned. Even the girls.'

Ned grinned and hugged the first mate.

'Here, I have something for you,' said Amaldus.

Ned was speechless as Amaldus reached into a pouch on his belt and pulled out a short length of braided silk.

'You've earned this over and over again,' said Amaldus, hanging the warrior's talisman round Ned's neck. 'You look after that now, won't you? It belonged to my brother, but you deserve to wear it, and it deserves to be worn by you.'

'Thank you, Amaldus. Thank you so much,' gasped Ned, cupping the exquisitely carved piece of amber in his hands.

'Ned! Come on over here.'

'Bryn! How are you? What happened to you?' said Ned, running up to the craftsman, who lay stretched out on a bench, a large mug of tea beside him.

'Oh, nothing much, nothing much. Just a few cuts and bruises,' he said, reaching out and swallowing Ned up in his huge arms.

Putting Ned back down, Bryn held him at arm's length.

'I'm so proud of you, Ned, you've done so well. And look at you now, I swear you've grown a foot. You're not the same scared little boy who came through the stone all by himself.'

'Just a second, I nearly forgot. I brought these over for you,' said Ned, slipping his rucksack off and pulling out a slightly crumpled red and green cardboard box.

'Yorkshire Tea. You wonderful boy. These will see me along the road to recovery without a doubt. Bless you.'

For a brief moment, Bryn's garden was cast into dark shadow as the sun was blotted from the sky and a hot, sandy breeze wafted through the garden.

'Hello, Ned. Delighted to see you again,' said Marganth, poking her head over Bryn's roof.

'Wow. Are you a real dragon? Did you really fly on her, Ned? Did you?' said Sam, struggling to pull free of Gretta and Peggy, who had been taking turns in clucking over him.

'It's so good to see you all again,' said Ned, looking at his friends. 'I really thought it was over when Malverfuhren pointed his wand at me. It was horrible, I'd never been so scared in my whole life, but then you all arrived and saved me. How did you find his castle? What happened after Marganth and I flew from the Hideout? How did the battle end?'

'Oh, Ned I was terrified when Marganth flew off with you,' said Grace. 'I thought you were going to fall off and I was shouting at Marganth to bring you back and then the roof of the cave collapsed and I was trapped. I couldn't even get down the tunnel to tell the others.'

'Not that we needed telling,' said Amaldus, 'Marganth's departure wasn't exactly quiet, nor was the sound of half the cliff face falling into the sea.'

'So how did you get out of the cave?' said Ned.

'We spent hours trying to clear fallen rocks out of the way, Amaldus and the crew of the *Lampwing* on one side and me on the other. Captain Ruby guessed what had happened and gave battle orders to the Outcasts.'

'I didn't know they were ready,' said Ned.

'They weren't anywhere near ready,' said Captain Ruby. 'I called everyone together and asked for volunteers to follow me into battle. I'm proud to say that without any hesitation, every one of them stepped forward.'

'How did you get out of the cave, Grace?' said Ned.

'Mairwen arrived on Mr Swanson's carpet and blasted the rocks away until I could crawl free. That's when we went looking for you and Marganth. When Mairwen and I found her and you weren't there – I, I…'

'She cried an awful lot until Marganth told us where you'd gone. And then she became really quite cross and gave Marganth an absolute roasting. Called her an ungrateful and irresponsible lump of rock, amongst other things. Some quite colourful language too, I can tell you,' said Great-Aunt Gail looking at Grace sternly but with the slightest hint of a smile.

Grace shrugged and smiled at Ned, while Marganth gave Grace a wary look.

'I've never seen a dragon with its tail between its legs before. She was quite ashamed of herself by the time Grace finished with her,' continued Great-Aunt Gail. 'But what a way to travel! Beats carpets any day of the week.'

'Anyway,' said Grace, 'after that Captain Ruby and all the others arrived. Marganth took Mairwen and led us to the castle, and I flew with Amaldus. He's not a bad flyer, but could do with a bit more practice. You know the rest.'

'What happened to Malverfuhren?'

'Well, after the lampwings saved us from the Gravemen, the svartelves' spirit broke and they turned and fled back into their tunnels. Unfortunately, Malverfuhren had the same idea and he sealed the tunnel behind him. He's probably fled to Belastung by now. He'll be grovelling for weeks to get back in favour. Out of all the Circle's treasures, Belastung would have wanted the ring the most.'

'Will they be back? Will they come looking for the ring?'

'Almost certainly, I'm afraid,' said Mr Swanson, his face sombre.

'Come on, Ned, don't look so worried. We're safe for now and you've got an army of Outcasts, mages and pirates behind you. And a dragon. Let's enjoy ourselves a bit,' said Grace.

Ned grinned.

'Yeah, you've got a point. Come on, grab your carpet. Let's have a race.'

Made in the USA
Charleston, SC
04 May 2016